DemiGod

Volume 7 of the Vellhor Saga

BY
MARK STANLEY

Contents

Prologue 4
Chapter 1 7
Chapter 2 16
Chapter 3 27
Chapter 4 31
Chapter 5 43
Chapter 6 54
Chapter 7 59
Chapter 8 70
Chapter 9 79
Chapter 10 83
Chapter 11 95
Chapter 12 108
Chapter 13 112
Chapter 14 128
Chapter 15 148
Chapter 16 152
Chapter 17 161
Chapter 18 170
Chapter 19 174
Chapter 20 180
Chapter 21 193

Chapter 22	204
Chapter 23	208
Chapter 24	214
Chapter 25	223
Chapter 26	228
Chapter 27	240
Chapter 28	250
Chapter 29	259
Chapter 30	265
Chapter 31	271
Chapter 32	274
Chapter 33	279
Chapter 34	287
Chapter 35	297
Chapter 36	305
Chapter 37	313
Chapter 38	323
Chapter 39	338
Chapter 40	351
Chapter 41	365
Chapter 42	376
Epilogue	384

Prologue

Gunnar woke to the clash of steel and the screams of the dying. The sound was distant at first, an old song carried on the wind, before sharpening into the present. His fingers tightened around the haft of his axe, calloused skin meeting cold frosteel.

He did not question why he was here. There was battle, and so he fought.

Smoke coiled thick in the air, tainted with blood and something else—something metallic, ancient. It clung to his tongue, seeping into his lungs with every breath. The battlefield stretched beyond sight, a wasteland of shattered ruins and statues eroded to anonymity. A place long forgotten, save by those who now warred upon it.

Then they came.

Shapes moved in the distance, first shadows, then forms. They advanced in silence, save for the whisper of their weapons sliding against ancient armor. He knew them before they stepped into the light. Every warrior did.

The Karvashi.

Their name was a wound in his mind, a scar left by old tales told in low voices over dying fires. He had never seen them—no one had. Yet they were known to him. They should not exist. They were what remained of an army that refused to die, twisted by the weight of their defiance. Once mortal, now something else—something bound by war alone.

The first emerged from the ruins, its body a fractured sculpture of obsidian and iron, glowing veins of molten gold coursing through the cracks in its limbs. A low groan rolled from its throat, the sound of breaking rock, and then it moved. Others followed. Some still wore the remnants of armor, plates melted into flesh, their mouths frozen in the silent echoes of final screams. Their weapons belonged to another age—scimitars that flickered like mirages, spears that drank the light from the air.

They did not speak. They did not call for surrender. The Karvashi did not parley.

So Gunnar did not wait. He lifted his axe and rushed to meet them.

The first fell beneath his swing, its head splitting with a sound like shattered glass. The second was faster, its blade a blur. Pain bloomed across his ribs, but he did not slow. He turned the axe, drove the blade through the thing's throat. It did not bleed.

None of them bled.

But they kept coming.

He hacked through them, breaking bone, splitting rusted metal, his muscles burning, his breath ragged. For every one he felled, another rose. Some pulled themselves back together, molten veins knitting their wounds as if the axe was nothing more than an inconvenience.

His own wounds closed as fast as they were made. He should have been dead, but the battle did not end. The Karvashi did not allow it.

He gritted his teeth, planted his boots in the blood-drenched earth, and fought on.

The axe became weightless in his hands, its arc precise, its bite absolute. He fought as though the battle had always been, as though it would always be. There was nothing beyond the swing of his blade, the crash of steel, the endless tide of foes who would never die.

Perhaps he was one of them now.

Perhaps he always had been.

Chapter 1

Anwyn

The battlefield seemed to stretch on forever. In that scorched wasteland, a choking mist clung like a cursed shroud, and every twitching shadow whispered of betrayal and the sudden, brutal violence lurking just beyond sight.

The clash of steel rang out like the echo of thunder, mingled with the raw, breathless screams of warriors falling in agony. Blood stained the earth, and the air thickened with the stench of death—a horrific, endless symphony, played by the damned and the dying, with no end to the slaughter in sight.

Anwyn stood at the fringe of it all, her breath shallow and rapid, her heart thumping so hard it felt like it might burst. There was a pungent mix in the air—blood, sharp iron, and a faint tang of decay—even though no lifeless bodies lay scattered before her.

Then she caught sight of him.

Gunnar.

He tore through them like a storm, his axe flashing in brutal arcs, cleaving through the faceless horde. His armor, battered and scarred, clung to him like some cursed second skin, streaked with the blood of those he'd left shattered in his wake. He fought with the fury of someone who feared *nothing—unyielding, unstoppable—a warrior condemned to fight until the earth itself crumbled beneath him.*

Suddenly, another wave of shadowy figures surged toward him. He pivoted quickly; his blade found its mark on the throat of the first assailant. As another foe lunged in, he deflected and countered—but they kept coming. His stance faltered ever so slightly, the weight of endless combat pressing down.

Anwyn tried to step forward, to do something, but her body felt frozen, as if it wouldn't obey her desperate commands.

Then, in a moment that made her heart lurch, Gunnar's eyes locked onto hers. His face contorted in a mix of determination and something almost tender. His lips moved—just one word, maybe her name or a dire warning— but the sound was lost in the clamor.

In the blink of an eye, a sword pierced his gut. He staggered, his teeth clenching in pain, and another brutal strike slashed his shoulder until his knees buckled and he hit the ground.

Anwyn wanted to scream, but no sound emerged—her cry was trapped inside her.

Reaching out with trembling fingers toward his bloodied hand, she watched as the mist thickened, swirling around him until he was swallowed whole.

And then everything went dark.

She jolted awake, gasping for air, sweat soaking her skin. In the dim light of her chamber, the stone walls blurred and firelight danced erratically, casting uneven shadows that seemed to pulse with her racing heartbeat.

For a long moment, she lay still, her pulse a drumbeat against the silence. The truth struck her like a winter storm—Gunnar was gone, swallowed by the brutal tide of battle. And yet the dream gnawed at her, a relentless whisper in the dark. A warning, perhaps? But of what? She could not say, only that it felt real, and that it would shape everything to come.

With a heavy heart, she surrendered to the darkness once more, letting sleep reclaim her weary soul. In that fragile, haunted slumber, the oncoming storm whispered its dire promise: the battles ahead would spare no one.

The first light of dawn crept into Anwyn's chamber like an unspoken promise, its soft light brushing against timeworn tapestries and bare, enduring walls. Faded velvet drapes guarded the full arrival of morning, permitting only wisps of light to mingle with the gentle flicker of candles. In the hush, every creak of the ancient structure murmured echoes of long-fought battles and sorrows buried in the deep creases of time.

Anwyn's eyes opened slowly, as if reluctant to leave the half-dream, half-nightmare where Gunnar's cries still echoed. The space next to her, once warm with his steady presence, was now a void, a silent testament to his absence. Each shallow breath carried with it the sting of loss, a raw ache that pulsed like a wound freshly reopened. In that heart-wrenching moment, her mind spun with memories of his gentle smile and the fierce determination in his eyes—a memory now shrouded in the mist of dawn and sorrow.

As she lay there, grappling with the grief, a chorus of cries broke through the silence of her solitude. From the far, shadowed recess of the chamber came the fragile sound of new life—tender yet unyielding, as if daring the gloom to persist. Though soft, the cries sliced through the melancholy like a lone hawk's cry echoing across a long, dark night.

Lorelei fluttered over and landed beside her, folding her wings with a quiet sigh. She didn't say anything. She didn't need to. They had long since learned to share their burdens in silence.

Nearby, next to a rough-hewn wooden table, her mother and Elara moved with the deliberate precision of seasoned nursemaids. Their hands, calloused yet gentle, cradled two tiny infants swaddled in cloth dyed with deep indigo and silver thread. The babies' cries were not merely sounds; they were a reminder of a world that, despite suffering and loss, refused to stand still.

Eira, her face lined with quiet resolve, set one of the babes upon a worn quilt embroidered with faded symbols of ancient lore. "Come now, Anwyn," she said, her voice a low murmur that carried both command and care. The tone was reminiscent of a battlefield order softened by the touch of a mother's compassion. "We cannot lose ourselves when there is life to nurture." Her eyes, fierce and kind in equal measure, searched Anwyn's face for the spark of resilience hidden beneath the veil of sorrow.

Across the room, Elara's fingers moved with quiet precision, adjusting the small cap on the infant's head. Her actions bore the weight of countless years of knowledge, passed down through blood and bone, honed by the passage of time. "Every ending births a beginning," she murmured, her voice gravelly like the distant roar of a mountain stream.

Outside, the air was heavy with the bitter tang of smoke—a grim reminder of fires that had scorched the city. Beyond the stone ramparts of the keep, the clamor of battle had faded into the persistent sound of repair: the ringing strike of tools against shattered stone, the measured tread of boots over broken earth, and the low, sorrowful murmur of soldiers tending to the fallen. Far off, dark plumes ascended toward the heavens, while the ruins of once-proud structures stood as mute witnesses to a day rent asunder by fury and flame.

Anwyn's heart pounded as she tried to reconcile the surge of grief with the undeniable pull of life that surrounded her. She reached out slowly, her fingertips trembling as they brushed against the cool fabric of the quilt. In that touch, she felt the echo of Gunnar's warmth, a phantom sensation that made her both ache and yearn.

Inside, her soul was a battleground where grief waged war against her duty to those who still relied on her. In that quiet room, the soft cries of the babies blended with the steady presence of her mother and Elara, filling the space with a muted strength that defied the shadow of her despair.

A shiver ran down her spine as her eyes locked with her reflection in the brass mirror hanging on the wall. The gaze staring back was hollow, marked by the wounds of past wars and the unknown future ahead. In that fleeting moment, she felt Gunnar's absence not just as a personal loss, but as a warning… an omen that the fragile peace of the world was fraying at the edges.

Lorelei's small form settled softly on Anwyn's shoulder, offering comfort, but it felt as fleeting as sunlight lost in heavy cloud. "There is strength in caring," she whispered, the words gentle, yet unable to erase the weight of the world pressing down on Anwyn. "Even in the endless night, the light of new life can guide us."

From beyond the walls, the distant call of a horn carried on the wind, a sound that seemed to speak of trials yet to come. Anwyn felt it then—the heavy hand of fate, urging her forward, asking her to rise from the grip of sorrow and face an uncertain future with courage. She nodded, slow and reluctant, understanding the road ahead would be one of pain, a journey marred by the loss of what had been. And as she breathed, a brief flicker of hope whispered faintly, cradled by the cries of the newborn—but the pain of Gunnar's absence, a wound too deep and raw, overshadowed it all. The ache in her heart was too great, far too great. In that moment, grief snuffed out the faint flickering of hope. She knew it then—no matter how fragile the light, the darkness had already taken its toll.

Elara cradled the babies, her soft hums weaving through their tiny cries that filled the small room. Above them, Lorelei hovered, her delicate voice a cascade of tinkling shushing sounds as she tried to lull them into calm.

Eira moved toward Anwyn, her gentle voice breaking through the silence. "Time for a bath, love," she said, her cool hands brushing Anwyn's forehead. A damp cloth, freshly wrung, pressed against her clammy skin, and with it came a flood of memories.

Anwyn's eyes closed, grief crashing over her like a storm. Every time her gaze fell on the babies, she saw Gunnar—his laughter, his unwavering strength—and it twisted her heart. The thought of holding them, of caring for them in his absence, filled her with a gnawing fear. How could she be the mother they needed without him beside her? How could she guide them, shape them into something strong when all she felt was broken?

Her voice trembled as she confessed, "I can't do this. I'm not enough... I can't even hold my children without feeling him all over again." The words fell like a curse in the heavy air, mingling with the soft rustle of cloth and the distant murmur of rebuilding beyond the walls.

Eira's hand found Anwyn's, soft but resolute, her fingers steady with the weight of truth. "My dear," she said, her voice low but unwavering, "you are not alone in this. Grief has its hold on you, and that is only natural. But you are stronger than you think, even now. It doesn't take perfection—only the willingness to try. This... all of this... it's more than you should bear in one lifetime. But one step, one breath at a time, and you'll find your way. Your love for them, for Gunnar—those are your strength. You are not alone." Her hand then gently cupped Anwyn's chin, guiding her daughter's gaze up with tender, unspoken strength. "Even in this storm, your love will guide you."

Anwyn choked back her sobs, tears streaming as she whispered, "Thank you, mother." Her voice was raw with grief. She turned her gaze to the children, a sudden pang of guilt twisting inside her. In that bitter moment, she realized she had barely seen them at all—her babies, the living promise of a future that now felt so distant. With slow, measured steps, she rose. The pain of birth still throbbed in her bones, yet she knew she must hold them. Their innocent love was the one strength she clung to.

Drawing near, the boy looked up. His soft blond hair danced in the light, and his blue eyes held a quiet, steely resolve that reminded her so much of Gunnar. A fragile laugh, half mirth and half mourning, escaped her as she reached out to stroke his smooth cheek. For a fleeting second, his tiny laugh eased the crushing weight of her sorrow.

Her eyes then wandered to her daughter. The little one, with longer, lighter hair and eyes like melted honey, gazed up at her with a searching innocence. The sight of her stirred both fierce tenderness and a deep, unyielding ache. As Anwyn extended her hand, tears welled anew when the child began to suckle at her thumb.

"They're hungry," Elara murmured softly at her side, her voice a quiet thread of observation amidst the morning air.

"Hungry?" Anwyn asked, her voice trembling as disbelief surged within her. "Didn't I just feed them?"

Her mother appeared then, her presence a balm amid the storm of Anwyn's thoughts. Calm, unhurried, and with a knowing smile, she spoke. "Aye, dear," Eira said gently, a faint chuckle rising from her chest. "They've certainly inherited a dwarven appetite, those two."

A choked laugh escaped Anwyn's lips—a fleeting reprieve. "Like Gunnar," she said, the image of him in his prime flashing in her mind. "I once witnessed him eat a whole lamb."

Eira's chuckle was warm and full of affection, yet beneath it lay the echo of Gunnar's absence. "Aye, they'll be eating like that too, I suspect. Elven babes eat far less, that's for sure."

She smiled softly at the children, her eyes crinkling with bittersweet affection. For a moment, a fragile peace flickered in the air—a brief respite before the heavy weight of the world outside returned.

In the silence of the keep, Eira broke the quiet with a voice both gentle and unyielding. "You haven't named them yet," she said, each word resonating like a steadfast drumbeat.

Anwyn exhaled sharply, a breath heavy with grief and the muddled haze of recent days. She knew the truth, yet every moment had blurred into the relentless march of sorrow.

A soft laugh from Eira cut through the gloom, an attempt to lighten the burden. "We can't keep calling them 'the babies' forever," she teased, her tone both tender and firm.

Anwyn's nod was slow and laden with silent grief, her face a quiet map of sorrow. In a soft, careful whisper, she promised, "I'll choose strong names that their father would have been proud of."

Chapter 2

Kemp

The cold hit first.

A sharp bite in the air, slicing through the thin remnants of sleep, creeping past the seams of Kemp's cloak and sinking into his bones. He stirred, his breath misting in the grey dawn, curling and fading like ghosts in the thin mountain air. His body ached from the night spent on hard earth, every muscle stiff, as though his very bones resisted the day to come.

Another day. Another battle.

Kemp forced his eyes open. The peaks loomed high, jagged and merciless, their dark tips knifing into the dull sky. Below, the desert remained smothered in shadow, waiting for the sun to drag it into the light.

He could see the remains of the fire smoldering nearby, little more than a scattering of embers, its meagre heat long stolen by the wind.

Ruiha was already awake.

She sat on a flat rock, sharpening her dagger with slow, deliberate strokes. Steel rasped against whetstone, the rhythm cutting through the silence like the promise of a blade finding flesh. She did not look at him, but she didn't need to. The stiffness in her shoulders, the tight set of her jaw, spoke louder than words. She was waiting—for him, for Vaelthys, for whatever this day would bring.

Beyond her, the dragon stood motionless.

Vaelthys' scales shimmered with a shifting interplay of deep purple and green, their edges darkened and charred, remnants of the fire that had seared him at birth. His wings lay folded, draped around him like the lingering shadow of a dying ember, refusing to fade into the light. His golden eyes burned, unblinking, fixed on the horizon beyond the mountains. Watching. Waiting. Judging.

Kemp swallowed, his throat dry. He knew what was coming.

Vaelthys exhaled. The sound was low, a deep rumble in his chest, like the distant growl of a coming storm. Mist curled from his nostrils, twisting into the air before vanishing into nothing.

"Today, you are unmade."

The words landed heavy in Kemp's chest, dragging down into his gut like stone tossed into a lake.

Vaelthys turned his gaze on him, and Kemp fought the instinct to look away.

"Tomorrow, you rise anew."

Ruiha stood, sliding the whetstone into her belt, the dagger back into its sheath. Her dark eyes found Kemp's, expression unreadable, then she nodded once. No sympathy. No words of comfort. Only acknowledgment.

He clenched his jaw, pushing himself upright. Pain flared through his back, his shoulders—every piece of him protesting, but he swallowed it down. The time for weakness was over.

Vaelthys moved, slow and deliberate, like a predator descending from its perch. Each step sent a tremor through the earth, his talons biting into the frost-kissed stone. He did not speak again. He did not need to.

Kemp followed.

The morning light sharpened, washing over the mountains in pale gold, painting long shadows that stretched across the valley. Ruiha trailed behind them, silent but present, her watchful gaze a weight at Kemp's back.

They walked until they reached a clearing of bare stone, wind-scoured and cold. Scattered among the rock were old scars—deep gouges in the stone, charred marks where dragonfire had blackened the earth. Kemp had seen them before, but today, they felt different. More than relics of past lessons. More than a warning.

Vaelthys turned, wings unfurling slightly, casting a shadow over the clearing.

"Begin," the dragon commanded.

Kemp hesitated. "What—"

The blow came too fast to react.

Vaelthys moved like a thunderclap, a wing lashing out in a blur of motion. Kemp barely had time to brace before it struck his chest, launching him backwards. The breath tore from his lungs as he hit the ground, skidding across stone. Pain lanced through his ribs, air scraping his throat as he gasped for breath.

He rolled onto his hands and knees, coughing, trying to find solid footing beneath him.

"Too slow," Vaelthys rumbled. "Too weak."

Kemp gritted his teeth, forcing himself up. His limbs shook, but he stood. Barely.

Another movement. Another strike.

This time, a tail lashed out, sweeping his legs from beneath him. He crashed down again, pain flaring through his side. The taste of blood filled his mouth.

"Again," Vaelthys growled.

Kemp pushed himself up.

The next blow came, and he *tried* to move—tried to roll, to shift his weight—but the dragon's claws clipped his shoulder, sending him sprawling once more.

He pressed his hands to the stone, fingers curling into fists. The world blurred at the edges, his vision pulsing with every throb of pain.

This is what you wanted.

The thought came unbidden, cutting through the haze.

This is what you asked for.

He breathed deep, his chest burning, his body screaming in protest. And yet—somewhere beneath the pain, beneath the exhaustion—was something else. A flicker of something that had once belonged to him.

He clenched his jaw.

And he stood.

Vaelthys studied him, golden eyes unreadable.

Another attack came. Kemp moved.

Not fast enough, not clean enough—but he moved. The blow still sent him down, but this time, he didn't stay there.

The training continued. Strike after strike. Fall after fall. Until the sun had fully risen, until the sky turned a pale and distant blue. Until the taste of blood and sweat became the only thing he knew.

He did not win. But he did not break.

As he lay there, staring at the sky, chest rising and falling in ragged breaths, he felt a shadow fall over him.

Vaelthys loomed above, his gaze sharp.

"You are unmade."

Kemp closed his eyes and knew Vaelthys had been right. *Tomorrow, he would rise anew.*

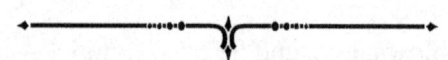

"You mortals believe strength is power," Vaelthys rumbled.

His golden eyes gleamed in the half-light, unblinking, unwavering. He stood at the edge of the plateau, wings half-unfurled, the wind whipping at his scales, a thing of molten shadow and fire. He did not look at Kemp. Instead, his gaze was set beyond, to the peaks and dunes stretching into the horizon.

"You think strength is a weapon. A force to be wielded, to carve the world into your own shape." He exhaled, a slow breath that sent ripples of heat curling through the morning air. "But strength without control is destruction."

Kemp clenched his jaw, fists balling at his sides.

"I have controlled it," he said.

The words tasted hollow.

Because they were a lie.

He had not controlled it. He had feared it. Feared what it might do. Feared *what he might do* if he let it loose. Ever since the darkness had been torn from him, he had held back, caged the fire rather than dared to use it.

Vaelthys turned his gaze on him then, golden and piercing.

"Have you?"

The silence stretched between them, thick as a blade pressed to the throat.

Kemp swallowed.

And said nothing.

"No," the dragon said. "You wielded it. You burned dark and hot, but fire without a master consumes all—friend, foe, and self alike." His wings twitched, the edges dragging through the dust. "Tell me, Kemp. What did your flames give you?"

Kemp's breath caught in his throat. His fingers twitched at his side.

Death. Pain. Regret.

The faces swam behind his eyes before he could stop them—the ones he had lost, the ones he had killed. The cities he had left in ruin. The darkness that had coiled in his veins, whispering, feeding, taking.

He forced the memories down.

"I didn't have a choice," he murmured.

Vaelthys watched him for a long moment, then nodded once.

"No," he said. "But you do now."

Kemp swallowed. He felt Ruiha's presence beside him, silent, waiting. She had not spoken since the lesson had begun, but he could feel her watching. Judging.

The dragon stepped back.

"Control the fire," Vaelthys said. "Or it will control you."

Kemp stared into the flickering embers at his fingertips, feeling the heat coil and writhe beneath his skin. It was not fire in the way he had once known it. Shadowfire was something else entirely—alive, hungry, a force that both obeyed and defied him in equal measure.

He clenched his fists, forcing the flames to retreat. They guttered, resisting, then vanished. The cold absence of them left his shadow hand trembling.

Vaelthys watched in silence. The great dragon's golden eyes gleamed like twin suns, unblinking in the half-light. His wings shifted, rustling like a distant storm.

"Again," he said.

Kemp exhaled. He opened his hands, let the power flow. Shadowfire bloomed between his palms, licking at his skin, whispering promises in the void. He tried to shape it, to bend it to his will, but it bucked like a wild thing, twisting and writhing against his control. It wanted to consume. It wanted to destroy.

His breath hitched. The flicker of doubt was enough. The flames surged outward, snapping toward the dry earth.

A great gust of wind slammed into him. Vaelthys's wings flared wide, and with a single powerful beat, he extinguished the errant fire before it could spread. The dragon stepped forward, lowering his head until Kemp could see his own reflection in those molten eyes.

"Remember," Vaelthys rumbled. "Strength without control is destruction."

Kemp's hands curled into fists. "I am trying."

Vaelthys studied him, the weight of his gaze pressing down like a mountain. "No. You are fighting it. There is a difference."

Kemp gritted his teeth. "Then what do you want me to do?"

The dragon's gaze softened, but only slightly. "Stop fearing it."

Kemp faltered. Fear?

He did not deny it. The power unnerved him. Not just because of what it was, but because of what it could make him.

Vaelthys tilted his head. "I am a force of pure destruction," he said. "A weapon wielded without care. When my bonded partner calls, I answer. When he commands, I obey. It does not matter what the command is—whether to burn cities to cinders or to cradle a wounded child in my claws."

His voice dropped lower, a growl edged with something ancient. "We are bonded, Kemp. And you wield my power now." His golden eyes narrowed. "You must control it."

Kemp swallowed. He felt Ruiha shift beside him. He had nearly forgotten she was there, watching in silence.

"So, what happens if he doesn't learn?" she asked, her voice quiet but firm. "What if he never controls it? Like you said. You are already bonded, Vaelthys. If Kemp cannot master his own power—if he chooses destruction instead of restraint—what then?"

The dragon did not look at her. He kept his eyes on Kemp, as if weighing something unseen. Then he exhaled, a slow, measured breath.

"Then I will have failed," he said. "But I will not be able to stop it from happening."

Silence stretched between them. Kemp's heart pounded. He wanted to deny it, to claim that he would never let himself become that monster again. But doubt gnawed at him. He had seen what unchecked power could do. Had lived it. Had lost everything to it.

Vaelthys let the silence settle before he spoke again. "You must choose, Kemp. Not once, but every moment. Power does not shape the wielder. The wielder shapes the power."

The dragon stepped back, wings folding. "Now. We go again."

Kemp flexed his fingers. He reached for his fire.

And this time, when it surged, he braced himself. The heat seared, the shadowfire twisted, wild and ravenous—but he took it anyway. Fear still coiled in his gut, a silent specter at the edge of his mind. But fear was not the choice.

He stepped forward.

Kemp exhaled, measured and steady, as the power stirred within him. Shadowfire curled around his fingers, hungry tendrils of black flame that pulsed in time with his heartbeat. It didn't just cling to him—it was part of him, an extension of his will. His left hand, the real one, trembled at the heat, but his right...

His shadow hand manifested in a slow unfurling of darkness, a spectral limb woven from the remnants of a shadowwing. Ethereal fingers flexed, insubstantial yet solid, their edges flickering like dying embers. It was neither flesh nor spirit, but something in between. And it ached—not with pain, but with need. The power wanted out.

Kemp curled his shadow-forged fingers into a fist. He wasn't ready to let it loose. Not yet.

Control it. Or it will control you.

He willed it into shape, forced his mind to focus, to command rather than fear. But the flame resisted, slipping through his grasp like water through cupped hands. His breath hitched. He could feel it turning, pushing back against him, seeking a way out.

The darkness always seeks a way out.

A flicker of doubt.

A crack in his resolve.

And suddenly, the fire was no longer in his hands.

It erupted.

The air split with a roar as purple-black flames tore from him, streaking across the plateau like a serpent unchained. The dry earth ignited where it struck, flames crawling across the stone, searing a jagged scar into the world.

Ruiha moved.

She was fast—faster than thought, faster than instinct. A blur of motion as she twisted away, the heat searing the space where she had stood. Kemp barely registered her leap, barely saw the way her body tensed for a counter before she caught herself.

The fire raged.

The sky darkened.

A shape moved through the flames.

Vaelthys.

The dragon did not flinch. Did not retreat.

Instead, he walked through the dark inferno, his molten eyes fixed on Kemp, his wings folding tightly to his back. Flames licked at his talons but did not burn him. They parted around him like a tide, as if they knew their master had come.

Kemp staggered backward, breath heaving.

"Again," Vaelthys rumbled.

Kemp's heart thundered. His body trembled. "I—I can't—"

"You can," the dragon growled, stepping closer. "You will."

Kemp clenched his fists. Shadowfire still coiled at his fingertips, restless, waiting. He felt Ruiha's gaze on him, unrelenting.

His throat was dry. He swallowed hard.

"I don't know how," he admitted, the words barely a whisper.

Vaelthys huffed, the sound a rumble of distant thunder. "Then you will learn."

The dragon lowered his head, pressing his snout close enough that Kemp could feel the heat of his breath, the scent of cinders and earth. "Fire is not a weapon," Vaelthys murmured, "until you make it one. Fear is not a weakness, unless you let it be."

Kemp gritted his teeth.

Control it. Or it will control you.

He closed his eyes.

The fire surged.

He let it.

Not as a force of destruction, but as something else. As a part of him. As breath in his lungs, blood in his veins. He did not fight it. Did not force it into submission.

He let it burn.

And when he opened his eyes, the flames were still there—but they no longer raged.

They no longer devoured.

They coiled around him, gentle as a tide, waiting.

Kemp exhaled.

Vaelthys studied him for a long moment, then nodded.

Ruiha lowered her blade.

The fire whispered, smoldered, and then—at last—faded.

And Kemp stood, for the first time, unafraid.

Chapter 3

Gunnar

Gunnar's breath burned in his chest, raw, scraped by iron. His axe was heavy, but he would not loosen his grip.

The battlefield sprawled before him, endless and broken. Ruins jutted from the earth like shattered bones, the shadows swallowing what little remained. The sky twisted in unnatural currents. Smoke and ash thickened the air. It clung to his skin, choked him with the taste of scorched metal.

There were no banners. No horns. He was alone.

The dead lay where they had fallen, stiff and silent. Empty eyes stared at the sky, clouded with dust and death, their final moments frozen in silent accusation.

A war fought long ago. And yet, it had never truly ended.

They came without sound. A grotesque hoarde, flowing like a shadowed tide, countless and unrelenting. The air itself seemed to recoil from them, thick with the scent of scorched metal and something older, something wrong.

Some moved with the heavy certainty of old warriors, others with the jagged grace of things shattered and reforged too many times. The darkness clung to them, splitting where cracks of raw energy pulsed, searing through the gloom like the embers of a dying forge.

The Kavarshi.

They knew him now. And they wanted him dead.

Gunnar set his stance, axe raised, and met the first charge.

His steel blade flared green as it tore through the nearest Karvashi, splitting it from shoulder to waist. No blood, just shards of blackened stone scattering like shattered glass. The thing shuddered, molten veins flickering, fighting to knit its ruin back together.

He twisted, severing an arm. It hit the ground still grasping, fingers twitching as if unwilling to admit they were no longer attached. His back foot skidded against the scorched earth, muscles raw with exhaustion. Another came for him, its blade rusted but deadly, swallowing the light as it swung. He stepped into the arc, felt the rush of air past his cheek, and turned its momentum against it—his axe buried deep, ribs splintering, heat licking at his hands.

They fell in droves, bodies torn and broken. But it didn't matter. The tide did not break. More came. More always came.

No matter how many he hacked down, they kept surging forward. He cut, he shattered—one fell, two took its place. His axe sang. Bodies broke. The horde did not thin.

His arms burned. His legs felt like lead. Each breath was a ragged, tearing thing in his chest.

Still, he fought. What else was there?

They did not stop.

The sky darkened. The ground cracked. The broken lay strewn across the battlefield, their silent witness a heavier weight than the axe in his grip. His foot slipped on filth, his own blood mixed with whatever foul substance leaked from the Karvashi.

How long had he fought? Minutes? Hours? Days?

His body screamed. His wounds, torn open again and again, mended just enough to keep him standing. The pain never faded, only deepened, a slow knife carving into his marrow.

One of the creatures lunged. He raised his axe—but too slow. The blow struck deep, searing pain down his side. He staggered. Another came. Then another. Claws raked his chest, tore into his shoulder, and the axe slipped from his fingers. He reached for it, but another strike sent him to his knees.

The world blurred. His vision wavered.

A voice whispered, low and cold.

"Why do you fight?"

It did not come from the Karvashi. It did not belong to the dead. It was the wind, the ruin, the very bones of this forsaken battlefield.

"You cannot win. Lay down your axe."

His hands were slick with blood, his own or theirs. It no longer mattered.

He could kneel. He could let it end.

But there was a reason. He could feel it, clawing at the edges of his mind, slipping between his fingers like mist. Close enough to taste, yet just beyond his grasp.

He had a purpose. He knew that much. And it wasn't to die here. Not today.

With a growl that scraped his throat raw, he grasped his axe and pushed himself upright. His legs trembled, his arms burned, but he stood. The Karvashi moved as one, a single wave of darkness, rising to swallow him.

Gunnar charged.

The first fell beneath his axe. Then another. And another. He fought knowing he would fall. He fought anyway. He had to.

The final blow took him in the gut, steel biting deep. His breath hitched. The axe slipped from his fingers. His knees struck the earth, the world blurring, the Karvashi dissolving into a haze of shadow.

A second strike. Blinding pain. Then nothing but silence.

He waited for death, but it did not come. The pain faded. The battlefield was gone.

He stood alone in the dark, unbroken. His axe was in his grip once more.

Before him, a path stretched into the void, endless. Waiting.

He did not know it yet… but this was only the beginning.

Chapter 4

Anwyn

Anwyn sat by the window, the pale light of morning stretching weak fingers across the wooden floor. The air was still, thick with quiet, broken only by the soft, steady breaths of the two babes nestled against her. One stirred in her arms, his tiny mouth seeking, and she guided her breast to him. He drank greedily, unaware of what had been lost. His sister slept, nestled in the crook of her arm, peaceful in the way only those untouched by sorrow could be.

Her mind wandered as she fed him. What names would suit them? Names worthy of Gunnar. Strong names. Names with weight, with history, with meaning. She imagined his voice, deep and steady, rolling through suggestions. He would have wanted something fierce, something noble, something that would stand large like the mountains he once climbed.

But then, a thought struck her, sharp and sudden. Would it have mattered to him? Gunnar would have loved the names, not for what they meant, but because she had chosen them. The realization settled in her chest like the last embers of a dying fire—warm, yet aching. That was the truth of it. He would have trusted her, as he always had.

The door groaned on its hinges. A draft curled through the room, stirring the heavy air. Eira stepped in first, swift and sure, the scent of fresh linen and crushed lavender trailing her like a whisper of home. Laoch followed, his steps slower, uneven. A fresh scar carved a path down his cheek, the skin around it red and raw, a wound not yet settled into memory. His limp was slight but there, a reminder of the battle that had cost them too much.

Eira knelt beside Anwyn, fussing over the babes, fingers tracing their delicate cheeks with a grandmother's tenderness.

"I swear, they're growing already," Eira murmured, wonder softening her voice. "Such quiet little things. You were the same, Anwyn—silent as a shadow, yet trouble at every turn."

Anwyn managed a small smile, watching her mother work. It was Laoch, though, who caught her attention. He lowered himself beside her, the weight of him shifting the bench beneath them, a slow smile creeping across his face as he leaned toward the babes.

"I need to tell you both something," Laoch said, his voice low, rich with warmth as he looked down at the twins. A small smile tugged at his lips. "Your mother was the fiercest child I ever met."

His gaze lifted to Anwyn, something unspoken lingering in his eyes. "Had to keep a tight grip on her just to stop her from climbing higher than any sense would allow. And when she wasn't halfway up a tree, she was out swinging a wooden sword, telling us that she'd be the greatest warrior the world had ever known."

Anwyn huffed a quiet laugh. She could picture it—the wild-haired girl she had been, stubborn and reckless, with more will than wisdom.

Laoch grinned. "Your mother tried to steer her toward something sensible, you know. A healer, a scholar—gods, even a merchant would've been easier on my heart. But that look in her eyes…" He shook his head, voice dipping low. "She was always meant for something greater." His gaze found hers again. "Still is."

Something thick and heavy lodged in her throat. She knew what he was doing, and he knew she knew. He was telling the babes of her strength, her determination. But it wasn't for them. Not truly. It was for her. A reminder, gentle but firm, that she was not so easily broken.

She swallowed, nodding slightly. She understood.

The silence stretched, comfortable at first, then heavier, weighted with something unspoken. She hesitated before breaking it. "The funeral? Gunnar's—"

Eira's hands stilled over the babes, her fingers resting lightly against the soft swaddling. She glanced at Laoch, something unspoken passing between them. For a moment, neither spoke. Then, at last, Eira sighed.

"Karl's handling it," she said, her voice quiet but steady. "He wants to know if you'd agree to hold it in a few days, then take Gunnar's body back to Draegoor for burial. He's asked if you'd be willing to honor him with a dwarven ritual."

"It's what Gunnar would have wanted," Anwyn said, the words quiet, but certain. She hesitated, gaze flicking between her mother and father, before asking, "Do you know what a dwarven ritual entails?"

Laoch turned from the babes, his expression thoughtful, solemn. "It's different from an elven funeral, love," he said.

"Dwarves do not bury their dead for the forest to reclaim. They honor them in stone, in flame, in story."

He exhaled, shifting his weight as if carrying the weight of the words themselves. "There is a procession first," he began, his voice low, reverent.

"A torch-lit march through the night. Friends, kin, shield-brothers—they walk together, their voices raised in remembrance. They will speak of Gunnar's deeds, his triumphs, his courage. For most, this lasts an hour or so, but for someone like him… it could stretch long into the night."

His brow furrowed, a ghost of sorrow flickering across his face. "His body will be carried on a bier of forged frosteel, draped in his battle-armour, his weapon laid upon his chest. The dwarves believe a warrior should meet the afterlife as he was in life—ready to fight, should the gods demand it." His eyes met Anwyn's, steady. "This part can be done here, in Tempsford."

A breath. Then his voice dropped lower.

"For the first and only prince of Dreynas, it will not end there. His body will be taken to the mountains. A tomb will be carved into the heart of the rock, its walls etched with runes, its halls lined with reliefs of battles fought and won. His deeds, immortalized in stone." Laoch's jaw tightened. "The dwarves do not forget their heroes, Anwyn. They return to their tombs, to kneel, to remember, to draw strength from those who came before."

His hands curled into fists at his sides. "It will be a shrine," he murmured. "A place where his name will never fade."

He looked away for a moment, gathering himself. Then, when he spoke again, his voice was steady.

"A pyre will be set. Not to destroy, but to transform. Fire is sacred to the dwarves—it is the forge, the heart of creation, the means by which steel is made strong." He exhaled. "They believe that as the flames rise, so too does the spirit, carried by ember and smoke to Aerithordor, the eternal forges of their ancestors."

A long pause followed, the weight of it settling deep in Anwyn's chest. But Laoch wasn't done.

"And then... they feast." His lips twitched, though there was little humor in it. "The last part of the rite. A gathering, a great meal, where stories are told and drinks are raised. Every dwarf will take part—each of them ensuring that Gunnar's name is woven into their shared history, spoken for generations to come."

Silence stretched between them, thick, heavy.

Then Laoch's gaze found hers, his voice quieter now. "This is how the dwarves honor their dead. With fire, with stone, with memory that never fades."

Anwyn swallowed hard. The tears came freely now, hot against her skin, but she made no move to wipe them away. Her grip tightened around the babes in her arms, her fingers curling protectively against the soft swaddle.

Gunnar deserved no less.

She nodded, her gaze falling to the tiny faces resting against her. Guilt coiled in her chest, sharp and unyielding. She should have been the one to arrange it. To honor him. But she had barely found the strength to rise each morning.

"I will tell Karl to proceed," she said, her voice steadier than she felt. "But I want to help him."

Eira's hand was warm on her shoulder, grounding her, though the weight of grief still pressed heavy. "Only if you're ready," she said softly.

Anwyn nodded again, slower this time. It was a lie. She would never be ready. But some things had to be done, whether she was or not.

She hesitated before speaking again. "How is Karl?" The words were little more than breath, fragile in the space between them.

Laoch exhaled, long and deep. His jaw tightened. "Not good."

Anwyn closed her eyes for a moment, the ache settling deeper in her chest. Karl and Gunnar had been more than comrades. More than friends. They had been brothers, bound not by blood but by battle, by hardship, by steel and trust. Losing Gunnar was like losing a limb—something vital, irreplaceable.

"But he'll survive," Eira said. There was certainty in her voice, quiet and unwavering, like stone beneath shifting sand. A truth Anwyn had to cling to.

She didn't answer. There was nothing to say. The world had grown quieter, its edges softer, but not with kindness. Only with loss.

Karl

Karl had fought in a hundred battles, faced things that would have made lesser dwarves curl up into the fetal position and rethink their life choices. He had seen warriors torn apart by beasts with too many teeth and even more claws, watched comrades dragged into the depths by things that slithered, things that whispered. But he had never been so reluctant to push open a bloody door.

And yet, here he stood, his hand hovering just above the worn brass handle. The weight of things unsaid pressed down on his shoulders. It had been there since Gunnar fell, heavy as a mountain, silent as snowfall. He was good at carrying weight—his own, other people's, the occasional wounded dwarf—but this was different. This was the weight of absence. And that, Karl thought grimly, was the heaviest of all.

He took a breath. It didn't help. He pushed the door open anyway.

The chamber was dimly lit, all shadowed corners and muted candlelight. Anwyn sat by the window, moonlight stretching across the floor in long fingers of pale light. The twins lay against her, warm and oblivious, wrapped in swaddling cloth.

Karl had always thought babies looked a bit like old dwarves—small, wrinkly, prone to unexpected noises. But these two... these two were different. Because these weren't just any children. These were Gunnar's.

His throat tightened. It was a ridiculous thing, really. They weren't warriors. They hadn't fought at his side, hadn't bled for the same cause. And yet, in the small fist curled against Anwyn's chest, in the slow rise and fall of their breath, Karl felt something shift inside him.

Anwyn looked up, exhaustion shadowing her face, but her eyes—those sharp, elven eyes—were steady. "You look like hell," she murmured. It was the closest thing to warmth he had heard in days.

Karl huffed, something like a laugh. "You've seen the mirror lately?"

She almost smiled. Almost.

He stepped forward, awkward at first, until he was close enough to see them properly. One of the babes stirred, stretching a hand out as if reaching for something unseen. Before he could stop himself, Karl extended a finger.

Tiny fingers curled around his own. Held tight.

The breath left him. His chest ached, but for the first time in days, it wasn't the kind of ache that hollowed him out.

"Greedy little thing," he muttered, his voice rough. "Just like his father."

Anwyn let out a quiet chuckle.

"So—" Karl started, then hesitated. "What do I call 'em? Got names yet?"

Anwyn exhaled, the sound soft and weary. "Don't tell me you've come to pester me about names too. You sound like my mother."

Karl gave a lopsided grin. "Dwarves take names seriously. A name is a history, a battle cry, a burden, and an honor all at once. Gunnar was named for his grandfather, you know. A legend in his own right."

Anwyn's fingers drifted absently over the child's downy head. "Should I name him Erik, then? After Gunnar's father?"

Karl thought for a moment. Then he shook his head. "No. Gunnar surpassed his father when he united the clans and became Prince of Dreynas. If he's to carry a name, let it be one that speaks of something new."

She considered that, and Karl continued, voice quieter now. "There are names worth carrying, names that echo through time. Owen Battleborn—one of the greatest dwarven commanders in our history. He never lost a battle, for it was said the gods guided his hand. Sigmund Thunderaxe—took down a troll king with a single strike. Dain Fireheart—led the charge against the Draken Lords when no one else dared."

Anwyn raised a brow. "Only males, then?"

Karl grunted. "There are women, too. Yrsa the She-Wolf, who led a rebellion with nothing but wit and sheer stubbornness. Hilda Snow-Maiden, who walked alone through an avalanche to save her people. And Freya, sister of Dreyna, whose very touch mended flesh and spirit alike. It was said the land bloomed in her footsteps, and no wound, no sorrow, could withstand her grace."

"I feel like I need her here with me now," Anwyn said. "The pain of losing Gunnar is—" She stopped, exhaled sharply. "It's unbearable at times."

Karl cleared his throat, because that was what dwarven warriors did when faced with emotions too large to shove into words. "Aye," he muttered, rubbing the back of his neck. "A right pain in the arse at times, but that dwarf was the best of us all."

He looked down. The baby stared up at him, round-eyed and solemn, the way infants often look at people they suspect of being idiots. A curious thing happened then—somewhere in the tangle of grief that had taken up residence in his chest, a small, stubborn bloom of hope pushed through.

He glanced at Anwyn. "You know—maybe you do have her here with you." His eyes flickered toward the babe.

Anwyn considered this, the silence stretching just enough to be uncomfortable. Then, softly, she said, "Freya."

She rolled the name around in her mouth, tasting it. Then her fingers tightened, just a little, around the fabric of the swaddle.

"I was going to wait until after the funeral to name them." Her hand traced a slow, careful path along her daughter's cheek. "But I like it. I think Gunnar would like it, too."

Karl nodded. "Well, Freya it is then."

A pause. A hesitation.

His gaze drifted to the other tiny bundle in Anwyn's arms. He cleared his throat again—twice this time, just to be sure.

"And the boy? Can't have a name for one bairn and not the other."

Anwyn's brow creased as the moment stretched, long enough for Karl to start wondering if she'd fallen asleep with her eyes open—or if he should clear his throat just to check. Then, at last, her gaze settled on him.

"If the gods once guided Owen's hand," she said slowly, deliberately, "then perhaps they will be willing to guide it again in this life."

Karl gave a firm nod. "A strong name. A true warrior's name."

He watched as Anwyn looked down at her children, Freya and Owen. The silence stretched again, but this time, it didn't feel like something waiting to strangle the air out of the room.

Eventually, Anwyn broke it.

"The funeral," she said, her voice steady. "Tell me what needs to be done."

Karl straightened, rolling his shoulders, slipping into the role he knew best—the dwarf who got things done. "The bier is being forged from frosteel. The procession will begin in three days. I've sent word to Magnus in Draegoor. His tomb is nearly ready. The pyre will be lit beneath the night sky. He'll go to the forges of Aerithordor, as all great warriors do."

Anwyn nodded. No hesitation. No breaking voice. Just quiet, tired acceptance.

Then, softer: "I want his axe. For Owen."

Karl hesitated. Then nodded.

"And a lock of my hair. Bound with his. For Freya."

That, he did not expect. He stiffened. Not because it was strange, but because it was right.

A warrior's send-off, yes. But also a father's farewell.

"He'd like that," Karl said finally, his voice hoarse. "And for you? Is there anything you would like?"

A tear slipped down Anwyn's cheek, but her voice was steady. "A bag of his ashes."

Karl's breath slowed. She wasn't finished.

"I want to lay some in Luxyyr. And the rest..." Her fingers curled slightly, as if already gripping a hilt. "I want them forged into my katana. So he's always with me when I need him."

Karl exhaled slowly. But as the words settled between them, he realized—Gunnar would have liked that too. He nodded.

Anwyn looked down at the twins. "Will you be the one to carry him?"

Karl hesitated. Not because he wasn't willing. But because it would break something in him. "If that's what you want."

She didn't answer immediately. But she didn't say no, either.

The silence stretched once more, heavier this time. Karl lingered, his gaze flickering back to the twins.

He would not let them forget Gunnar. That much he swore.

Before he left, he placed a firm hand on Anwyn's shoulder. "I won't let them forget him."

Anwyn exhaled. Nodded. "Neither will I."

Karl stepped out. The grief was still there. But somehow, it sat differently now. As if, perhaps, he no longer carried it alone.

Chapter 5

Ruiha

The fire cast flickering shadows across the rocky ground of the sanctuary, dancing and twisting like restless spirits. The open clearing atop the mountains was still, save for the occasional snap of embers and the distant howl of the wind sweeping through the peaks. The sky stretched vast and endless above them, streaked with the fading hues of dusk, while the jagged ridges of the mountains loomed like silent sentinels.

Vaelthys stood near the edge of the clearing, his massive, sinuous form outlined against the darkening horizon. The dragon shifted, flexing his wings before folding them close to his body. His molten-gold eyes flicked toward Ruiha and Kemp, lingering for a moment before he spoke.

"I will hunt," he announced, his voice a low rumble that echoed through the clearing. "Kemp, your strength is returning. With it comes appetite. I will be gone at least two days."

Ruiha watched Kemp nod, running a hand through his unkempt hair. His voice came rough when he spoke, still hoarse from the earlier training. The strain of channeling his shadowfire showed in the heaviness of his movements, the sluggishness in his gaze.

Vaelthys inclined his head, then turned, moving with a grace that belied his immense size. A moment later, he leaped into the night, his wings unfurling in a great sweep that sent dust swirling through the sanctuary. The rush of air tugged at Ruiha's hair, and she watched him disappear into the dark sky, leaving them alone in the vast chamber.

Silence stretched between them, thick and charged. Kemp exhaled heavily and sank onto the furs near the fire, rolling his shoulders with a wince. Ruiha's gaze lingered on him—the sharp lines of his face, the way the firelight caught the faint sheen of sweat along his collarbone. He had pushed himself hard today, forcing more from his body than it was ready to give. She hesitated, then moved behind him, settling onto her knees.

"Here," she murmured, placing her hands on his shoulders. "You're stiff as stone."

He let out a low chuckle, though it was laced with exhaustion. "Feels like it."

Ruiha's fingers pressed into his muscles, kneading the tension there. He sucked in a breath as she worked through the knots, his head tipping forward. Minutes passed in comfortable quiet, the only sounds their slow, measured breathing and the soft crackling of the fire.

Then, almost imperceptibly, his hand found her wrist, his thumb brushing against her skin. A slow, deliberate touch. Her pulse quickened. Kemp turned his head slightly, his gaze finding hers over his shoulder. There was something raw in his expression, something unguarded.

She didn't resist when he twisted, shifting to face her. The space between them shrank until there was none at all. His breath was warm against her lips, his fingers trailing the barest touch along her jaw, down the column of her throat. A slow drag, igniting sparks beneath her skin.

Ruiha shivered—not from the cold, but from the quiet, simmering hunger in his gaze. Kemp studied her like she was something precious, something he was afraid to break but desperate to consume.

Then he kissed her.

Time unraveled between them. Soft at first, almost hesitant, before restraint slipped. His fingers tangled in her hair, drawing her closer, his heat pressing against hers. Ruiha let him. Let the tension coil in her stomach. Let herself sink beneath him, his weight pinning her to the earth.

His hands traced her, slow and deliberate, memorizing every inch. Every brush of his lips sent a shiver through her. Every touch a promise. His fingers skimmed the curve of her hip, lower, and she arched, a moan slipping free before she could stop it.

Time blurred. The fire crackled somewhere distant, a weak rival to the heat between them. He was everywhere. His touch. His breath. His name on her lips.

When he pulled her fully into his embrace, she shattered, clutching his shoulders.

No man had ever made her feel like this. Owned her like this. His grip in her hair sent pain spiraling into pleasure, tearing through her, merciless and consuming.

The press of his body. The rasp of his breath. The low growl of her name against her skin. It was too much, yet not enough all at once.

She couldn't think. Couldn't speak. Only feel.

The world beyond them ceased to exist. No past. No future. Only him. Only this.

Her nails dug into his shoulders. Her lips parted, a sound she barely recognized escaping. And when the pleasure crested, stealing the last of her breath, she wasn't sure if she was falling or flying. Only that she never wanted to land.

By the time they lay tangled in the furs, the fire had burned low, leaving only the embers of what they'd ignited between them. Their breath still came uneven, their bodies thrumming with a shared warmth. Ruiha traced idle patterns along Kemp's collarbone, feeling the steady rise and fall of his chest beneath her fingers.

Neither of them spoke. Words would be too small for what had just passed between them.

Instead, she curled against him, and for the first time in a long time, she let herself feel safe.

"What now?" he asked, his voice quieter than before.

Ruiha hesitated. The sanctuary felt smaller in that moment, pressing in with unspoken truths. She stared at the mountainside, at the soot-darkened rock, before answering. "We keep moving forward."

Kemp shifted beside her, propping himself on one elbow. "Not good enough." His expression was thoughtful, determined. "I want to be stronger. As strong as you."

A pang of something close to regret curled in Ruiha's stomach, settling like a stone. She exhaled slowly, searching for words that might soften the weight pressing against her ribs.

"Kemp…" His name barely left her lips before she hesitated, the confession catching like a hook in her throat. She closed her eyes for the briefest moment, then turned to face him fully. He deserved that much.

"I've done things to get here." The words felt heavy, unwieldy. "Hard things. Things I'm not proud of."

The past pressed against her, unbidden. She could still see Faisal standing behind her as a child, feel his gaze. Her hands, small and shaking, slick with blood that was not her own. The moment hovered at the edges of her mind, as real as the chill in the air.

She drew in a sharp breath, steadying herself, forcing the past back into the shadows where it belonged. She would not let the tear slip. She couldn't.

When she looked up, Kemp's gaze was steady, unwavering. "So have I," he said.

The words landed like a blow. Ruiha flinched, though she masked it quickly. Still, the past surged—memories like an old wound torn open, aching and raw. She saw the understanding in his eyes, the quiet recognition of something broken, something neither of them could erase. For a heartbeat, neither spoke.

Then, slowly, she nodded. The silence between them thickened, stretched—not uncomfortable, but heavy with something unspoken. A quiet accord, forged in fire and shadow, in all the things they could never take back.

"Then I'll help you," she said at last, her voice steady.

A sudden growl from her stomach broke the silence. Ruiha blinked, then huffed a quiet laugh, pressing a hand to her abdomen as if that might still it.

She met Kemp's gaze, a wry smile tugging at her lips. "As soon as we eat."

Kemp

Minutes bled into hours. Hours into days.

Kemp ran until his lungs burned. Dodged until his legs trembled. Climbed until his fingers bled.

Ruiha made him fight against the mountain itself. Every step a battle, every breath a test. The stone beneath him crumbled. The ice threatened to send him plummeting. One wrong move meant death.

Maybe that was the point.

The air bit at his skin, sharp as a blade, thin as a whisper. His fingers ached from gripping jagged rock, his boots scraped raw against the mountainside. His muscles burned, each movement sluggish, as if the cold had seeped into his very bones. And still, she did not let up.

Ruiha struck without warning. A blur of motion, her blade flashing silver in the pale mountain light.

Kemp barely twisted in time. Metal bit into the leather of his shoulder guard, a shallow scrape but a reminder that hesitation meant pain. She did not hold back. She never had.

He stumbled. She caught him.

Then shoved him forward.

"You keep up, or you die," she said, voice flat, offering no comfort. No sympathy.

Kemp swallowed the anger rising in his throat. Anger at himself. At her. At how she made it look so damn easy.

He pressed on.

His muscles screamed. His vision blurred.

He fell. Again.

And again.

And again.

But each time, he forced himself back to his feet. Each time, the fire inside him slipped further from his grasp.

High above, Vaelthys stood at the peak, watching. Measuring. Offering nothing. No sympathy, no encouragement—only silent judgment, the kind that spoke of expectations Kemp had yet to meet.

The wind roared through the peaks, a ceaseless howl that swallowed breath and thought alike. Kemp staggered, his breath ragged, his limbs shaking. He had nothing left. No strength. No fire.

But still, he stood.

And for the first time, Vaelthys gave the smallest of nods. Not approval. But perhaps acknowledgment.

But the trial was far from over.

Ruiha moved again, faster this time, testing him. Hunting him. Kemp barely dodged the first strike, but the second caught him across the shoulder, sending him sprawling. Instinct flared. His magic rose, shadowfire flickering to life beneath his skin.

He doused it immediately, cursing himself. Not here. Not now.

His breath came hard and fast, body on the verge of collapse. But failure was not an option. Weakness was not an option. He had to keep going. Had to be better.

He caught the next strike on the flat of his blade. A small victory, but a victory nonetheless.

Ruiha's face gave nothing away. Then, in a blur of movement, she twisted, feinted, and swept his legs out from under him.

Kemp hit the ground hard, cursing as he landed on his hands and knees. He spat dust from his mouth, eyes narrowing. "You're stronger than me. Better than me. I'll never catch up."

Ruiha stood over him, her expression unreadable, save for the slight furrow of her brow. "Strength isn't about being better, Kemp. It's about learning from failure. I've made more mistakes than you. That's the only difference."

Kemp had barely found his footing before the sky darkened, a shadow plunging toward him with terrifying speed.

Vaelthys.

The wind struck like a hammer, a force so sudden and overwhelming that he barely registered the moment his boots left solid ground. The cliff edge vanished beneath him, and then—nothing.

The fall ripped the breath from his lungs, the world turning weightless in an instant. For a single, stomach-twisting heartbeat, he plummeted unchecked, the wind screaming past his ears like the lash of a cruel master.

Above, Ruiha's voice rang out, sharp and urgent—but the wind swallowed her words, leaving only the roar of the abyss below.

Then came movement.

Vaelthys dove, wings flaring wide, the dragon's immense form cutting through the sky with terrifying grace. But before he could reach him, Kemp's shadowfire ignited.

The world twisted. The air thickened, charged with something unnatural.

Panic flared, but instinct was faster. Magic roared in his veins, heat surging, colliding with the biting cold of the mountain air. His shadowfire flared to life—but this time, it was different. Less raw destruction, more control. It twisted, merged with something deeper.

Wind.

He knew wind. Had spent years studying its currents, its nature. How heat affected it. How it could be shaped.

Now, he felt it. The heat of his magic clashed with the mountain chill, forcing the air to shift, to churn. The currents bent, warped, responded to him.

The fall slowed.

He wasn't flying—not truly—but it felt like it. The wind no longer lashed at him like a beast trying to tear him apart. It obeyed.

He had stopped plummeting.

Still falling, yes, but now it was different. A gentle descent, like a leaf drifting from a branch.

For the first time, he understood.

He had always thought of fire as destruction. As something that consumed, devoured. But fire could shape, could rise, could bend the world to its will.

The ground rushed to meet him, but at the last moment, the wind swelled beneath him, and he landed hard but not broken.

Silence.

Then, above, Vaelthys let out a low rumble, something between approval and amusement, his wings stirring the air in slow, deliberate beats.

Kemp lay sprawled on his back, chest heaving, limbs trembling with the aftershock of what he had just done. The wind still whispered around him, a lingering echo of something vast and untamed. Something waiting.

Then Ruiha was there. Standing over him, silhouetted against the sky, her expression unreadable.

"Looks like you learned something," she said, offering her hand.

Kemp stared at it for a moment, then grasped it, his grip firm despite the way his muscles shook. He rose, the ground solid beneath him, but something in him had changed.

His breath came fast. His heart pounded. And yet, beneath it all, there was a certainty. A knowing.

"Yeah," he said, voice rough, steady. "I think I did."

Far above, Vaelthys let out another low rumble, wings shifting as if sensing the weight of the moment. The dragon dipped his head, something like respect in his molten gaze.

Kemp met his stare, his pulse still thrumming. And he smiled.

But the moment did not linger. Vaelthys exhaled, a slow, deliberate sound, and his gaze sharpened.

"You will need to prove yourself another three times," the dragon said.

Kemp's smile faded. "Three?"

Ruiha frowned, stepping closer. "Why?" she asked. "He's already bonded with you."

Vaelthys held her gaze, unblinking. "Because a bond is not enough." His voice was calm, yet it carried a weight that settled over them like a stormcloud before the first crack of thunder. "Should he fail, it will be up to you, Ruiha."

She stiffened. "Up to me to do what?"

Vaelthys' molten eyes did not waver. "To attempt to prevent him from leaving this sanctuary with me. In any way you can."

Silence fell between them. A silence filled with understanding. With the heavy knowledge of what that meant.

Kemp swallowed, his throat dry. Ruiha said nothing, but her fingers curled into fists at her sides.

MARK STANLEY

The wind whispered again, but this time, it carried no comfort.

Chapter 6

Gunnar

Gunnar's mind sharpened as he stepped forward, his boots sinking into blood-soaked earth. It was as if a fog had just lifted, the world coming into focus all at once.

Before him, a battlefield sprawled in ruin, a wasteland of shattered steel and lifeless flesh. The air hung heavy with the iron tang of blood, the stench of burnt meat and rot curling in his lungs, thick as smoke from a dying fire.

A banner, torn and blackened, fluttered weakly in the wind, its sigil unrecognisable beneath the soot. He barely felt the weight of his axe now. After so much killing, the burden of steel had become second to the burden of memory.

Then—a movement amongst the dead.

His grip tightened as he turned.

A body stirred. Not the erratic twitch of the dying, nor the hollow reflex of someone clinging to his final breath. This was different—slow, deliberate. Purposeful.

Gunnar watched. Unmoved. Unfeeling. He had waded too deep in blood for anything to matter now. The dead were the dead. The dying, not far behind. And him? He was something in between.

Through the ruin and blood, a figure rose. A broken thing, barely a dwarf anymore.

General Bjorn.

Gunnar knew the shape of his stance before he knew his face, the way he held his shoulders, the weight in his gaze. But this was not the Bjorn he had fought beside. Shadows coiled through his flesh, seeping through the rents in his armour like ink spilled across stone. His veins pulsed with something black and slow, thick as tar. And his eyes—

Gods, his eyes.

Flickering with something ancient. Something vast.

Yet the voice was the same.

"You look like you've seen a ghost, Gunnar."

Gunnar did not lower his axe. "You should be dead."

Bjorn smiled, though there was no warmth in it. "Oh, I was. Perhaps I still am. Does it matter?"

The wind howled between them, a hollow sound, empty as the battlefield. Bjorn took a step closer, and Gunnar caught the scent of him—iron and fire, the reek of something burnt beyond recognition.

"We bled together once," Bjorn said. "We can do so again."

A flicker of memory—fighting side by side, shoulder to shoulder, laughter between battles, the shared weight of survival. The memory turned to ash in Gunnar's mouth.

"I fight for the living," he said. "Not whatever you are."

Bjorn exhaled sharply, something like a laugh. "The living? You stand alone in a field of corpses. How many times will you fight, Gunnar? How many battles until you realise death is the only thing that remains?"

He gestured at the ruin around them, at the bodies strewn like fallen leaves.

"Death is not the end," Bjorn continued. "Not for you. Not for me. But there is a way out. A path beyond this endless struggle. You need only take it."

Gunnar said nothing.

Bjorn tilted his head, as if considering. "One life. That is all. One death for your freedom."

A beat of silence.

"Kemp," Bjorn whispered, a slow smile curling at the edges of his lips.

The name fell between them like a stone into deep water.

Gunnar's grip on his axe tightened. "He is innocent. I do not kill innocent men."

"No?" Bjorn's voice was almost gentle. "He killed your father. You know this. He chose his own ambitions over your kin. He is the reason your blade will never rest. But you can end this. You can walk away. A single act of justice. A single moment of truth."

Gunnar said nothing.

Bjorn stepped closer. "One life. That is all."

The battlefield groaned. The earth itself seemed to shift beneath Gunnar's feet. For a moment, doubt pressed against his ribs, cold as a knife. The fighting was never-ending. The dead all consuming. And Bjorn was not wrong. Kemp had killed his father.

But then—a whisper. A voice not of the battlefield, not of war. Not of *death*.

"It wasn't Kemp who truly killed your father... it was the darkness which corrupted him..."

The words struck him like a hammer, shattering the ice forming in his bones. He could not remember whose voice it was. A woman? A promise?

Bjorn's gaze darkened. "What will you do, brother? Will you choose freedom, or will you choose to fight forever?"

Gunnar did not answer.

He raised his axe.

Bjorn's face twisted. In rage. In disappointment. In something deep and hollow. "You were always a fool, Gunnar. Always bound by the weight of your word. You could have been more."

Bjorn swung his axe.

The fight was not of brute force. Bjorn knew him, knew his movements, his weaknesses. Every blow came precise, deliberate, aimed not to kill but to wear him down, to make him doubt. It was a test of resolve, not strength.

Gunnar fought through the ache in his limbs, through the doubt pressing against his ribs. He parried, dodged, struck where he could. And still, Bjorn did not relent.

They had fought together once. Now, they fought for the last time.

A gap in Bjorn's guard. A single moment.

Gunnar took it.

The axe found rotting flesh. A clean strike. A killing strike.

Bjorn staggered, his breath hitching. He looked down at the wound, black blood seeping through his fingers. When he met Gunnar's gaze, his lips parted—not in a snarl, not in pain, but in something close to understanding.

"I would have done the same."

The battlefield trembled. The bodies dissolved into shadow, the ground splitting beneath them. The world itself unraveled, falling away like smoke in the wind.

Gunnar stood alone in the dark. His axe was still in his grip. His heart was heavier than ever.

The path ahead was waiting.

Chapter 7

Anwyn

The babe stirred, little fingers grasping at the empty air. Anwyn traced a slow hand over Freya's soft cheek, breathing in the faint scent of milk and warmth. Beside her, Owen slept on, undisturbed. A knot twisted in her chest. Too soon. She wasn't ready to leave them, not yet.

Eira adjusted the blanket around Freya, her hands gentle but firm. "They'll be fine, Anwyn," she murmured, her voice laced with quiet reassurance. "Go. Do what must be done."

Laoch stood by the hearth, arms crossed, saying nothing. But his eyes followed her, measuring, knowing. He saw the war within her, the battle between duty and grief.

She moved because she had to, though each step felt like wading through thick, cloying mud. The days before had blurred together, slipping from her grasp like water, leaving only exhaustion in their wake. Sleep came in restless snatches, never enough to quiet the ache in her chest. And always, Gunnar's absence gnawed at her, a shadow she could never outrun. At the doorway, she hesitated, glancing back at the babes wrapped in swaddling. Her breath caught. Duty waited, cold and unyielding. She turned and walked away.

Boots scuffed against stone, armor clinking as weary guards trudged past. Voices murmured in shadowed alcoves, hushed and uncertain. Smoke and damp clung to the air, the lingering ghosts of battle. The walls bore scars—blackened stone where fire had licked and seared. A torn tapestry sagged from the wall, its center split, unraveling thread by thread.

Anwyn walked on, catching whispers as she passed.

"...Cahir's men never saw them coming."

"...The Sand Dragons turned the whole battle."

"...I heard Cahir died at Dakarai's hand."

She shut it out, pressing forward. A chill curled through the corridors, a whisper of wind slipping through cracked stone. Her boots struck the floor in steady rhythm, each step pulling her further from the past and deeper into what lay ahead. The keep loomed around her, vast and bruised, a wounded beast licking its wounds in the dark.

She flexed her fingers, aching to grip the hilt of her katana, though no steel would cut through the grief that coiled in her chest. Words and whispers flitted past like autumn leaves, swirling in unseen currents. None of it mattered. Not yet.

The doors to the queen's chamber stood ahead, tall and unyielding. Anwyn took a breath, straightened her shoulders. No more hesitation. She placed a hand against the cold wood, exhaled, and stepped inside.

Queen Kathrynne stood by the window, the city stretched beyond her, scarred and smouldering. A battlefield after the storm. The pale morning light caught in the strands of her hair, turning them to dull gold. She turned slightly at Anwyn's approach.

"I appreciate you coming on such short notice," the queen said, her voice measured, though weariness laced the edges. "You could have rested longer."

Anwyn studied her, the tension in her shoulders, the shadows that clung beneath her eyes. She could have said the same to Kathrynne.

She exhaled, the words bitter as iron. "Rest is for those who have time to spare. You and I both know we are not among them."

Kathrynne turned, her gaze steady. For a fleeting moment, Anwyn did not see a queen—only a woman. A woman who had already lost too much and knew the gods were not done taking from her yet.

"How are you, Anwyn? And the babes?" Kathrynne asked.

Anwyn drew in a slow breath. *How was she?* She wasn't even certain herself. "They are well. My mother and father watch over them now. And... I gave them names."

Kathrynne's eyes flickered, the smallest sign of surprise. "Names?" she repeated. "Tell me."

A rare smile touched Anwyn's lips. "Owen and Freya."

Kathrynne nodded, the tension in her shoulders easing just a fraction. "Strong names."

"They are named for dwarven gods," Anwyn admitted.

Kathrynne's voice softened. "Names Gunnar would be proud of."

Anwyn swallowed, but the ache remained. "Yes," she said quietly. "He would have loved them." A single tear traced a path down her cheek.

Kathrynne's next words were a quiet, unwavering truth. "Gunnar saved us."

The words landed like a blade to the ribs. Anwyn closed her eyes against the grief, but it was always there, waiting.

She forced steel into her spine, into her voice. "He died saving his children, Kathrynne. It was the Sand Dragons and the Shadow Hawks who turned the tide at Tempsford."

Kathrynne held her gaze, unflinching. "It was Gunnar's actions—his foresight—that brought them here in time. Without him, we wouldn't have made it. As far as I'm concerned, it was Gunnar who saved Tempsford."

Silence thickened between them, heavy as the weight in Anwyn's chest. The memory of battle still clung to the air, an unseen specter neither of them could shake.

Then Kathrynne inhaled, shoulders squaring, mask slipping back into place. "Cahir is in the dungeons."

Anwyn went still.

"He lives?" The words were sharp, bitter.

The queen held her gaze. "He will die. But not yet."

Anwyn's fingers twitched at her side, as if reaching for her katana. "He deserves nothing but a blade to the throat."

"And he will have one—once we have what we need." Kathrynne's voice was calm, measured, a steady breeze against Anwyn's fury. "He knows of Junak's plans."

The name burned in Anwyn's mind, stirring unease beneath her anger. Junak. A specter lurking at the edge of every battle, always one step ahead. If Cahir had answers, if he could reveal even a sliver of what lay ahead—

She exhaled, forcing the anger down, burying it beneath colder, sharper things. "Then he had best start talking."

A pause. The weight of it hung between them. Anwyn watched Kathrynne, searching for any flicker of hesitation, any sign that the queen was holding something back.

Nothing.

But there were other battles yet to be fought.

She inhaled, steadying herself. "Luthar and his army? What of the fight against Junak?"

Kathrynne's mask of control slipped, just for an instant. A flicker of something in her gaze—something fragile.

"We don't know."

Silence stretched between them.

Kathrynne looked away first. Anwyn saw it then, the thing hidden beneath all the rest—the quiet, gnawing fear. Not just for the war. For her husband.

Anwyn understood.

She stepped forward, setting a hand lightly on Kathrynne's arm. The queen did not pull away.

"He's alive," Anwyn murmured. "He has the dragons and the elves at his side."

Kathrynne said nothing. But her shoulders eased, just slightly.

The queen recovered quickly. "A council meeting will be held this afternoon. Will you be in attendance, Anwyn?"

Anwyn nodded. "I will be there."

She turned to leave, pausing at the threshold. A final glance at Kathrynne.

For the first time, she truly saw herself reflected there.

Two women standing on the edge of loss, holding the line.

And neither could afford to fall.

Anwyn

The great hall of Tempsford's keep bore the scars of hardship, the air thick with the lingering heat of battle and the press of too many bodies. Firelight danced along the stone walls, throwing long shadows that flickered like wraiths. The sharp tang of sweat, damp earth, and woodsmoke coiled in the rafters, a reminder of the struggle that had brought them here.

Anwyn sat at the war table, its scarred surface worn by time and conflict. Maps lay sprawled across the oak surface, edges curling from heat and use. Reports of the battle's cost—men lost, provisions burned, defenses weakened—were stacked in uneven piles, ink smudged from the hands that had gripped them too tightly.

She ached. Not from wounds but from exhaustion, from the heaviness of decisions yet to be made. Queen Kathrynne sat beside her, expression unreadable save for the tightness at the corners of her mouth. They had held Tempsford. Barely.

The council gathered, a restless energy shifting among them. No one spoke at first. Not until Kathrynne exhaled sharply and broke the silence.

"There has been no word from Luthar." Her voice was clipped, controlled, but the concern there was sharp enough to cut. "Nor the elves. Nor the dragons."

The room stiffened.

Dakarai leaned forward, forearms braced on the table, his face lined with exhaustion. "No response means one of two things." His voice was sandpaper rough, scraping against the quiet. "Either they're too deep in battle to send word, or there's no one left to send it."

A grim truth.

Baron Roderic cleared his throat. "We could send a rider, but it would be reckless. We know nothing of what awaits beyond our walls."

Anwyn's fingers curled into fists. Doing nothing gnawed at her, coiling tight in her chest. Every second of silence from Luthar's forces fed the worst possibilities. She forced herself to breathe through it, to keep her face as still as the stone beneath them.

Laoch pushed back from his chair. "Then I'll go." His voice was steady, but beneath it, Anwyn heard something deeper—duty, tempered with personal resolve. The elves were his command. If any of them still stood, he needed to know.

Kathrynne studied him, jaw set. "Not alone."

Laoch inclined his head. "If she can be spared, I'd have Ignara at my side. She'd cut the journey in half, and if the worst comes to pass, a dragon's presence could turn the tide."

Silence stretched. Then Kathrynne inclined her head. "Agreed."

The decision settled, but the weight in the room did not ease. The city still bled from the siege, its people hanging by a thread.

Roderic shifted the discussion. "Our walls are compromised. We need stonework, proper dwarven work."

Draeg grunted. "I can oversee that."

"Water and supplies?" Kathrynne pressed.

"Low," Roderic admitted. "We need to ration carefully. The fields outside the walls were torched in the attack."

A slow breath passed through the chamber. The cost of survival was always higher than expected.

"The dead," Kathrynne murmured, rubbing at her temple. "We need them buried."

Anwyn glanced at her. There was no need for the question. Kathrynne already knew the answer: burning the enemy dead was the only way to prevent sickness from taking root.

Kris, usually quiet, lifted his head. "We should hold a procession. For our fallen."

Anwyn spoke at last, her voice steady. "It would be an honor to have it at the same time as Gunnar's."

Kathrynne glanced her way, a flicker of softness breaking through the hard set of her features. Karl rubbed the back of his neck, casting her a sidelong look before nodding his agreement.

No one argued. It was a small thing, but right now, small things were all they had to hold onto.

Then Karl cleared his throat, breaking the solemnity with a grin that did not belong in this room. He reached into his pack and pulled out something wrapped in cloth. With deliberate theatrics, he set it on the table and pulled back the fabric.

A tankard.

Silence.

Kathrynne frowned. "A... tankard?"

Karl beamed. "Not just any tankard."

Thraxos exhaled through his nose, long-suffering.

Karl, undeterred, launched into his explanation with the enthusiasm of a dwarf who had just struck gold. He extolled the metal's virtues—light enough to wield without effort yet so unbreakable it would probably survive the end of days, which, he assured them, was *very* handy in a drinking vessel.

It shimmered with a natural luster, catching the light in a way that suggested it had been polished by the gods themselves.

Draeg, despite himself, gave a nod here and there, though it was the sort of nod that suggested he was simply indulging Karl rather than being entirely convinced.

And then Karl got to *the handle*. Oh, the handle. Forged to fit the hand so perfectly that lesser cups might as well have been fashioned from damp clay by blindfolded children. The *balance*, the *weight*—neither too top-heavy nor so bottom-heavy that it would tip precariously like a drunkard on his fifth ale.

"And the thermal retention!" Karl declared, eyes gleaming with the passion of a dwarf who valued both metalwork and drink temperature with equal reverence. "Keeps yer drink warm in winter, cool in summer, an' just right in that awkward in-between weather when ye can't decide if ye want a stout or a lager."

He finished with a flourish, pausing just long enough for the sheer genius of dwarven craftsmanship to truly settle over his audience. Then, with a final, self-satisfied nod, he added, "Pretty proud of it, to be honest."

The room stared at him as if he had lost the plot completely—not just misplaced it, but taken it outside, set it on fire, and danced around the flames singing drinking songs.

Thraxos, however, finally reached his limit. With a sigh that carried the weight of a thousand past disappointments, he grabbed the tankard from Karl's grasp and turned it over in his hands.

"It's a *vessel*, Karl," he muttered. "Not a bloody drinking cup."

Karl shrugged. "Aye. But if I'm going to trap the darkest evil this world has ever seen, I'd at least like to do it in style."

Laughter rippled through the chamber. Even Anwyn's lips twitched. And beneath it, a truth settled among them. The vessel existed. The next step in their fight had begun.

Then Kathrynne straightened, and just like that, the moment passed. "One last matter." Her gaze cut to Anwyn. "Duke Cahir is in the dungeons."

Anwyn's pulse spiked. Her fingers twitched, aching for a blade.

Laoch's voice was quiet steel. "You're too close to this, Anwyn."

She turned to him, lips parting, but Karl leaned back, arms crossed, before she could argue. "I'll go."

She met his gaze. Something unspoken passed between them. Karl was many things—reckless, infuriating—but never a fool. If there was truth to be dragged from Cahir's throat, Karl would find it.

Kathrynne nodded. "Karl. Handle the interrogation. We need to know what he knows."

The council adjourned, but no one rushed to leave.

Draeg clapped Karl's shoulder, still chuckling at the tankard. Kris lingered by Kathrynne's side, voice low as he spoke of the city's morale. Dakarai stood near the window, staring at the dark horizon where Luthar and the elves had marched.

Anwyn was the last to rise. She caught Karl's eye as he turned for the door.

"Don't go easy on him."

Karl smirked, but there was steel in his gaze. "Wouldn't dream of it."

The chamber emptied, but Kathrynne remained at the head of the table, staring down at the map of Vellhor. Her fingers tightened against the wood. Outside, the city still smoldered, and somewhere beyond the horizon, war still loomed.

Chapter 8

Ruiha

The past pressed down on Ruiha, thick as the dust clinging to her throat. She had felt it before. She felt it now.

The chamber swallowed them whole. Shadows stretched beyond the torchlight. Columns loomed in fractured lines, their tops sheared off. The ground was uneven, paved with remnants of a world long crumbled to dust.

Kemp walked ahead, shoulders tight, jaw set. Ruiha knew his silence well enough to recognize the battle behind his eyes.

Vaelthys had given him three trials. This was the first.

And if he failed…

She swallowed. If he failed, he would not lose his power. That was the problem. He would still walk away with the strength of a dragon at his back, the force of Vaelthys' power in his hands.

She trusted Kemp. Had fought for him, bled for him. But trust was not certainty. Passing these trials meant proof—proof he would wield his power for Vellhor, for the people who needed him. But if he failed…

She clenched her fists.

Failure meant doubt. Doubt meant risk. If Kemp failed, there would be no promise of what he would become.

To stop him—she didn't know if she could.

And yet, she had not argued. Had not told Vaelthys no. This was no mere test of will. It was a reckoning. If Kemp could not wield the bond, if the power consumed rather than strengthened him, the cost would be too high.

A prickle ran down her spine.

The air shifted.

A whisper on the wind.

Then movement.

Ruiha heard it before she saw it—the scrape of bone on stone, the rasp of something long dead stirring to life.

The corpses rose.

At first, they were little more than shifting shapes, clawing their way up from the broken stone. But then, the details formed—solid, sharp, *real*.

They were *dwarves*.

And Ruiha understood.

These were not the dead left behind in battle, not soldiers who had fallen with a blade in their hands, not foes who had met their deaths in the dance of war. These were the ones Kemp had butchered.

Ruthlessly. Without hesitation.

Their eyes burned with hatred. The wounds that had killed them still glowed at the edges, charred and cracked where unnatural flames had eaten through flesh and bone.

A boy, no older than twelve, his face frozen in horror, his small hands curled in agony. His beard had barely begun to grow, and yet darkness had carved into him, splitting him apart from the inside out.

A dwarven scholar, wrapped in tattered grey robes, her fingers still twisted around the remains of a book, its pages turned to ash. Her mouth was open in a scream that had never faded.

A warrior, his armor melted into his flesh, the heat of the fire having fused steel to bone. He still clutched his weapon, but his stance was twisted, ruined. A dwarf who had *burned* rather than fallen.

And there were *more*.

Dozens. Maybe hundreds.

Ruiha had seen men stand before death, had seen warriors hold their ground against impossible odds. But she had never seen a man so utterly *still* as Kemp was now.

She did not need to look at him to know what he was feeling.

He had spent the past months running from this. From *them*.

Then another shape stepped forward.

Not a dwarf.

Kemp.

But not as he was now.

This one was younger. His face unlined, his hands unscarred. His cloak unburned. No hesitation in his stance. No pain in his eyes.

No shadow curling where his arm should be. No storm churning behind his gaze.

"You do not belong here," his younger self said. The voice was Kemp's, but cold, empty of regret. "You were never meant to be here."

Ruiha's breath stilled.

Something was shifting beneath the surface of her thoughts, curling into place. The trial was his—of course it was. The ghosts were *his*.

But as the corpses stood waiting, she knew—this was her trial, too.

Because she had left bodies behind.

She had killed before she knew what killing meant. A child of the streets, blade in hand, death a necessity rather than a choice. And later—when it *had* become a choice—she had not hesitated.

She had killed for coin. For survival. For *reasons*.

But it had never been *this*.

She had never burned people alive, never turned flesh into something unrecognizable, never left behind *monsters*.

And yet—

She had been no better than him, once.

Kemp's breath shuddered out of him. His fingers curled into fists.

She saw it then—the thing he had never let himself say aloud.

He had not just *killed* these dwarves. He had *become something else* when he did it.

A weapon. A monster.

And he feared, even now, that he still was.

Ruiha exhaled, slow and careful.

"You see them," she said. It was not a question.

Kemp did not answer.

But he took a step forward.

Ruiha watched the struggle carve itself into him—the past pressing against the present, the pull of what he had been against what he might yet become. Shadows curled at the edges of his form, restless, waiting.

The dead did not speak. But they lingered. In the scorch marks on the stone. In the silence that followed. In the eyes of the man who had made them.

Another step.

The storm in his gaze did not clear, but it did not deepen either. His fists loosened. His breath steadied.

He moved forward—not away, not past, but through.

And for the first time, Ruiha thought, perhaps that was enough.

Kemp

Kemp's throat was dry. The weight of the dead pressed against his chest, heavy as the air before a storm. Their eyes—what remained of them—held him in place. An accusation, a reckoning.

His voice, when it came, was barely more than a breath. "I see you."

The words scraped from his throat, raw, unwanted. He had spent too long denying them. He had spent too long pretending the past could be outrun.

But the past did not forget.

It stood before him now, waiting.

His gaze swept across them. The scholar, her book turned to ash. The boy, too young to have met such an end. The warrior, steel melted into flesh. Their pain had not faded. It never would.

"I have not forgotten you," he said.

It was not an apology. Apologies were for the living. It was a truth. The only one he had to give.

The air hummed. The corpses did not move, but something in them... changed. Not forgiveness. Not peace. But recognition.

A shudder ran through him, cold as the grave.

Beside him, Ruiha stepped forward.

He felt her presence before he saw her. Solid. Unwavering. A blade honed against the same whetstone of regret.

She turned to face them—the dead.

Her fingers twitched at her sides, the instinct to turn away coiling through her. He saw it. He knew it. The urge to keep walking, to push forward without looking back.

But she did not.

Instead, she met their gazes, one by one.

"I see you, too," she said.

No magic answered. No great force swept through the chamber to take them away. And yet, they began to fade. Not in an instant. Not with fire or wind or light. But softly, as if they had never been there at all.

Ash on the wind.

And then—only silence.

Ruiha exhaled, her breath uneven. The tightness in her shoulders eased, just slightly.

Kemp turned to her.

She was already watching him.

For a moment, they simply stood, the past still lingering, still pressing. But lighter now. Not gone. Never gone. But carried differently.

Her hand lifted before he could think to stop her. Fingers brushing against his scarred face—Karl's attack that had nearly taken him. They still ached, even now.

He did not flinch.

Her touch was light, tracing the uneven edge of his cheek, as if mapping the ruin he had become.

"The pain is still there," she murmured.

A truth. A wound. A reminder.

His lips parted. He found himself breathing too shallowly, her touch searing through him in ways he could not name.

"Some things are meant to be," he said.

The silence between them was not empty. It was thick with all they had not said, weighted by the glances they had exchanged but never explained.

She had not spoken of what had passed between them on those nights. Neither had he. Yet it had been there, woven into the quiet spaces between words, settled into the way they moved around each other.

The cavern air was cold, damp with the scent of old stone and lingering magic. Beyond them, the heavy doors groaned, shuddering open to reveal the next trial.

But neither of them moved. Not yet.

"I never meant to leave it unspoken," he said at last, voice quieter than he had intended.

Her fingers stilled where they rested against his scar, a touch so light he might have imagined it.

"Neither did I," she murmured, though she did not meet his gaze.

She traced the jagged ridge along his cheek. Her touch did not shy away from it, nor did he flinch beneath it.

For a long moment, they stood there, poised between past and present, between the doors that had opened and the words they had finally dared to say.

A shadow stirred at the threshold of the chamber.

The air thickened, a low, resonant hum filled the space—not a sound, but a presence.

Vaelthys stepped forward, his massive form folding into the cavern's dim light. His scales shimmered like liquid metal beneath the flickering torchlight.

His gaze settled on Kemp.

"You see them now," he said, voice deep, edged with something unreadable.

Kemp's jaw tightened, but he did not look away. "Yes."

Vaelthys studied him a moment longer before exhaling, a breath like embers stirring in a dying fire.

"And still, you resist what is," he rumbled. "You look at the past as though it is a wound to be erased. As if shame will rewrite the stone."

Kemp's hands curled at his sides. "If I could undo it, I would."

Vaelthys' molten gaze did not waver. "Then you have learned nothing."

Ruiha stiffened beside Kemp, but Vaelthys remained focused on him.

"Perfection is a myth," the dragon said. "A thing men chase when they refuse to face their own reflection. But what is broken is not worthless. A scarred blade still cuts. A shattered mountain still stands. Ruin does not make a thing lesser."

His voice, low and measured, filled the chamber, pressing against the silence left in the wake of the dead.

"The past does not unmake you. It shapes you. The stone does not fight the wind that weathers it—it becomes something new beneath its touch."

Kemp's breath came slow, measured.

Ruiha saw the way his shoulders shifted—not in defeat, but in something else. Not resignation. Not surrender.

Understanding.

Vaelthys turned his gaze to her now, those molten eyes weighing her as heavily as they had Kemp.

"You both carry your past as chains," he said. "But what has been broken is not lost. What has been scarred is not ruined. There is beauty in what endures."

His great wings shifted, sending a ripple of air through the chamber.

"The first trial is passed," he said.

Then he turned, stepping into the darkness beyond. But his voice lingered, a final ember in the air.

"You are not what you have done. You are what you choose to become."

Chapter 9

Gunnar

Gunnar kept moving forward, the battlefield had dissolved behind him. The scent of blood faded, replaced by damp stone and the lingering trace of something ancient. Long shadows stretched across the ground, cast by flickering torches that burned without warmth. The air was stagnant, thick with the weight of ages. No wind, no sound beyond his own breath.

Tall ruins loomed around him, pillars broken but defiant, walls half-crumbled yet still standing. A place built for warriors, for trials. He did not trust it. His grip tightened around the axe haft, muscles tensed. This was not a battlefield where brute strength would carry him. He felt it in his bones.

Then, a sound.

Low, guttural. Not the snarl of any beast he knew. It slithered between the stone, reverberated through the air like something half-formed, caught between this world and another.

He turned, and it emerged.

A shape neither beast nor man, bleeding shadow, shifting stone. It was not alive, yet it moved. Not dead, yet it learned.

It had no eyes, but Gunnar felt its gaze burrowing into him, stripping him bare. Studying. Calculating.

He had fought monsters before. Creatures of fang and claw, creatures that tore flesh from bone. But this was different. This was no beast. No mindless horror.

This was a demon. And it knew him.

And it was watching.

He moved first, closing the distance in a burst of speed. His axe cut true, blade singing through the air.

Impact. Stone met steel, unyielding.

The moment his axe struck, its flesh hardened, shifting to meet the force of the blow. The demon did not flinch. It did not bleed. It reacted. It adapted.

Gunnar wrenched his axe free, retreating a step as the creature changed. Its stance adjusted, mirroring his own. A slow, deliberate mimicry. A measured response.

He attacked again, faster, sharper. Feints, real strikes, a brutal rhythm honed through years of war. It countered everything. Its movements refined, precise. It was learning him.

A blow came too close. He barely dodged, rolling aside as the stone fist crashed into the ground where he had stood. Dust and shattered rock filled the air.

It was getting ahead of him.

Gunnar's breath came harder now. Not from exhaustion, but from something worse. Instinct screamed to fight harder, to push forward with more force. That was how he won. That was how he always won.

But brute strength was failing him.

The creature did not grow tired. It did not hesitate. It did not fear. It only watched. And learned.

It was patient. Unfaltering. A thing without doubt or exhaustion.

Gunnar saw it now—not in the blur of movement, not in the clash of steel, but in the silence between. A fraction of a second, the way it moved—too precise, too measured. Not just countering. Following. Adapting.

This was not an enemy. It was a mirror.

A reflection of himself, shaped by his instincts. A trap forged in his own shadow.

Most warriors would have fought harder. Fought faster. They would have tried to break it. But winning here was not about strength. Nor speed.

His father had told him once, "A fool fights because he must. A wise dwarf fights because he chooses. And the wisest of all know when not to fight at all."

Gunnar had not truly understood then. He had thought it the words of someone who had seen too many council meetings. But now, standing in the ruin of this fight, the truth of it settled deep in his bones.

So he stopped.

Gunnar stilled.

The creature did not.

It hovered on the edge of motion, waiting—expecting his next move. When it did not come, it hesitated. A fraction of uncertainty. The first and only flaw in its design.

That was his opening.

He moved—not with power, not with intent, but with error. He moved wrong.

A step too soon. A weight shift too deep. A mistake no warrior would ever make.

It struck for an opening that did not exist, overextending in its own perfect imitation.

Gunnar turned, swift as a breaking current, redirecting the motion. His axe found its neck—not with brute force, but with timing. The demon's own momentum sealed its fate.

Stone cracked.

For the first time, it faltered.

Gunnar did not hesitate. He shifted, using its own weight, forcing it into itself. It resisted, but not enough. It could not. It had never learned to resist what it was.

It had never learned to stop.

The thing collapsed, unraveling in slow, crumbling dissolution. No scream. No thrash of dying limbs.

Only silence.

And the lingering impression that it understood.

And then, the ruins vanished.

Darkness swallowed the world for an instant before parting like mist. The ground beneath him was solid once more. The torches still burned, but the air felt lighter. His axe was in his hand, but it no longer felt the same.

No voice declared his victory. No sign marked the battles end.

But the path before him opened.

He moved forward.

Chapter 10

Anwyn

The sky hung low, bruised in shades of red and grey, as if the world itself had taken a wound. A chill bit through the morning air, damp with the scent of rain that had yet to fall. In the courtyard soldiers moved with quiet efficiency—sharpening blades, checking armour, tightening the straps on their war gear. The sound of whetstones scraping against steel filled the silence between them, a rhythm of preparation, of necessity.

Anwyn barely heard it.

She stood stiff-backed, watching as her father adjusted the straps of his cloak. Laoch's armour, once polished to a sheen, was dulled with wear, the edges of his pauldrons scuffed from countless battles. His katana hung at his hip, the hilt worn smooth by his grip. Behind him, Ignara crouched low, her golden eyes half-lidded as she exhaled slow plumes of steam into the cold air. She was waiting.

Anwyn wasn't ready.

She clenched her fingers around the leather of her gloves, the tension in her chest twisting tight.

"You'll miss his funeral," she said, voice steady but thin, stretched too tight.

Laoch's hands stilled.

Guilt flickered across his face, a shadow passing over the hard lines of his features. He opened his mouth, then shut it, exhaling instead through his nose. His jaw worked.

"I know," he said at last.

A silence settled between them, heavy with things left unsaid.

"I should stay," Laoch murmured, though there was no conviction in his voice. Just longing. Just grief. "I should—"

"No." Anwyn's breath trembled, but she forced the words out. "You can't."

She swallowed hard. Gunnar's loss sat like a blade lodged deep, but there was no more time for grief. Not yet.

"Gunnar would understand," she said, softer now. "He would *want* you to go. The elves, the dragons, King Luthar—they need you, Father. And I—"

She hesitated. Not because she doubted, but because saying it aloud made it real.

"I will be as I have always been," she finished, forcing a small smile. "My father's daughter."

Laoch's throat bobbed. He looked at her as though memorising every line of her face, like he might never see her again. His hands twitched at his sides.

Then, without warning, he stepped forward and pulled her into his arms.

Anwyn stiffened, surprised, then melted into the embrace. Her father was solid, unyielding, yet his grip trembled, just slightly.

"I am so proud of you, Anwyn," he whispered against her hair.

Something inside her cracked. She gripped him tighter.

When he pulled away, his hands lingered on her shoulders. He looked at her for a long moment, searching, as if trying to etch her into his memory.

"Lead them well," he said. "Make him proud."

And then he turned.

The loss of his warmth left her cold.

Laoch climbed onto Ignara's back with the ease of someone who had done so a thousand times before. The dragon let out a low rumble, almost a sigh, then spread her wings.

Anwyn held his gaze until the last moment.

Then, with a final beat of mighty wings, they were gone.

She stood there long after they had vanished beyond the clouds, the wind from their departure still stirring her hair.

A breath shuddered from her lungs.

Eira stepped beside her. She didn't speak, not at first. Just placed a hand on Anwyn's arm. A grounding touch. A mother's comfort.

"He will return," Eira said.

Anwyn nodded, but her throat felt thick. "I know. It's just…"

Her breath hitched. She clenched her jaw against it, but the words came anyway.

"I have lost so much already."

Eira didn't speak. Instead, she reached up, brushing a stray strand of hair from Anwyn's face—light, fleeting. Then, she wrapped her in her arms. The warmth of it, the quiet strength, was nearly enough to undo her completely.

The sky rumbled above, a low growl of something restless and unseen. Then, the first drop struck Anwyn's cheek—cold, trailing down like a tear that wasn't hers.

And as mother and daughter stood together, one truth settled over them like a shroud:

The dead do not wait for the living. But the living—they carry their ghosts, whether they wish to or not.

Laoch

The wind clawed at Laoch's cloak, whipping the edges against his armour as Ignara cut through the grey-streaked sky. She flew with an easy grace, wings stretching wide, muscles shifting beneath her scaled hide. Beneath them, Tempsford Keep grew smaller with each passing beat of her wings, its stone walls dark with soot, its banners torn and limp from the battle. It looked less like a fortress now and more like a wound.

Laoch didn't look back.

He kept his eyes forward, scanning the horizon where mountains rose like jagged teeth, half-swallowed by mist. The ache in his chest, though, refused to be ignored. It sat heavy beneath his ribs, pressing deeper with every breath.

He had left them. Again.

His hands tightened around the small horns on Ignara's, though he barely needed them. She knew what was weighing him down.

"You're thinking too much." She rumbled, her words curled through the wind, carrying the deep, resonant timbre of the dragon's voice.

Laoch exhaled sharply, shifting his grip. Though he said nothing in reply.

Ignara rumbled beneath him, the sound more felt than heard.

They flew in silence for a time, the cold tightening around them. Tempsford had long faded behind the mist, swallowed by distance. Before them, the land stretched out in rolling hills and thick forests, painted dull under the heavy sky. Somewhere ahead, Luthar and the elves had vanished.

The thought coiled in his gut.

"No response means one of two things." Dakarai's voice echoed from the war table, dry as stone. *"Either they're too deep in battle to send word, or there's no one left to send it."*

Laoch's jaw tightened.

The air thinned as Ignara climbed higher, breaking through the lowest stretch of cloud. Far below, the world blurred into shadows and pale light.

His mind, however, trailed behind him.

Eira.

Her warmth still clung to his memory, her embrace pressed into his skin like a brand. She had said nothing when he pulled her close, only held him too tightly, too long—as if she knew this would be the last time. He didn't tell her otherwise.

And then Anwyn.

He had seen the steel in her eyes, the way she forced herself to stand straight when she spoke. The weight she carried in her silence.

"Gunnar would understand."

Would he?

Laoch wanted to believe it. Needed to.

But war had a way of breaking what people *should* understand.

A gust of wind tore through them, rattling his pauldrons. He adjusted his seat, gripping Ignara's ridged spine for balance.

Ahead, the mountains grew closer, their peaks wreathed in mist. A place where shadows moved when they shouldn't. Where silence stretched too far.

Laoch narrowed his eyes. No fires. No movement. No sign of anything.

"The elves should have patrols." The words passed between them, sharper now.

"They should." Ignara's voice was quiet.

The wind carried nothing. No birds. No distant horns. Just silence.

Laoch reached for his katana.

And in silence, the weight of farewell pressed down like a blade against his ribs.

Karl hesitated at the door.

It wasn't hesitation of the usual kind—like when you weren't sure if the ale in the tankard was the good stuff or the stuff that might make you go blind for a few hours, or the hesitation before stepping into a room where a very large, very angry dwarf had just discovered that you'd been seeing his sister.

No. This was the hesitation of a dwarf standing before a door he wasn't quite sure he wanted to open. *Again.*

He was beginning to worry about how many doors in his life had done this to him. Given him pause. Made him think. That wasn't normal. Doors were meant to be opened, walked through, shut behind you. They were not meant to loom.

And yet—here he stood.

His fingers curled into a fist, then loosened again. He exhaled through his nose. The real reason, of course, wasn't the door.

It was what waited behind it.

Because inside was grief.

And grief had a way of making even the strongest warrior hesitate.

Still, he knocked.

"Come in," Anwyn's voice called. Steady. Measured.

Karl pushed the door open, stepping inside. The room was dimly lit, the fire low, throwing shadows that flickered against stone. Anwyn sat beside the cradle, her fingers tracing slow, absent patterns in the carved wood. The twins slept, wrapped in linen, impossibly small, impossibly new, in a world that had already taken too much from them.

Karl exhaled through his nose. *Too small. Too fragile for a world like this.*

"You look terrible," Anwyn murmured, not looking up.

Karl snorted. "Good. I was worried I'd been getting too pretty."

Anwyn made a sound—not quite a laugh, not quite anything at all. Just breath, shaped into something that might have been amusement if the world had been kinder.

Her fingers kept moving against the wood. A nervous tic, maybe. Or maybe something to do with the fact that if she kept her hands busy, she wouldn't have to think.

Karl stepped further into the room, resting a hand against the back of a chair. He didn't sit. Sitting felt like it would make things too real.

"I'm heading to the dungeons," he said.

Anwyn nodded. Still watching the twins. "I know."

A pause.

"Are you ready for this?" she asked.

Karl let out a slow breath, rubbing a hand over his face. "No. But I'm going anyway."

Another pause. This time, she looked at him, and for the first time since he'd stepped into the room, he saw it—the thing she wasn't letting show.

Grief clung to her like a second skin. Tight, inescapable. And gods, he knew the feeling.

"Make him suffer," she said, voice quiet.

Karl flexed his fingers, jaw clenching. "That's not my job."

Anwyn studied him. Not with judgment, not even with expectation. Just looking.

"But you want to," she said.

Karl's jaw tightened. "Yes."

She nodded. Looked away.

They understood each other, even in silence.

He sighed, staring at the flames curling in the hearth. "If I'm honest, I don't know what I'll do when I see him. I tell myself I'll be professional, that I'll do what needs to be done." His voice dropped, something raw threading through it. "But I also know that if he smirks, if he acts like none of this matters—" He broke off, shaking his head.

Anwyn didn't look away this time. Didn't blink. "You'll do what needs to be done."

Karl let out a dry laugh, though it didn't hold any humour. "You sound sure of that."

She turned back to the twins, reaching out, brushing a lock of fine hair from one of their impossibly small faces.

Her voice was quiet, measured—the kind of steady that took effort to hold.

"Because Gunnar wasn't just your prince, Karl. And he wasn't just your friend."

She hesitated, but only for a moment. Then, softer, "He was your brother. If not in blood, then in everything that mattered."

Even though he knew the words to be true, they landed heavy in his chest. He wasn't sure why.

A beat of silence. The fire crackled.

Karl swallowed, something thick in his throat. "And you? How are you...?" He trailed off, because what was the point in finishing? It was a useless question.

Anwyn didn't answer right away. She just adjusted the blankets around the twins.

When she finally spoke, her voice was quiet. "I still expect him to walk through that door."

Karl closed his eyes. Exhaled.

He understood. Too well.

There weren't any words for this. No clever remarks, no wisdom stolen from old soldiers.

So he reached forward, just briefly, and squeezed her shoulder. Not hard. Just enough.

Anwyn didn't pull away.

And for now, that was enough.

The stairs groaned under Karl's boots, each step dragging him further down into the belly of the keep.

He rolled his shoulders, stretching out the tightness there, but it wasn't leaving him. Wouldn't. The weight sat deep, pressing in.

Anwyn's voice echoed in his head. Not the strong, commanding one she used in council meetings, nor the sharp, measured one she used to cut men down with words alone. The other voice. The one that cracked, just a little.

"Gunnar was your brother."

A muscle twitched in his jaw.

Justice. That's what he was after, wasn't it?

Problem was, justice had never been his trade. Justice was measured. Justice was fragile. Karl had never been good at handling fragile things.

The air thickened the further he went. Cold. Stale. Heavy with the stink of sweat, piss, and the kind of blood that had long dried to the stone.

The dungeon door loomed ahead.

He shoved it open.

Duke Cahir sat slouched in the chair, shackled wrists raw from struggling against iron. His fine clothes were ruined, stained with filth, one sleeve torn clean off. He looked small. Not in size, but in presence.

And yet—

The bastard still found the strength to smirk.

"I was wondering when someone would come," he said, voice mild. "I assumed they'd send the Queen. But instead, I get… a dwarf…"

Karl shut the door behind him. Hard.

"Lucky you."

He pulled up a stool, but didn't sit. Instead, he folded his arms, watching, waiting.

Cahir tilted his head, all slow amusement, like a man pretending he wasn't chained to a chair in a dungeon beneath a ruined city.

"You don't belong here, you know." His tone was light, conversational. The kind of voice a man uses when he's got nothing left but words. "You're just a soldier. No family name worth a damn, no title, no claim. You're—what is the word?—replaceable."

Karl leaned forward, resting his hands on the table between them. Not reacting. Not yet.

"You know nothing about me." Karl growled.

"I know you're not important." Cahir smirked.

"Then it's a good thing I don't need to be important to kill you."

Cahir's smirk twitched.

Karl let the silence sit between them. Let the Duke stew in it.

Then—calm, measured—"The attack on Tempsford. The orders you gave. They were to burn, to destroy. Why?"

The Duke shrugged. Casual. Indifferent.

"Because it was war."

Karl shook his head.

"No. War is taking a city and keeping it. War is breaking your enemy's army. What you ordered? That was slaughter. That was the kind of thing a man does when there's nothing to be had after victory."

A flicker of something in Cahir's expression. Not fear. No, this bastard wasn't afraid. Not yet.

But frustration.

Karl pressed. Dug in.

"You weren't trying to win. You were covering something up."

Cahir laughed. Thin.

"Clever boy."

Karl didn't speak. Just let the silence stretch.

Long enough for Cahir to fill it.

And he did.

"It was never about the city."

Karl felt it then. A shift.

The way Cahir's smirk had gone tight, like the joke wasn't funny anymore. Like he knew the power wasn't truly his to wield.

"Who gave the order, Cahir?"

The Duke exhaled through his nose. Wet, bloody.

"You think you'll live long enough for the answer to matter?"

Karl punched him.

Not out of rage. Not out of hatred. Just because it needed doing.

The Duke's head snapped sideways. Blood dripped slow from his lip. He grinned through red-stained teeth.

"You think I'm afraid of you?"

Karl grabbed his collar, dragged him forward.

"Say it."

Cahir's breath ghosted over his face, ragged, damp, reeking of copper.

"You're already too late."

The torches flickered.

And for the first time, Karl felt something else.

Dread.

Chapter 11

Ruiha

Ruiha stood at the threshold of the trial, her breath shallow, muscles tensed. Beside her, Kemp hesitated, the eyes of the dead pressing down on both of them. The cavern held its silence close, thick with the ghosts of their last struggle. She could feel the stillness like a held breath, as if the world itself was waiting.

A heartbeat. A breath.

Then fire swallowed the air.

Heat surged forward like a living thing, searing against her skin before thought could catch up. The air thickened—cloying, suffocating, dense with the acrid stench of burning flesh and charred steel. Beneath her feet, the ground trembled, a slow, pulsing shudder, like the ribs of a beast rousing from uneasy sleep.

Smoke bled into the sky, black as spilled ink, curling in slow, insidious coils that devoured the horizon. Embers drifted like dying stars, flickering as they rose on unseen currents. The taste of ash clung to her tongue—dry, bitter. She exhaled ruin.

And then, beneath it all, a sound.

At first, a low murmur, lost beneath the howling wind. Then rising. A wail, stretched thin and sorrowful—a war horn, long and hollow, carrying its dirge across the battlefield.

The trial had begun.

Kemp

Kemp blinked against the glare, his mind catching up to what his body already knew: this was a war zone.

Flaming wreckage littered the land—siege engines torn apart by something far stronger than trebuchet fire, their wooden limbs clawing uselessly at the air. The ground was slick with blood, bodies strewn across it in tangled heaps. Some still twitched. The dying, indistinguishable from the dead.

And ahead, armies clashed.

Steel screamed against steel. Shields splintered under the weight of brutal blows. The air shuddered with battle cries and dying gasps, thick with the iron-stench of blood and churned earth.

Beside him, Ruiha shifted. He felt the movement more than saw it, the faint scrape of her boots against stone, the whisper of steel as she drew her blades. She was taut with purpose, her focus locked on the battlefield.

"A battlefield," she said, voice steady. "Another fight. Is this the trial?"

Kemp narrowed his eyes. "Not just any battle. Look at them."

He pointed to the enemy ranks, and Ruiha followed his gaze. There, among the chaos, a man with a melted face turned toward them, his features twisted beyond recognition. Kemp knew him. He had burned him alive.

Further down, a boy stood frozen mid-charge, no older than thirteen. His sword was too big for him, the tip dragging, his knuckles white around the hilt. Fear pinned him in place, his breath misting in the cold air.

Ruiha inhaled sharply, her body going still as if struck. "I knew him." Her voice was low, tight. She raised a hand, pointing. "He stole from one of the Sand Dragons. I caught him." A pause. The battle roared around them, but she was staring at the boy, lost in the memory. "I spared him."

Her grip on her blades tightened.

Kemp looked around at the other faces from his past. "This battlefield is not just a war. It is our past, come to haunt us."

Ruiha set her jaw. "Maybe we just have to win. End the battle, end the trial."

Kemp nodded. He had fought in wars before, seen battlefields where only one truth mattered: kill or be killed. That was the way of things.

His pulse steadied. Power surged through him.

Shadowfire roared from his fingertips, black flames twisting into a storm of destruction. The heat bit at his skin, but he welcomed it. He did not hesitate. He became the storm.

Blades melted before him. Bodies crumbled to ash. He carved through the battlefield, his power ripping through enemies like they were nothing.

And for a moment—it worked.

The battlefield fell silent. The fighting stopped. The enemy lay still.

Then—

They rose again.

Kemp staggered back, breath caught in his throat. The things before him were not the enemies he had cut down.

Their bodies blackened where his flames had touched them, their limbs twisted, grotesque. Wounds that should have ended them glowed with unnatural fire. Their eyes—empty, hollow pits—burned with something he did not understand.

The more he destroyed, the stronger they returned.

A hiss of frustration escaped him. He hurled another wave of shadowfire, but this time, the creatures didn't burn. They absorbed it. Their bodies cracked and pulsed with dark energy, their movements sharpening, accelerating.

Kemp cursed. "That's not—"

A blade flashed past his vision. Ruiha.

She was already moving, cutting through the twisted creatures with practiced precision. Her daggers sliced clean, severing limbs, impaling skulls. One lurched toward her, its fingers clawing for her throat. She ducked low, swept its legs from beneath it, and drove a blade into its chest before twisting sharply, sending another enemy stumbling back with a well-placed kick.

"It's getting worse," she said through gritted teeth, her eyes darting toward him.

Kemp gritted his teeth. He couldn't stop. If he hesitated, they'd be overwhelmed.

Another creature lunged at him. Kemp reacted instinctively, his magic surging to meet it. Shadowfire coalesced into a jagged spear in his hands—pure, lethal, decisive. He drove it forward with all his strength, impaling the beast through the chest. A clean kill.

Or so he thought.

The creature did not fall.

It snarled, blackened claws raking across the ground as it pulled itself forward, impaled but undeterred. Inch by grueling inch, it dragged its body along the length of the spear, its burning eyes locked onto his. Not fading. Not weakening.

Kemp's breath stilled. His fingers tightened around his weapon, as if willing it to finish the job. But the thing would not die. It clung to life with terrifying resolve.

His first instinct was to push more power into it. Burn it away. End it before it reached him.

But something about the way it moved—relentless, inevitable—sent a chill through him.

His magic had skewered its body, the wound should have been fatal. And yet it crawled forward, dragging itself along the length of his own weapon, undeterred.

Suddenly, a memory surfaced, unbidden, dragging him back through the years.

He was a boy again, crouched by the riverbank in the cool shade of his father's house. The sun dappled the water, and he had a stone in his hand, smooth and round. He cast it out, hopeful, only to watch it vanish beneath the surface without a trace. A failure. He reached for a bigger stone.

His father had been there, watching. A quiet man, stern but fair, his wisdom shaped by the land and the toil of his years. He crouched beside his son, picked up a smaller stone, and placed it in his palm.

"It's the little things, son. The small choices, the small changes—those are what shape the world."

Again, he threw, and again the stone sank. Another, and another, until at last, one skipped. Once. Twice. Three times. His heart had swelled, not from the small victory itself, but from the knowing. That if he kept at it, if he refined his hand and learned from his failures, he would succeed.

A single stone did not shape a river.

But many?

Many could carve through mountains.

Small steps. Tiny discoveries. They had built toward something greater.

He hadn't understood then how important that lesson was.

But now, standing amidst the charred ruin of the battlefield, watching the creature drag itself along his spear, refusing to die, he understood.

He had tried to end this in one stroke, one decisive act, as if power alone could cut the thread and unravel the whole tapestry. But the world did not work that way.

Vaelthys' voice rolled through the air like distant thunder. "Destruction feeds destruction. Did you think fire would burn only what you chose?"

Kemp staggered back, breath shallow. His gaze lifted from the corpse at his feet to the wasteland beyond. Not a battlefield—no, not anymore. The ground where his power had touched was blackened, stripped bare. Bodies twisted in unnatural shapes, some still smoldering, smoke curling from flesh. He had meant to end this quickly. Instead, he had only begun something worse.

One act of destruction was never just one act. It spread. Like fire. Like rot.

He had been a fool. He had believed—arrogantly—that if he burned away enough enemies, he could force change. That power, wielded in a single decisive moment, could rewrite everything.

But fire was never precise. It devoured without thought.

His hands trembled at his sides. His magic still simmered in his veins, eager to be called upon again, but he resisted.

This was no victory. This was a lesson. And he was only beginning to learn it.

Ruiha

Ruiha had always known battle. It was in her blood, in the marrow of her bones, a truth carved by hardship and sharpened by steel. She had fought and bled on the pitiless streets of Gecit, where only the strong ate and the weak were left to rot. She had endured the brutality of the gladiator pits, where survival only meant one step closer to death. She had marched across the war-scarred fields of Vellhor, where fate's cruel hand struck down countless before her eyes. She had made choices, hard as iron, sharp as a blade, and each had left its mark.

But now, amidst the clash of steel and the screams of the dying, something felt *wrong*.

This wasn't just another battle.

It was a reckoning.

A figure caught her eye—a boy in the ranks, too small to wield a sword, too thin to withstand a blow. His knuckles were white where they gripped the hilt, his arms trembling beneath the weight of iron. His face was streaked with dirt, his ribs sharp beneath the threadbare tunic. His eyes—hollow, starving—held nothing but the will to survive.

A memory surfaced, unbidden.

Rain. Cold, relentless. The alley reeked of rotting fish and unwashed bodies. A boy, half-buried in tattered blankets, huddled in the doorway of a butcher's shop.

Please. His voice was hoarse, his breath shallow. A single hand stretched toward her, fingers curled like claws.

Ruiha had stopped. Just for a moment.

She had coin. She had food. But she had also learned, long ago, that kindness had a price. That mercy, in Gecit, was another word for weakness.

So she had kept walking.

Not out of cruelty. Not even indifference. Survival had no room for kindness.

Now, years later, he stood before her, blade shaking, breath ragged, caught between life and death as surely as he had been all those years ago.

A cry split the air.

The boy's head snapped toward the sound. His hesitation cost him.

Steel flashed.

The enemy soldier moved with precision, cutting down the boy as easily as a farmer scything wheat.

Ruiha felt herself moving before she knew why.

Too slow.

The boy collapsed.

For a breath, no one else seemed to notice. The battle raged on, steel ringing, men screaming, the world shaking beneath the weight of war. The boy gasped once, his body curling inward. His fingers twitched, reaching for something unseen.

His sword lay just out of reach.

She dropped to a knee beside him.

His lips parted, but no sound came. Only his eyes moved—still wide, still hollow, still afraid.

And then, nothing.

A street orphan. A child of the alleys. One she had walked past long ago.

One she had let die a second time.

Ruiha's breath caught.

Her fingers clenched around her weapons, but for the first time in years, they felt like dead weight.

"We thought this was a battle," she murmured. "But this isn't about fighting. It's about the cost." She exhaled, her voice barely above the din of war. "Every moment. Every action. Every choice I ever made."

Her gaze swept the battlefield, and at last, she saw it.

The bodies strewn across the mud, the broken weapons, the blood pooling in the earth—it was more than carnage. More than victory or defeat.

It was the weight of every decision. The echoes of lives taken, lives spared.

This *was* war.

Not of swords and steel.

But of consequence.

And consequence had no mercy.

Kemp

The battlefield did not fade.

It lingered.

The scent of charred flesh clung to the air, thick and unshaken. The twisted corpses remained where they had fallen, their scorched limbs frozen in grotesque angles. The ground beneath Kemp's feet was blackened, stripped of life, the earth itself wounded by his fire.

He had tried to end the battle with a decisive stroke. But there were no endings, only consequences.

His breath was slow, measured, but his chest felt heavy. Beside him, Ruiha stood rigid, staring at the fallen boy. Her grip on her blades was tight enough that her knuckles had gone pale. She did not move. She did not speak.

Kemp looked away. He understood that silence.

He had been wrong.

Power was not an answer, only an echo of what had already been done. He had set the field ablaze, believing he could burn away the past, but fire did not choose what it destroyed.

A shadow loomed ahead.

Vaelthys.

The air grew thick, pressing down like a storm about to break. A weight—ancient, immense—settled on Kemp's skin, sinking into his bones.

The dragon moved with purpose, slow, deliberate, each step pressing deep into the scorched ground. His gaze dragged over them, cold and knowing, as if he had already judged them and found them lacking.

Kemp straightened, forcing himself to meet the dragon's eyes.

Vaelthys' wings shifted, stirring the ash in slow, whispering eddies, the fine dust curling like dying breath across the charred ground.

His eyes burned—deep, endless. But his expression remained unchanged.

No fury. No pride. Just the patience of something older than steel and war, watching as another empire tottered toward ruin, as it always had. As it always would.

The dragon halted beside them.

The battlefield sprawled in every direction, a graveyard of the broken and burned. Silence hung heavy, thick as the stench of charred flesh and blood-soaked earth.

Kemp swallowed. His hands trembled at his sides, fingers still itching for power he dared not call upon. He had wanted to believe this was a trial. A test to be won.

A soft rasp of breath came from beside him. Ruiha shifted, rolling her shoulders as if shaking off a thought that had settled too deep. She hadn't spoken since the boy had fallen. Hadn't so much as looked at Kemp.

Her blades, still slick with blackened ichor, hung loose in her hands, her grip uncertain for the first time since the fighting had begun. But she did not sheathe them.

She was waiting. Not for another enemy—there were none left.

For the lesson neither could ignore.

Kemp exhaled, meeting Ruiha's gaze. There was no anger in it, no sharp edge, only a quiet sadness. A knowing.

Kemp swallowed. Ruiha had seen it.

This had never been about victory.

He looked down at the ruin before him.

But now, standing in the wreckage of his own making, he wondered.

Had this ever been a trial at all?

Or had it been a reckoning?

Vaelthys did not look at the dead. Only at Kemp.

"A blade is swung in a moment. A fire is lit in an instant. But neither battle nor ruin is shaped in a single act."

Kemp swallowed, his throat dry. The battlefield lay still, but he could feel it—the weight of every choice that had led them here, pressing down on his shoulders.

Vaelthys watched him, unmoving, vast and unreadable. Then the dragon spoke again, his voice like distant thunder, low and absolute.

"Power alone does not change the world. It only marks it."

Kemp clenched his fists. He had wanted to end this, to burn it all away, but fire did not choose what it destroyed. His gaze flickered to Ruiha—her knuckles white around her blades, her breath slow, measured. She understood. Had understood before him.

Vaelthys shifted, the air thickening with his presence. "It is the small choices—over years, over lifetimes—that carve the path of history. That build or break empires. That shape gods or monsters."

The words settled over them like falling ash.

Kemp's fingers twitched at his sides. He had spent so long wielding his power, worrying that it could change everything in a single moment. But that had been a lie.

Vaelthys' golden eyes burned into his.

"A kingdom is not lost in one day, nor is it built in one. The weight of every act, every choice, lingers long after the fire has burned out."

Silence.

The battlefield around them began to fade, swallowed by shadow, the dead sinking into the earth like embers winking out. But Kemp knew they were not gone. Nothing was ever truly gone.

Not the fire. Not the wounds. Not the choices that had led them here.

And not the choices still to come.

He said nothing. There was nothing to say.

Vaelthys began to move again, his form shifting, breaking apart like mist in the wind. The battlefield quivered, the edges of the world fraying as if it had never been real at all.

And still, the lesson remained.

Ruiha exhaled beside him, the sound barely audible. Her shoulders lowered—just slightly—as if she had been carrying something unseen.

Kemp looked down at his hands.

The battlefield dissolved, and they stood once more in silence.

The trial was over.

But something told Kemp the real test had only just begun.

Chapter 12

Gunnar

Gunnar woke mid-stride, his breath a torn rasp in his throat. His legs burned, muscles tight with the kind of exhaustion that came from days, no… weeks of running. Yet his mind held no memory of the journey.

The ground seemed to betray him with every step, shifting and sliding, treacherous. It was not earth, nor stone—something more fickle, something that did not welcome him. The sand beneath his boots writhed, a restless tide of whispering grains, seeking to swallow him whole.

The wind raged through the dunes, a savage thing of heat and hunger, howling as it tore across the sand. It carved into his skin like a blade, peeling away what little protection remained. Each breath was an effort, the air thick with heat, searing his lungs with every inhale. The desert pressed against him like a living thing, not content to simply burn—it sought to burrow into him, to find the spaces between flesh and armor, to coil around his ribs like molten chains, tightening with every second.

He staggered once but did not fall. A second time. His footing slipped, the ground shifting beneath him, but still, he pressed forward.

Then came the feeling. Something was behind him.

He could not hear it. Nor could he see anything . It was something deeper. A presence, vast and patient, lurking at the edges of his senses. A thing that did not need to be seen to be known. A thing that had always been there.

Gunnar turned, axe raised, though he had no memory of drawing it. Shadows moved—no, they rippled, shifting in the wind like ink spilled in water. But when his eyes fixed upon them, they were gone.

But they had been there. He knew it as surely as he knew his own name.

His fingers flexed around the haft of his axe, the weight of the weapon grounding him, reminding him that he was still here. Still real. But that presence... it was watching. Waiting.

The wind shifted, carrying the faintest whisper—a voice, or something older than language itself.

A hunt had begun.

A sudden force slammed into his back, driving him forward. Pain lanced through him as sharp claws scraped across the unprotected flesh of his neck—not deep, but enough to set his nerves on fire.

He spun, axe cutting a vicious arc through the air. Nothing.

Only the wind, howling its laughter.

Whatever this thing was, it wasn't trying to kill him.

Not yet, anyway.

The land shifted beneath him. Heat vanished, torn away in an instant, replaced by a biting cold that cut to the bone. The dunes hardened beneath his feet, sand turning to ice. He stumbled, boots skidding across the slick surface, his breath rising in thick, misting clouds.

His limbs slowed, stiffening with the creeping frost. Each step a battle against the cold that gnawed at his bones. His wounds did not clot. Nor did they bleed. It remained—an open thing, neither healing nor worsening, just as the pain never dulled.

A second attack. This time, he saw it.

A blur of black against the snow. Fast. Unnaturally so. He barely raised his weapon before it struck, claws flashing, teeth bared in something almost like a grin. He lashed out, felt the axe connect, solid and true—only for the thing to vanish like mist dispersing in sunlight.

He was not sure if this thing could be killed.

Was it sent here purely to make him suffer?

The sky cracked. A storm howled into existence, the ice swallowed by wind and fire. Sand returned, then stone, then nothing at all. The world remade itself in chaos, landscapes forming and dissolving in the space between breaths.

And always, the shadow followed.

Time lost meaning. Minutes, hours, days—he no longer knew. Every time he collapsed, the world waited. The whispers came then, slithering through the shifting dark.

"Lie down."

"Rest."

"End it."

They did not command him. They did not beg. There was no deceit, no trickery.

They simply offered a release. A way out.

Their voices curled at the edges of his resolve, whispering through the fractures forming in his mind. Soft. Patient. Certain.

He wanted to listen.

He wanted to let go.

But then…

A voice. Not theirs.

It drifted through the darkness, as soft as a breath, as fragile as dying embers. So quiet he almost missed it. So weak it was almost swallowed whole.

Yet it found him.

Luck or fate? Gunnar didn't know. Maybe it didn't matter.

"Promise me you'll come back."

A memory, a ghost of warmth in the cold. A face he could not quite see, but the voice—he knew it. Someone who had mattered. Someone who still did.

He rose.

The storm screamed. The demons came again. Claws found flesh, teeth found bone. He did not fight back.

He endured.

The wind raged. The heat burned. The cold swallowed. He moved forward.

They struck again. He stumbled, but did not fall.

The world shifted once more, but this time, something changed.

The storm vanished.

The shadows were gone.

Gunnar stood, alone, his body whole once more. The pain lingered, the scars carved deep into flesh and bone, but he breathed. He was still here.

And before him, a path opened.

He moved forward.

Chapter 13

Anwyn

Anwyn sat stiff-backed in the Queen's waiting chamber, fingers laced tightly in her lap. The fire in the hearth crackled softly, sending waves of warmth against the stone walls, but it did little to thaw the cold knot in her chest. Outside, the corridors of the keep echoed with the distant clang of metal, the murmur of voices beyond the heavy doors.

Across from her, Baron Roderic sat with one hand resting against his bruised jaw. The deep purple swelling stood in sharp contrast against his otherwise pale skin, the remnants of Gunnar's furious act before his death. Anwyn's gaze kept flicking to it, no matter how she tried to focus on anything else. The guilt sat in her stomach like a stone.

She drew in a breath. "I'm sorry."

Roderic raised an eyebrow, his fingers brushing the bruising with a wry smirk. "For what? For your Gunnar punching me? Or for the fact I was too slow to stop it?"

Anwyn's lips pressed together. "For both." She hesitated, then met his gaze fully. "And for everything else. For what you did for my children. You saved their lives."

Roderic exhaled sharply through his nose. "I did what anyone would have."

She shook her head. "No. You didn't. You could've turned away. You could've left me to fate." Her voice was quiet, but it held weight. "You didn't."

For a long moment, he said nothing. Then, he gave a small shrug, his expression softening. "A man does what he can to protect what matters. I'm a father, I understand that much."

Anwyn swallowed. "Thank you."

Roderic simply nodded.

The silence between them stretched, this time more settled. The tension that had been there, the unspoken weight of Gunnar's blow, seemed to ease. It wasn't gone entirely, but it no longer sat like a wall between them.

After a moment, Roderic leaned back slightly, studying her with a quiet intensity. "And you?"

Anwyn blinked. "What about me?"

His gaze didn't waver. "How are you holding up?"

The question struck deeper than she expected. She let out a breath, staring down at her hands. "I feel like I should be stronger," she admitted. "Like I should have control of it by now. But it's..." She clenched her fingers tighter. "It's consuming. Like a storm I can't see through."

Roderic didn't speak, just let her continue.

"But," she said, voice steadier, "the twins. They keep me anchored. I have to be strong for them."

Roderic gave a small nod. "That's something."

She nodded too. "Karl and I will begin preparing Gunnar's funeral." The words came out even, but her chest ached as she said them. "It's the least I can do."

Roderic watched her for a beat before shifting the subject. "And the little ones? How are they?"

A small, almost wistful smile touched her lips. "Owen and Freya."

At their names, Roderic's brow lifted slightly. "Lovely names. Do they mean anything?"

Before she could answer, the door to the council chamber creaked open.

Karl stepped through, his presence tense, his expression unreadable. His gaze flickered between them. "You better come in."

Anwyn and Roderic exchanged a look. Whatever discussion had just happened inside, it was serious.

The war chamber was dimly lit, shadows pooling in the corners where torchlight failed to reach. The air carried the scent of old parchment, damp stone, and lingering battle. A map stretched across the table, its inked lines charting the fractures of a world on the verge of collapse. Queen Kathrynne sat at its head, her gaze as sharp as the ornamental sword mounted on the wall behind her. She was unreadable, a specter of control amidst the fraying edges of their war.

Karl wasted no time.

"Cahir is holding something back."

Anwyn's stomach tightened, though she kept her face still. The name alone was enough to summon the bitter taste of unease.

Karl planted his hands on the table, fingers pressing into the grain. His jaw was tight, his words measured. "He wasn't afraid. Not truly. He wanted us to think he was, but it was a performance. And he let something slip."

His gaze flicked to the Queen. "He said we were already too late."

Silence settled over the chamber, a thick, suffocating thing. Even the torches seemed to burn quieter.

Roderic, arms crossed, broke it first. "What does that mean?"

Karl exhaled through his nose. "I don't know. And that's the problem."

Kathrynne's fingers tapped against the table, slow and deliberate. "It could be anything. A trap. A force we haven't accounted for. A weapon we don't yet understand."

"Or something worse," Anwyn murmured.

Karl nodded, his gaze sharp. "Exactly. And we need to find out." He hesitated, just a fraction of a moment, then straightened. "But I need to know my limits."

Kathrynne's attention locked onto him, assessing. "Explain."

Karl's expression remained unreadable. "In Dreynas, things are different. You rule here. Your laws stand. I need to know exactly how far I can go to extract the truth."

A chill curled through the chamber, though the fire burned strong.

Kathrynne didn't blink. "There are no limits."

Anwyn spoke without hesitation. "Do what you must."

Karl studied them both, searching for doubt. He found none.

Then, he smiled.

Not a warm smile. Not cruel, either. Something in between—something sharp. Knowing.

The meeting was over.

As Karl stepped away from the table, the air shifted, the weight of unspoken agreement pressing into the stone walls. Whatever came next would not be clean.

Cahir was about to learn what it meant to run out of time.

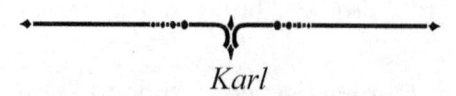

Karl

Karl rolled up his sleeves. Not that it was necessary, but it was a ritual. A good torturer needed rituals. Like a butcher sharpening his knives, like a surgeon washing his hands. Set the tone. Let the subject know this isn't some passing unpleasantness. This is precision work. This is art.

Duke Cahir watched with swollen eyes, his lips cracked, his once-pristine finery torn and soaked through with sweat. He'd pissed himself an hour ago. Maybe two. Time blurred in a room like this. He flinched when Karl stepped closer, the iron-shod heels of his boots ringing off the stone floor.

Karl grinned, all teeth. "Let's make this simple, eh? You tell me what I need to know, and I don't have to get creative."

Cahir tried to square his shoulders, but his body betrayed him with a shudder. His jaw worked before words stumbled out. "You—you want information? I can give you information. But I'll need assurances. A cell. A comfortable one. Books, a—"

Karl laughed. "You think we're negotiating?" He grabbed a dagger from the table behind him, turning it in his hands, watching how the torchlight danced along the edge. "I'm getting what I need either way, Duke. You can play the helpful little courtier and keep your tongue, or..." He pressed the dagger's tip just under Cahir's fingernail, pushing until a thin bead of blood welled up.

Cahir bit down on a scream.

Karl sighed. "That was the kind way." He set the dagger down and took up a set of iron tongs. "This next part? You're not going to like it."

Cahir's shrieks rang against the stone walls. Karl took his time. Torture wasn't about the tools. It was about the pacing. You had to let them taste the pain before drowning them in it. He started with the fingernails—nothing fancy, just the slow, deliberate pull of keratin from flesh. Then the fingers themselves, squeezed until the bones shattered like dry twigs. He worked through the joints with methodical precision, snapping knuckles, twisting sockets, peeling skin like the rind of an orange.

Cahir sobbed, blubbered, pleaded. He'd offer anything—titles, gold, his family's estates, all the wealth he had. Karl ignored it. Information was what mattered. Not deals. And besides, there was a certain joy in the work. A rhythm to it. By the time he reached the Duke's knees, he was humming to himself, elbow-deep in ruin.

Cahir had stopped screaming. Now he just whimpered, breath coming in hitching gasps. Karl leaned in close, his breath hot against Cahir's blood-slicked face. "You ready to talk?"

Cahir gagged on his own breath, chest heaving, hands twitching in their bindings. His throat convulsed, trying to swallow sobs that refused to be buried.

"Please," he rasped, voice breaking like shattered glass. "I'll talk—I'll tell you everything."

Karl crouched in front of him, rolling his shoulders, his gaze steady and unreadable. The torch beside them flickered, its glow licking across the blood stained walls.

Karl wiped his hands on a filthy rag, smearing away blood and grime. "Go on, then."

Cahir shuddered. His fingers curled into fists, ruined nails biting into the flesh of his palms. He wet his lips. Swallowed.

"They… they don't stay dead." His voice trembled.

Karl's brows knitted together. "What?"

"The Drogo." Cahir squeezed his eyes shut as if he could block out the memories. "They've—they've done something. The ones we kill… they come back."

Karl stilled. "What do you mean, 'come back'?"

Cahir let out a ragged exhale. "Not like ghosts. Not spirits. Their bodies—" His breath hitched. "They rise. Their limbs work again, their eyes are wrong, but they move. They *fight*. They *understand*—"

He made a strangled noise, rocking slightly where he sat.

Karl tilted his head. "You're saying the Drogo are raising their dead?"

"Not just theirs." Cahir's bloodshot eyes met Karl's, filled with something deeper than fear—something like horror. "Ours too."

The silence stretched taut.

Karl's jaw flexed. He slowly lowered himself onto a wooden crate, watching Cahir like a man measuring the weight of a blade. "You're telling me," he said evenly, "that the dead—*all* the dead—can be turned?"

Cahir gave a jerky nod, his breath coming in sharp gasps. "They—" His voice cracked. "They aren't gone. They're *repurposed*."

The word sat heavy between them.

Karl inhaled slowly. "How?"

Cahir flinched. "Magic."

Karl scoffed. "Of course it's magic, you shit stain. *What kind?*"

Cahir's throat bobbed, his breath hitched again, and his gaze darted around the tent as if afraid of being overheard. "Junak or Nergai. He's—he's something else now. I don't know if he was ever alive, if he ever *died*. But Nergai's the one pulling the strings. He bends them to his will. He *makes* them fight."

Karl's grip on his dagger tightened. "You're saying Nergai controls the dead?"

Cahir nodded frantically. "Like—like dolls on strings." He shivered violently, his skin slick with sweat. "I saw men I fought beside last week standing in the Drogo ranks. Their bodies cut open, their faces—" He bit his lip so hard it split. "They looked at me. *Looked at me*. But there was nothing behind their eyes. Nothing left of them."

Karl said nothing. His mind had already gone somewhere else.

To Gunnar.

His friend's body, broken and bloodied. Death with honour.

Gunnar, pale and empty-eyed, standing on the wrong side of the battlefield.

A slow chill settled over Karl's bones, seeping deeper than any winter wind.

"What if..." His voice was quiet. "What if he's not resting?"

Cahir let out a strangled sob. "No one is."

The torch sputtered. Outside, the wind howled.

Karl exhaled through his nose, slow and steady.

This wasn't war. War had rules, even the ugly kind. This was something else.

Nergai wasn't fighting battles. He was rewriting the laws of existence.

Cahir shuddered violently. "I've told you everything. Please. *Please*—just kill me."

Karl rose, rolling his shoulders as though shaking off a weight. His dagger gleamed in the firelight as he wiped it clean against his sleeve.

"Oh, I'll kill you," he murmured. "But only after I make sure I don't have any more questions."

Cahir's scream rang long into the night.

And Karl listened.

Anwyn

The chamber lay in the grip of flickering firelight, torches sputtering in their iron sconces, their glow licking at the rough-hewn stone walls. Shadows stretched and recoiled, twisting like restless wraiths. The air hung thick with the bitter scent of old smoke, the must of parchment, and the sharp bite of spiced wine soured in abandoned goblets. At the room's heart stood a great wooden table, its surface gouged and pitted from years of use. Maps lay sprawled across it, their edges curled, ink-stained with hurried notes and battle plans scrawled in an unsteady hand.

A hush lingered in the chamber, heavy with unspoken dread. Anwyn's gaze shifted to Dakarai and Kris, who stood stiff-backed, their faces carved from stone, waiting. The weight of what was left unsaid pressed against the walls, thick as the smoke curling from the torches.

At the head of the table, Queen Kathrynne sat in regal stillness, her expression unreadable, a pillar of authority amid the encroaching tension. To the side, Baron Roderic sifted through a stack of papers, the rustling an unwelcome intrusion into the quiet, his movements quick and restless.

Karl stepped forward, and the room stilled.

It wasn't just his words, though they carried enough weight to crush bones. It was him. The way he moved—slow, deliberate, a dwarf-shaped hammer that had already broken something to get here. His face was taut, lines carved deep, shadows heavy beneath his eyes. A warrior's face. A weary one.

And then there was the blood.

Not his.

It crusted his nails, flaked from the calloused ridges of his fingers. Dark, dry, too much of it. The smell curled in the space between them—iron, sweat, something deeper, something worse.

Anwyn didn't flinch. She kept her hands still, her breath even, though something deep in her gut twisted. He had made Cahir bleed for this truth. And he had not done it quickly.

Karl exhaled through his nose, thick shoulders rising, falling. A soundless sigh. "They're raising the dead," he said, voice like ground stone, rough and scraped clean of anything but certainty.

No one spoke.

The fire crackled in the pit behind him, throwing long shadows. The kind that stretched over faces, made them longer, hollower.

Karl let the silence fester. Let the words settle into them like a rusted axe buried in bone.

"Not just their own," he went on. His voice was hoarse, the edges frayed, but the steel beneath it was still sharp. A voice of command. A voice of war. "Ours too."

A sharp breath from someone behind her. A muttered curse.

Anwyn didn't move. She studied Karl instead, the way one might study a blade that's been bloodied one too many times.

The fire spat behind him, illuminating the deep lines in his face, the sharp cut of his thick brows, the old scars half-hidden beneath his red beard. Not an old dwarf. Not yet. But war had aged him faster than most.

He rolled his shoulders, flexed his hands—not in discomfort, not in guilt, but because even dwarves couldn't hold their muscles clenched forever.

"Anyone who falls in battle can be turned," Karl said. He ground his teeth for a moment, then spoke again. "Stripped of their will. Bound to Nergai."

The words should have felt impossible. Should have been the kind of thing that men laughed off, dismissed as battlefield ghost stories.

No one laughed.

Because Karl didn't say things he wasn't sure of. And because the blood on his hands told the truth.

"He commands them," Karl said finally. "Controls them."

Anwyn saw it then—just a flicker of something, a hesitation that wasn't quite hesitation. Not fear. Not shame. Just the momentary weight of what he'd done to get this truth.

It wasn't that he cared. It was that it hadn't been enough.

She exhaled slowly, careful to keep her voice measured. "You're sure?"

Karl's dark eyes flicked to hers, steady, unwavering.

"I made sure," he said.

And that was the end of it.

A silence settled over the chamber, thick as fog.

Baron Roderic exhaled sharply, his eyes flicking to Anwyn. Something unspoken passed between them.

"We knew they could do this," he murmured. "I—" He hesitated, his fingers curling into a fist on the table.

Anwyn held his gaze, her expression darkening before a single nod. "The assassin."

He nodded stiffly. "But whole armies? That... that is beyond anything I ever imagined."

The moment stretched, pressing down on them all. Then Roderic's hand slammed against the table. "By the gods, if this is true, then every battlefield feeds them. Every fight makes them stronger."

Kris cleared his throat. "And we're supposed to win how, exactly?"

Dakarai exhaled slowly through his nose, shaking his head. "No. The real question is how you win when every fight only makes your enemy stronger."

Another silence. The truth of it hung heavy in the room.

Anwyn sat with her hands clasped, her gaze moving across the assembled faces. "We don't know where Luthar's army is. No word from the elves. No sign of the dragons. And Ruiha—"

Her throat tightened. "No one has heard from her or Kemp in months. If they fail with the Elderflame—"

Karl's voice was flat. "We lose. No Elderflame, no war. Just a slow death."

Queen Kathrynne's fingers drummed against the table. "We are playing blindfolded against an enemy who sees everything. Every move we make, he will counter. Every warrior we send, he can turn."

Baron Roderic, ever pragmatic, shook his head. "Then we do not move until we can see."

Anwyn exhaled, pressing her fingers against her temples. "We need time. We don't have the numbers to strike blindly. If we engage now, we risk annihilation. Our best course is to prepare. Fortify Tempsford. Stockpile food and weapons. Train the people for siege warfare. If we are to make a stand, we must be ready for it."

Roderic nodded. "We wait for Laoch and Ignara to return. We send another team to find Ruiha and Kemp. We need to know where Luthar's forces are. The elves. The dragons. We cannot be alone in this."

"And the Drogo?" Kris asked, arms crossed. "If we can't fight them, what do we do? Sit here and wait to be overrun?"

"No," Anwyn said, shaking her head. "We engage only when necessary. Controlled skirmishes. We pick the time, the place, and the terms of battle."

Roderic scoffed. "That's assuming we even know where they are."

Anwyn met his gaze. "We will. We send out scouts. We track their movements. If they're advancing, we control how and where we meet them."

Dakarai exhaled slowly. "And if they're not advancing? What if they're waiting, gathering their forces, while we're out there wasting men on skirmishes?"

"Then we make sure every fight is on our terms," Anwyn countered. "We don't throw our people into the dark and hope for the best. We strike where we have an advantage—supply lines, vulnerable patrols, isolated groups. We don't let them settle. We don't let them prepare."

Kris let out a short breath, rubbing his jaw. "Fine. We harass them, weaken them where we can. But that still doesn't solve the bigger problem."

"The dead," Roderic muttered.

Anwyn nodded. "Exactly. Which is why we burn our fallen. Every battlefield must be cleansed before they can turn our dead against us."

"Easier said than done," Dakarai said grimly. "What if we're forced into a retreat? What if we don't have time?"

"Then we make time," Anwyn said, voice steady. "We use Ignara once she returns. Fire squads. Oil reserves at every outpost. Pre-set pyres if necessary. This isn't just about winning battles anymore. It's about denying them more bodies."

Silence stretched between them.

Kris sighed, arms still folded. "So no open war. Just bleeding them where we can until we know we have a way to win."

Anwyn nodded. "Exactly."

Dakarai exhaled through his nose, shaking his head. "Hard to win a war like this."

Anwyn met his gaze. "Harder still if we let them choose how this war is fought."

Another silence. The truth of it hung heavy in the room.

Queen Kathrynne cleared her throat. "Then it is decided. We hold. We prepare. We wait for word from Ruiha, Kemp, Laoch, and Ignara. But if they don't return—"

A heavy silence. No one wanted to say it.

Finally, Anwyn spoke. "Then we make our last stand here."

With reluctant nods and murmurs, the council disbanded. Chairs scraped against stone, the sound grating in the heavy silence. One by one, they rose, shadows stretching long beneath the flickering torchlight. Footsteps echoed through the chamber, uneven, hesitant, some quick with purpose, others slow with thought. One by one, they drifted into the dim corridors beyond, swallowed by the dark, carrying the weight of what had been decided—or what hadn't.

Anwyn remained seated, her gaze fixed on the maps before her. Thin lines carved across parchment—routes, strategies, defenses—meant to shape the course of this war. But battle meant nothing if the dead refused to stay dead. She traced a finger along the inked paths, each mark a shackle tightening around her throat.

Dakarai approached silently. For the first time that night, his voice softened. "How are the little ones?"

Anwyn blinked at the shift, her mind still tangled in battle plans. But the weight in her chest eased, if only for a breath. "They're with Elara now."

Dakarai nodded, his expression unreadable, but Anwyn caught the way his features softened at the mention of Elara's name.

For a moment, neither of them spoke. The quiet stretched, fragile and fleeting. Then the torches guttered in their sconces, their flames writhing, casting shadows that stretched like grasping fingers.

This war was no longer about victory.

It was about enduring long enough to witness the end.

Chapter 14

Ruiha

Stillness.

It stretched around Ruiha, vast and motionless, neither light nor dark. No breath of wind, no weight of presence—only silence, endless and unbroken. A place between moments, where nothing began and nothing ended.

She sat cross-legged on what should have been the ground, but it had no texture, no warmth, no weight beneath her. Across from her, Kemp mirrored her posture, elbows resting on his knees, gaze lost in the void around them.

Nothing had happened since the trial ended. No voice. No summons. No next trial.

And that thought gnawed at her.

"Did we fail?" she asked finally, her voice quieter than she intended.

Kemp didn't answer at first. Then, after a long pause, he sighed. "Feels like it, doesn't it?"

She flexed her fingers, but there was no sensation, no edge of steel, no tangible reminder that she still existed. It was as if they were floating in limbo, trapped in some forgotten place.

"Maybe this is it," she murmured.

Kemp frowned. "No."

"Then why are we just sitting here? Why isn't anything happening?"

"Because it's not over," he said, but his voice lacked conviction. He ran a hand through his hair, exhaling hard. "Maybe we just need to wait."

Ruiha let out a quiet laugh, bitter and low. "I've never been good at waiting."

He smirked faintly, but it didn't last. The silence stretched again, and it sat like lead in her chest.

She hesitated, the words forming before she could stop them. "I used to think... if I could just find one thing, one moment, that would redeem me, everything I did would be undone."

Kemp turned his head toward her.

She exhaled, tilting her face toward the void above them. "All those years in Sandarah, all the people I killed—the innocent ones, the ones who begged, the ones who never had a chance—I thought if I just did enough good, it would wipe it away."

She swallowed, the confession settling heavy in her throat.

"But it doesn't work like that."

Kemp was watching her now, his gaze unreadable. She forced a breath, fingers clenching against her knees.

"No matter what I do, no matter how many people I help, how many lives I try to save, it doesn't change the past. It doesn't—" She broke off, jaw tightening. "I've been chasing something I can never catch. And I don't know if that means I'll never be free of it."

Kemp shifted forward, leaning his arms against his knees. "You're wrong."

She scoffed, shaking her head. "Kemp—"

"No, listen," he interrupted, voice firm.

She frowned, but he continued.

"The moment you left Sandarah, you started down a different path. And every step, every decision, has brought you here. You saved me. You fought for the dwarves. You fought in this war not because you were ordered to, but because you believed in it."

His voice softened.

"You severed your bond with Ignara to save *me*, Ruiha. You lost something that meant everything to you, because it was the *right* thing to do. *You* chose that."

Her breath caught in her throat.

"If you were still the person you were back then," Kemp said, "you wouldn't be sitting here, asking if redemption is possible. You wouldn't care."

She swallowed hard. The words should have felt like an empty reassurance. They should have felt hollow, the way all justifications did when the weight of the past pressed too heavily against her ribs.

But somehow, they didn't.

Because they were true.

She had spent so long trying to erase the past, to find the one act that would undo it all—but that wasn't how it worked. Nothing was erased. But everything built upon what came before.

She blinked hard, looking down at her hands, then back at him.

Kemp met her gaze. The truth settled between them, solid and unshakable.

And then—

A shift in the air.

Ruiha inhaled sharply, head snapping up as the void shuddered.

A deep, familiar presence coiled around them, vast and timeless, and when she turned, Vaelthys was standing before them.

Golden eyes burned in the darkness, watching them with something unreadable—something ancient.

"You begin to understand," the dragon rumbled.

Kemp rose slowly, muscles taut. Ruiha followed, the stillness folding inward—as if the moment itself had been waiting.

Vaelthys studied him.

"You believe your past has shaped you into something monstrous," he said, voice low and thunder-wrought. "And it has. But a monster does not wonder if he is one. A monster does not question the path he treads. It simply destroys."

Kemp's breath caught.

The dragon stepped forward, vast and coiled with power. "You have walked the edge of ruin. Held in your hands the kind of strength that could shatter empires. But true power is not in destruction. It is in restraint."

Kemp's fists curled.

Vaelthys' voice hardened, striking like hammer against iron. "You have committed atrocities. But you are not the sum of them. Peace is not the absence of violence. It is the mastery of it."

Ruiha watched Kemp's expression shift — the same quiet war she had once fought, now carved across his face. Shame. Doubt. Fear.

And then... stillness.

His fists eased. His breath slowed.

Their eyes met.

Vaelthys exhaled. The darkness stirred.

"You are capable of great destruction," he said. "But you will not be remembered for what you broke. You will be remembered for what you chose to protect."

Then—silence.

And with it, the final trial began.

Vaelthys vanished.

The void shattered.

And the world changed.

Kemp

Kemp stepped forward—and the world swallowed the sound.

No crunch of earth beneath his boots. No rustle of fabric as he moved. Even his own breath felt stolen, pulled into a silence that was not absence but something wrong, something held in place.

This was not the stillness of an empty battlefield, thick with the scent of iron and rot. Not the quiet of death, when the last breath faded from broken lips.

This was something else. A silence imposed.

He stood at the edge of a vast city, stretching before him in golden light, something almost familiar but... not quite right. The sky arched overhead, too blue, its color *too perfect*, as if it had never known a storm. The air was warm, but it carried no scent of fire, no trace of blood, no breath of war. He flexed his fingers at his sides, expecting soot, expecting burns, but his hands were clean.

Kemp stepped forward. The ground beneath his feet was solid, but wrong—when he pressed his heel into the dirt, it did not give, did not shift. It felt permanent, untouched, *unreal.*

There were no ruins. No scars of war, no toppled siege engines, no remnants of what had been.

The city stood whole, unbroken. Towering walls gleamed in the distance, strong and unmarred. The streets bustled with movement, people walking past in smooth, effortless steps. They spoke, smiled, traded goods—but something was wrong.

Too smooth. Too orchestrated. Their faces blurred at the edges, as if they were half-formed.

Kemp's breath shuddered out.

His magic stirred at his call, answering instantly, effortlessly. There was no strain, no pain, no darkness clawing at him like it always had. He barely had to think before shadows flickered at his fingertips, controlled and whole.

The war was over.

There was nothing left to fight.

But as he moved, a splinter of unease settled between his ribs.

He wandered into the marketplace, weaving through the clusters of people moving in perfect, rhythmic steps. The scent of roasted meat and fresh bread curled through the air, but when he inhaled, he tasted nothing.

He slowed.

A vendor stacked fruit onto a stall, moving with the same practiced motion, again and again—as if on a loop.

Kemp cleared his throat. "Excuse me—"

The vendor did not look up.

Kemp stepped closer. "Can you hear me?"

No reaction.

His voice did not carry.

It was swallowed by the air, vanishing before it could land.

Something cold curled through his chest.

He turned toward the nearest window, the glass reflecting the city, the people, the marketplace.

But his own reflection was barely there.

Faint. Transparent.

The first sliver of doubt stabbed deep.

Why doesn't anyone see me?

Kemp moved faster now, weaving through the crowd.

He knew where to go. Instinct pulled him toward a tavern, where men shared their war stories, whispered rumors, and raised tankards to their dead.

Inside, voices filled the air—Ellis and Addy's voices.

They were there, seated at a table, laughing between swigs of ale. Kemp's breath hitched, a wave of relief surging forward—until he stepped closer.

They were talking about the war.

About the battles. About the dead. About victories hard won and losses suffered.

But they did not say his name.

Not once.

His chest clenched. "Ellis."

No response.

Kemp moved closer. "Addy."

Nothing.

He reached out, his fingers brushing Ellis' shoulder—

His hand passed through him.

A blink, a flicker, and the world snapped back into place, Ellis still laughing, still drinking, as if Kemp had never been there.

Kemp staggered back, his heart hammering.

I was here. I fought. I bled for this.

But the world did not remember.

Then, through the numbing stillness, he heard it.

A whisper.

"Kemp...?"

He turned sharply, scanning the empty space behind him.

Nothing.

The world around him continued, unbroken.

But the voice had been real.

Hadn't it?

He walked through the streets, faster now, pushing past people who didn't feel him, whose faces blurred when he looked too closely. Every step felt wrong, like he was walking deeper into something that was falling apart.

The colors dulled. The buildings lost their edges, fading into sketches.

Overhead, the sun hung frozen, unmoving, as if time itself had stopped.

"Kemp, wake up."

The voice was clearer now, cutting through the unraveling dream.

A sharp pang of recognition hit his chest.

Ruiha.

He ran.

He ran toward the palace, toward where Vaelthys should be, where his allies should be—where someone should remember him.

The grand doors loomed before him, untouched, whole. He slammed his hands against them—

They crumbled to dust.

The city began to dissolve, the people on the streets breaking apart into drifting motes of sand.

He looked down at his hands—they were fading, vanishing, just like the world around him.

"This is not real."

The thought formed fully now—and the world reacted.

The ground cracked beneath him, the sky above fracturing like shattered glass.

The dream was ending.

Ruiha's voice cut through the collapse, stronger now, urgent.

"Kemp! If you stay here, you will be nothing!"

Through the ruins of the illusion, a door appeared.

A simple thing. Wooden, plain, standing alone among the falling city.

A path back into oblivion.

A voice—not Ruiha's—whispered from beyond it.

"There is no suffering here. No failure. No burden. Step through, and you will know peace."

Kemp turned, and there she was.

Ruiha.

She was real, but fading, as if the void was pulling at her. She did not reach for him. Did not command him to leave.

She only looked at him and asked, *"do you want to be remembered, or do you want to be nothing?"*

The door stood open.

The void waited.

Kemp's fingers tightened into fists.

He had a choice.

Silence.

Not the quiet of an empty battlefield, heavy with the weight of the dead. Not the hushed reverence of a temple or the muffled stillness before a storm.

This was true silence.

Kemp stood in nothing.

No sky, no ground beneath his feet. Just a vast, endless void, pressing against him with something that was not weight but absence.

He reached out, but his hand faded into the dark, swallowed before it could touch anything.

There was nothing here.

And neither was he.

The thought came slow, creeping through his mind like ink bleeding into water.

I was here. I fought. I bled for this.

And yet—the world had moved on without him.

There was no battlefield. No ruined cities. No monuments carved in remembrance. No one had spoken his name.

Had it ever mattered?

A voice—not spoken, but felt, curling in the quiet like smoke.

"It does not have to be a fight."

It was not a command. Not a plea. Just a truth, laid bare.

"You can stop. You can rest."

For a moment, the thought was tempting.

His body had known nothing but struggle. His mind had been torn in a thousand directions, clawing for answers that never came, fighting battles that only led to more. If he let go—

Would it be so bad?

A breath shuddered from his lips.

If he stayed here, in this place of nothing, there would be no war. No burdens.

No expectations.

No one left to save.

No one left to fail.

The weight of it pressed into him, but there was no pain.

No pain.

No feeling at all.

A flicker of panic stirred in his chest.

He had always carried something. Rage. Grief. Determination. He had wielded fire, had felt the pull of magic, the sting of wounds, the ache of exhaustion.

But now—there was nothing.

Nothing to hold onto.

Nothing to pull him back.

Nothing—

"Kemp."

The voice cut through the void like a blade.

Familiar.

Steady.

He turned sharply, searching. Nothing was there.

But the voice had been real.

"Kemp, you have to decide."

He swallowed. His throat was dry, though there was no air to parch it.

Ruiha.

She was here. Somewhere.

Faint, distant—but real.

"You have to fight."

Fight? There was nothing to fight. No swords, no enemies. Only this endless abyss, waiting for him to surrender.

He felt the pull again. Not a force, not a command—just an invitation.

"Let go. Step forward. There is no suffering here."

And that was the moment it hit him.

No suffering.

No pain.

No weight.

But also—no purpose.

His fingers curled into fists.

"I am still here."

The void rippled around him.

"I won't be forgotten."

The words solidified in his chest, taking root.

The void pushed against him, urging him back into its grasp.

"Kemp." Ruiha's voice again, stronger this time. Closer.

"Come back."

And for the first time, he pushed back.

His foot moved. Not into the void, but away from it.

The silence shuddered.

A crack split through the air—not sound, but the absence of it breaking apart.

And then—he fell.

The void shattered around him.

Kemp landed hard.

Not on stone. Not on earth. Not on anything real.

The ground beneath him was smooth, cold, endless—a vast expanse of something not quite solid, not quite air. Like the surface of a lake frozen so thin it might shatter beneath his weight.

He pushed himself upright, his breath coming ragged, chest rising and falling as if he'd just sprinted into battle. But there was no battle here.

Just silence.

And a door.

It stood alone in the vast emptiness, unremarkable and plain. Wooden, slightly worn, as if it had been used before.

It was open.

Beyond it, darkness. But not the cold, devouring void he had come to associate with darkness—this was something else completely. Something calm. Quiet. Peaceful.

A figure stood beside it.

It was him.

But not quite.

This version of himself was whole. He stood relaxed, his expression one of contentment, his face unmarked by burden. He did not carry the ghosts of war in his eyes, nor wear the scars of his past upon his skin.

When he spoke, his voice was smooth, untroubled.

"You don't have to fight anymore."

Kemp's jaw tightened.

"The war is over," his other self continued. "You've done enough. You don't have to carry this burden anymore. Just walk through. No more pain. No more loss. No more weight upon your shoulders."

Kemp took a slow step forward.

The air around the door was warm, carrying a faint scent of something comforting—fresh rain, woodsmoke, home.

For a brief, shuddering moment, he wanted to believe it.

No more war. No more battle. No more fighting.

It would be so easy.

The last place had offered him similar, but it had tried to erase him, but this... this was different. This was a choice.

"You have suffered enough," the other Kemp said gently. "You deserve peace."

The words settled in his chest, thick, cloying.

Hadn't he?

Hadn't he earned that?

He took another step toward the door.

Then—a shift in the air.

Not an attack. Not a warning.

Something stronger.

Something real.

"Kemp."

Her voice.

He turned sharply, and there she was.

Ruiha.

She stood at the edge of the emptiness, solid, yet flickering at the edges, as if the void were trying to pull her away.

She wasn't reaching for him.

She wasn't pleading.

She just watched.

"I won't stop you," she said. "But if you go, answer me this—"

She took a step forward, her gaze steady.

"If you walk through that door… will you still be you?"

Silence.

Kemp's heart slowed.

The warmth of the door faded.

His other self—the version of him that had never suffered, never struggled, never fought for anything—watched him with a patient, knowing smile.

"There is nothing left for you out there," his reflection said.

Kemp swallowed.

Was that true?

He thought of everything he had lost. Everything he had failed to do.

Then he thought of everything he had fought for.

Ruiha.

The people who still needed him.

The battles still to come.

His fingers curled into fists.

"I will not give up," he said.

His reflection's smile faltered.

"I will not abandon them."

The door trembled.

The warm, inviting air vanished, replaced by something else—reality.

The void pushed against him, urging him forward.

But this time, he resisted.

Kemp turned away from the door.

"I choose to fight."

The moment the words left his lips, the illusion shattered.

The door splintered.

The other version of himself vanished, dissolving into dust.

The ground firmed beneath his feet. The world slammed back into him.

Ruiha was there, solid and real. She caught him as he staggered forward.

He gripped her shoulder, chest heaving.

She breathed out, steady. Unshaken.

"Took you long enough," she said, voice rough.

Kemp gave a ragged breath, a crooked smile.

"I like to make an entrance."

She rolled her eyes, but didn't let go.

The void was gone.

The trial was over.

He'd made his choice.

To live.

To fight.

Not because it was easy, but because it was right.

Ruiha

The wind had returned.

Not fierce. Not cold.

Just there.

It stirred gently through the Sanctuary, curling around boulders and skimming across the dust like a breath finally released. Ruiha stood near the ridge overlooking the desert, arms crossed, cloak stirring at her calves. The sky stretched wide above her, bruised with dusk—gold fading into rust, rust giving way to deepening blue.

It should have felt like peace.

But peace had always sat uneasily in her bones.

Behind her, Kemp sat on a low stone, elbows on his knees, staring into the horizon like it might offer answers. Vaelthys rested further back, wings folded, the vast coils of his tail looped like a serpent asleep—but the dragon was not sleeping. He watched. Still. Present.

None of them had spoken since returning.

And yet, the silence between them wasn't empty. It was full. Weighty. Like a temple after prayer.

She turned to Vaelthys.

His scales no longer caught the light with their wild hues of violet and green. That brilliance was gone, swallowed by a sheen like storm-wet iron. Shadows clung to him now, and where colours once shimmered, only smudges of indigo lingered, like old bruises.

But it was his eyes that stole her breath.

The gold was gone. That burnished gleam—sunlight on steel—lost to shadow.

In its place: smoke and storm. Silver and ash, ever shifting, never still.

His eyes held the same churn, that restless drag, and it made her chest tighten, breath catch.

Like Kemp's.

She'd felt it before. That question, curling quietly at the edge of her thoughts.

But now, with silence settled and her heartbeat no longer thundering, she could finally give it shape.

She stepped closer, voice low. Barely hers.

"Vaelthys... what happened to you?"

The dragon lowered his head, slow and deliberate, like a mountain bowing to time.

"Kemp has passed the trials," he said. "And in doing so... part of him now dwells in me, as part of me now dwells in him."

Kemp followed her gaze, eyes narrowing. His voice, when it came, was tight. "What does that mean?"

Vaelthys shifted, dark scales catching the dim light. "It means the trials are done," he said. "And you are ready."

Ruiha's thoughts spun. One question rose above the rest.

"Vaelthys," she asked, "how can you be the Elderflame—hatched by us, by Kemp—and yet others have commanded you before?"

His eyes fixed on her. Unblinking.

She held her breath, wondering if she'd overstepped.

"Because none of them passed all three," he said at last. "The bond was never whole. They held sway over me, yes—but they were never part of me. Not truly."

Ruiha looked away. The ache of Ignara's absence sat heavy in her chest. She said nothing. Just nodded.

But Kemp... Kemp looked stricken. Pale, like he'd seen something rise from the grave.

"No one's ever passed all three?" he asked quietly.

The dragon shifted, wings rustling faintly. His voice rolled out, deep and solemn.

"None before you passed all three," Vaelthys said. "Not for lack of strength. But because they feared the truths buried deepest. You did not flinch. You looked—and still, you stepped forward. That is what sets you apart. That is why the world calls for you now."

Kemp dropped his gaze. The words didn't lift him—they settled on his shoulders like a new kind of armour, one forged not in fire but in truth. He nodded once. Slow. Steady.

Vaelthys turned.

His eyes met Ruiha's.

The air shifted. Not colder. Just heavier.

"And you," he said. "The trials were not meant for you. Yet you endured them. You walked alongside him—not as guide, not as witness—but as anchor. His burdens, you should not have carried. But you did."

Ruiha's spine held straight, though her fingers curled into her palms.

"Where others would have turned away, you stood in the fire. You bled for a bond already broken. You sacrificed without promise of return."

Her voice, when it came, was quiet.

"What does this mean?"

Vaelthys's mirrored gaze held her.

"Some say broken bonds are gone forever. But I have walked this world longer than most, and I tell you this—what is broken may still breathe. What is severed may still sing."

"The bond is not gone, Ruiha. It is… waiting."

He offered no more.

Kemp turned toward her, something like surprise flickering in his eyes. But Ruiha didn't speak.

Instead, her hand moved—slowly, without thought—to her chest. To the place where Ignara had once lived, blazing bright within her.

Where it had been severed.

And in that moment, the wind shifted.

Not stronger. Not colder.

Just *present*.

It curled through the stones, stirred her cloak, brushed past her ear.

And in its passing—

A whisper.

Not a voice. Not even sound.

Just a name.

Ignara.

Her breath caught—sharp and involuntary—even as she told herself it wasn't real. Just memory. Just longing.

She closed her eyes. Not from grief.

From reverence.

The wind moved on.

And the moment passed.

She opened her eyes to find Kemp watching her. He didn't ask. He didn't need to.

Vaelthys said nothing more.

They stood there in silence as the last light bled from the sky.

The trials had ended. But their echoes lingered.

In flesh. In flame. In the quiet where bonds still dared to breathe.

Chapter 15

Gunnar

Gunnar walked among the dead. His boots pressed into the brittle remains of warriors and demons alike, grinding them to dust. Bone and ash, honor and ruin—it was all the same to him now.

The silence pressed against him, a weight as heavy as the sky above. Not dawn. Not dusk. Just a bruised, dying thing caught between.

The battlefield had long been abandoned, yet death still clung to it, unwilling to let go.

Weapons lay rusted in skeletal grips, banners reduced to nothing but colourless rags, their purpose forgotten. The wind had forsaken this place. Time had turned its back.

Then—a sound.

Not the wind. Not the brittle shifting of old bones.

A breath. Ragged. Shallow. Alive.

He turned.

It slumped against the ruin of a shattered pillar—the remains of a demon.

Once, it had been terror made flesh. A thing of claw and fire, its eyes brimming with hunger, forged only to destroy. Its hide, now cracked and ruined, must have once gleamed like obsidian under moonlight, a thing not meant to be touched by mortal hands. Jagged horns curled from its skull, broken at the tips, their edges dulled by war.

Now, it's hunger was gone, hollowed out by wounds too deep to heal.

One arm missing. A trench carved through its chest. Blood, black and thick as tar, seeped from ruined flesh, pooling in the dust. Its once-mighty form, built for battle, was now a wreck of splintered bone and torn sinew.

Gunnar had fought demons before. Hadn't he?

The memory flickered at the edges of his mind, distant, blurred. He vaguely recalled their fury—the deafening roars, the relentless charge, the way they tore through battle like fire through dry grass. But this—this was something else.

A thing that should have been beyond pain, beyond suffering, slumped before him, struggling for breath.

Its eyes, dull and sunken, found his.

No rage. No defiance. Just silence. A deep, unsettling quiet, as if even death itself hesitated.

He should have felt triumph. Victory. But instead, there was something else.

Something cold.

Pity.

Its breath came slow. Labored.

Dying.

The hatred was gone from its eyes. What remained was something raw, something Gunnar could not name. It did not snarl. Did not curse him. It only watched.

Then, in a voice brittle as dead leaves, it spoke.

"End it."

Gunnar's hand found his axe without thought. A simple thing. A single swing. No witness. No consequence.

He had killed before. Too many times to count.

They had come for him in the heat of battle, screaming, howling, their madness carrying them forward like a tide. Others had crept through the dark, knives drawn, breath held. It hadn't mattered.

He had cut them all down. Because that was the way of things.

But this one did not lunge. Did not fight. It only sat in the ruins of war, its breath rattling in a chest that would not last much longer.

Would it be mercy to grant its wish? To let it die, swiftly and cleanly? Or was true mercy leaving it here, making it endure what all the others had not?

His grip tightened around the haft of the axe.

One swing. That was all it would take.

Quick. Clean. Easy.

But not right.

Mercy is strength. The words came unbidden, echoing in his mind, but they were more than that. Mercy was not just the absence of violence. It was a choice. A defiance of what the world had made him.

He did not swing.

The demon flinched, expecting the strike. When it did not come, its breath hitched—not in fear, but in something close to disbelief. Slowly, it lowered its head, shoulders sagging, as if the weight of war had finally left it.

Gunnar knelt.

He did not speak. There were no words for this. No explanations to give, no reasons that would matter.

The demon stared at him for a long while, its dull, sunken eyes searching—not for cruelty, not for mockery. For something else.

Understanding.

It released a breath. Shallow and final.

"Thank you," it whispered.

The demon looked up at him once more, then, slowly, it closed its eyes.

The silence pressed in again. The weight of death, the stillness of this place. But something had changed. Something had shifted.

When he finally stood, the demon was gone. Whether it had passed, or whether something greater had taken it away, he did not know.

But he was still standing.

And the world moved forward once more.

Chapter 16

Anwyn

The flames flickered, casting the night in shifting gold. Shadows stretched long across the stone, twisting with each step of the procession. The air smelled of burning oil and damp earth, of leather and sweat. Of grief.

Anwyn walked in silence, her boots scraping softly against the cobbled streets of Tempsford. Each step felt heavier than the last. Like she was sinking.

Ahead, Karl led the march, his broad shoulders squared beneath a burden none of them could see, but all of them felt. He had been Gunnar's shield-brother. His closest friend. Now, he was the one to carry him home.

It should not be Karl.

It should not be any of them.

Gunnar should be here. Walking beside her, his stride unhurried, his hand brushing against hers as if by accident. She could almost see him in the torchlight, just beyond the reach of her grasp. But when she blinked, there was only smoke.

Her throat tightened. She clenched her jaw and looked straight ahead.

She would not break.

The others spoke his name, telling stories of battle, of laughter, of a dwarf who had fought and won and fought again. Their voices rose and fell, rough and reverent, their grief carried in every syllable.

She said nothing.

She had thought herself prepared for this. She had been wrong.

Her nails pressed into her palms. A distraction. A way to ground herself. But the ache in her hands was nothing compared to the one in her chest.

Her breath hitched, just once. She swallowed hard, forcing it down.

Karl walked on, his steps steady. Hers wavered. Just for a moment.

No one saw. No one heard the breath she stole to steady herself.

She was still standing.

But gods, it hurt.

Beside Karl strode Draeg, silent as the grave, his usual booming words buried beneath the weight of the moment. Anwyn followed. She had earned her place in the procession. The battles fought side by side with Gunnar had seen to that. Dakarai and Kris marched behind her, warriors of different lands, different lives, now bound by the same truth—Gunnar had stood for them, and now they stood for him.

The torches burned high, their light chasing away the creeping dark. Yet grief lingered, a thing not so easily banished.

One by one, the voices rose. Soft at first. Then louder.

"He fought like a mountain, unyielding in the storm!" Havoc called.

"A warrior, a brother, a dwarf you'd want beside you when the sky turned black!" another voice rang out.

"He once drank an entire barrel of ale and still bested me," Karl muttered, half to himself.

A chuckle rippled through the mourners, brief but real. Laughter in mourning was no disrespect. It was remembrance.

Anwyn said nothing. She let the others speak, let the stories shape the air around them. A warrior is not truly gone while his name is spoken. And tonight, they would speak it loud enough for the gods to hear.

The procession wound its way to the courtyard, where the bier awaited. Forged from frosteel, cold and unyielding. As Gunnar had been. The metal gleamed in the firelight, strong even in death.

Karl stepped forward first, placing a hand upon Gunnar's chest. Draped in armor, scarred but whole, he looked as if he might wake. Ready to rise, take up his axe, and march into battle once more.

But the axe was gone.

She had saved it for Owen.

Their boy had lost much already. Too much. He would need something to hold onto. Something to remind him of the dwarf who had stood tall in the face of darkness.

Instead, another weapon lay across Gunnar's chest, placed by Karl's own hands. A gift. A tribute. A warrior's final offering.

One by one, the mourners came forward. Some placed a hand upon the armor, whispering their farewells. Others simply stood, heads bowed, words stolen by the weight of it all.

Anwyn did not step forward yet. Not yet.

Karl was the last. He exhaled, hands curling into fists before loosening again. A long breath. A short nod.

His voice, when it came, was hoarse. Stripped raw.

"He was a warrior."

The words settled over them, heavy as stone.

"He fought. For his people. For his kin. For those who could not fight for themselves."

Karl's fingers tightened around the hilt of his own axe. His voice did not waver.

"He did not flinch. He did not falter. He stood."

Silence followed. Then—

Steel struck steel.

Once.

Then again.

Then again.

The sound rippled outward, a wave of metal and mourning. A warrior's farewell.

The crowd lifted their drinking horns. Ale. Mead. Wine. Whatever could be spared. They drank deep, then poured the rest onto the earth at their feet.

A tribute. A parting. A farewell.

Then the moment passed, and the funeral turned to its final rites.

Anwyn stepped forward.

The torches burned low, their light flickering weakly against the night. The courtyard was silent now, save for the crackle of flame and the shifting of boots on stone. Karl stood nearby, watching her, arms crossed over his broad chest. His expression was unreadable, but his eyes carried the weight of what they both knew.

This was not her way.

She had no place in dwarven rituals, no right to stand among them as they bid farewell to one of their own. But she had fought beside Gunnar. Had bled beside him. Had loved him. And that was enough.

She knelt beside the bier, hands careful as she reached for her braid. Her fingers trembled, barely noticeable, but she felt it all the same. A weakness, a crack in the armor she had built around herself.

Slowly, she unsheathed her katana. The metal gleamed, silver and deadly, even in the dim light. She ran her fingers through Gunnar's hair, brushing strands from his forehead. His skin was cold.

A breath caught in her throat, but she did not stop. She could not.

The blade whispered as she sliced a long lock of his golden hair, severing it clean. It slipped through her fingers like silk, like something already lost.

"For Freya," she whispered. A vow, a promise. The words trembled, barely more than breath. A tear slid down her cheek, warm against the cold air, and she let it fall.

She clenched her jaw. Enough.

She exhaled slowly, forcing steel into her spine, and turned to Karl.

"Karl," she began, her voice raw, scraped down to nothing. She swallowed and tried again. "Remember the bag of his ashes. For me."

Karl's exhale was slow, measured. The kind of breath someone takes when words are useless, when the only thing left is duty. He nodded once.

She knew it was not dwarven custom. But the war had shattered enough traditions already.

The torches burned lower, their light failing. Shadows stretched long across the courtyard. The flames would die soon. And when they did, Gunnar would be gone. Taken back to Draegoor.

His body was prepared. His journey home awaited.

The mountain would take him now.

The gods would decide the rest.

The morning air hung heavy with the scent of damp stone and charred wood. The city of Tempsford stirred, but sluggishly, as if weighed down by the grief of the night before.

The funeral had been a warrior's farewell—loud, reverent, overflowing with stories and song. But for Anwyn, it had felt like the world was pressing in, the laughter and ale a poor salve for the wound left in her heart. She had listened as voices rose in tribute, as friends, old and new, spoke of Gunnar's courage, his fire, his love for his people— for her. Yet none of it could fill the silence he left behind. None of it could bring him back. Too much ale had drowned Karl's grief, but Anwyn's remained a blade lodged in her chest, unmoving, unyielding.

Anwyn approached Karl's quarters, her boots crunching against the frost-rimed cobbles. The door was slightly ajar, and from within came the unmistakable grumble of a dwarf who had overindulged.

"By the gods, does the sun have to be so damned bright?" Karl's voice was thick with grogginess as she stepped inside. He sat at the table, his face buried in his hands, a half-eaten chunk of bread and cheese on the plate before him. Draeg, Havoc, and Thraxos were already there, engaged in easy conversation.

"She's merciless, that one," Draeg rumbled, his voice as rich as rolling thunder. "Rises every day without fail. That's reliability, Karl. You could learn something."

Karl lifted his head just enough to glare at him. "Reliability can shove itself where the sun doesn't shine."

Havoc chuckled, lounging against the wall. "Come now, you got drunk, we mourned our friend, we honored his name. Small price to pay, eh?"

Karl sighed, rubbing a hand over his face. "Aye. He'd have wanted that." His tone softened, and for a brief moment, the weight of loss settled over them all again. Then he exhaled sharply, clapped his hands on the table, and pushed himself up. "Right, let's see what a city half-broken looks like."

Tempsford was alive with movement. Masons chipped away at broken walls, blacksmiths worked tirelessly, their forges glowing like embers against the cold. Civilians—those who had survived—patched roofs and hauled debris, rebuilding their home one stone at a time.

Karl nodded to a group of blacksmiths hammering out iron braces for the new gates. "I gave them a few tricks to make the metal stronger," he muttered. "No use fixing things only for them to break again."

Draeg took the lead, his bulk moving with surprising ease over the uneven ground. "Now, now, Karl. If anyone is an expert in lasting structures, it's me." He spread his arms wide as if presenting the city itself. "What you see before you is stonework reforged, improved! The weak points? Gone. The fractures? Sealed. This city won't fall as easily next time."

Thraxos, ever the tactician, surveyed the fortifications with a practiced eye. "Impressive. But walls alone won't stop an army."

Havoc sniffed. "You mean an army of the dead."

Thraxos exhaled through his nose—a weary sigh, the kind that came from years of expecting nothing but bad news. "Fine. Yes. An army of the dead." He dragged a broad hand down his face. "How's the watch?"

Havoc scratched his chin. "Oh, you know. Terrified. Mostly sober. Which, in my experience, makes for excellent cowardice but abysmal heroics."

Karl grunted. "We're doubling the rotations. No blind spots this time."

Thraxos nodded approvingly. "And supply chains? A siege isn't just about holding ground, it's about lasting longer than your enemy."

Havoc smirked. "Oh, listen to him, the strategist at work."

Thraxos ignored him. "Weapons? Food? Medical stockpiles?"

"Already in motion," Karl said. "I've made sure of it."

Anwyn listened, absorbing every detail. This wasn't just rebuilding. It was preparation. They were not fixing a city—they were fortifying it for the war to come.

They turned a corner and came upon the ruins of Baron Roderic's mansion. It had been beautiful once, grand and stately, before the flames had gutted it. It was where Gunnar had died. Where Owen and Freya had been born.

For a long moment, no one spoke. The laughter that had colored their earlier conversations faded into the cold morning air.

Karl exhaled, shaking his head. "The city will heal," he murmured. "But some scars stay."

Draeg in an attempt to lighten the mood clapped him on the back. "Aye, but stone is stronger than memory."

Anwyn looked at the burned ruins and then at the city beyond. Stronger than memory. Perhaps. But even stone could be broken.

As they reached the city's main gates, the sun crested over the horizon, bathing Tempsford in golden light. It was a new day, and despite everything, the city was still standing.

Anwyn squared her shoulders. The battle had taken much, but it had not taken everything. And whatever came next, they would be ready.

Chapter 17

Kemp

The Sanctuary stood quiet behind them, a hollow breath in the stone.

Before them, the world waited.

Kemp tightened his grip on the edge of his cloak as the wind stirred at his heels—not fierce, not cold, but present, insistent. A reminder that stillness was only ever the space between storms.

"We should go," he said.

Ruiha stood a step behind him, one hand resting lightly on the scorched ridge wall. She didn't answer right away. Her eyes swept the horizon where the desert met the sky, the bruised clouds stirring low like a beast yet to wake.

Kemp knew what she was thinking.

He was thinking it too.

Leaving the Sanctuary felt like stepping from a pyre into a world still burning.

Ruiha exhaled, low and steady. "Fenmark needs us."

A small nod passed between them. Agreement, heavy as a sword laid across the back.

Vaelthys shifted behind them, great coils grinding against stone. His new eyes, storm-bright and restless, watched them without blinking. No words passed between them—they were beyond the need.

Kemp swung up onto Vaelthys' back, muscles still sore from battles fought in places no blade could touch. Ruiha vaulted up behind him, light as breath. The dragon spread his wings, dark and vast, and the ground fell away beneath them.

They rose into the dying light, the desert sprawling endless and broken below.

The flight should have been freeing.

It wasn't.

Kemp felt it first—a wrongness prickling under his skin.

Not magic.

Something older.

As they crested the final ridge that cradled the Sanctuary, the world sharpened into sight—and the desert was no longer empty.

A battlefield lay sprawled before them. A boiling sea of Drogo warriors surged against a battered, sand-scoured line—the Sand Whisperers.

Steel flashed in the low light. Blood soaked the dunes.

The war had not waited for them.

Vaelthys snarled, the sound a rumbling quake that tore through the air.

Dark fire licked across Kemp's shadow hand before he even knew it.

Ruiha leaned forward, her voice low against his ear. "They're outnumbered."

Outnumbered—and falling.

Kemp's jaw tightened.

Vaelthys roared once—pure, fierce—then dove.

Wind shrieked past them as they plummeted toward the heart of the battle, fire gathering at the dragon's throat, magic flaring sharp and hungry along Kemp's veins.

Below, the Sand Whisperers broke under the Drogo assault.

Ruiha drew her blades.

Kemp shifted his stance, readying himself.

Vaelthys opened his jaws wide.

And the sky itself caught fire.

The world roared past them as Vaelthys hurtled into the fray.

Kemp tightened his grip against the dragon's scales, heart hammering a rhythm older than memory.

Below, Drogo blades tore into the dwindling Sand Whisperers. Blood darkened the sand, and the cries of the dying frayed the air.

Kemp lifted his hand, feeling the bond with Vaelthys surge—a river too vast to hold.

Shadow and flame answered him.

Not fire alone.

Not magic alone.

But something born of them both.

Kemp gathered it, wove it, shaped it with a will honed by pain and tempered by choice.

And when they struck—

They struck with fury enough to tear the world clean in two.

Vaelthys released a torrent of dragonfire, the blaze roaring like a newborn sun. Ruiha leapt from his back in a blur of steel and cloth, falling like a hawk into the thickest of the enemy ranks.

Kemp landed harder, boots slamming into sand and blood.

He barely felt it.

Magic boiled under his skin, a pressure so fierce it stole his breath. The bond with Vaelthys thrummed in every nerve, the dragon's power answering his call without hesitation.

Kemp strode forward, lifting his hand.

The Drogo turned to meet him—faces twisted with rage, spears and axes rising like a forest of death.

Kemp let the power loose.

The ground shattered beneath him.

A pulse of Varlthys' ancient magic erupted outward, rippling through the battlefield like a living thing.

For a breathless moment, the Drogo fell.

Whole ranks crumpled to the ground, smoke rising from charred armour and seared flesh.

Victory should have roared in his chest.

But instead—

Instead, a silence settled.

Not peace. Something worse.

Kemp's heart twisted as the first Drogo staggered upright.

Then another.

And another.

He noticed it then.

Their wounds gaped open—sword cuts, burns, even limbs hanging by slivers of sinew—and yet they rose.

Their faces blank.

Their movements jerky, inhuman.

Kemp took a step back, breath catching sharp in his throat.

Across the field, Ruiha froze mid-swing, staring as a Drogo she'd just gutted lunged at her with dead hands.

Vaelthys circled above, roaring in frustration.

Kemp spun, seeking answers, feeling dread sink into his bones like frostbite.

The Drogo didn't speak.

They didn't scream.

They just came.

Relentless.

Unstoppable.

The magic he had unleashed—the fury that should have turned the tide—had barely slowed them.

Kemp locked eyes with Ruiha across the battlefield.

In that single look, a thousand fears were exchanged.

And understood.

This was no longer a battle.

This was survival.

Ruiha

The Drogo should have stayed down.

The dead should have stayed dead.

Ruiha ducked under a sweeping axe, driving her blade hard into a Drogo's ribs. She twisted sharply, feeling the crunch of bone—but the warrior barely flinched, swinging again with a snarl that tore through dead lips.

She leapt back, cursing under her breath.

Across the battlefield, Kemp hurled shadowfire at a knot of enemies, disintegrating two where they stood. Vaelthys swept low, jaws snapping shut around a Drogo, hurling the limp body across the sand.

And still they came.

Ruiha sidestepped a spear thrust, dragging a dagger from her belt. She spun low, carving a line across the back of another Drogo's knee—but he only stumbled before straightening, moving with jerking, puppet-like stiffness.

Fear gripped her chest.

Not the clean fear of a battle fought and lost—a deeper, bone-rooted fear.

A war against something that should not be.

She caught movement from the corner of her eye—a Sand Whisperer, blade flashing.

He drove a sword upward, right into a Drogo's eye.

The body shuddered—and collapsed.

Dead. Truly dead.

Ruiha's breath caught.

The head.

It was the head.

Another Sand Whisperer slammed a blade clean through a Drogo's neck. The body dropped instantly, twitching once, then still.

Sever the brain. Sever the will.

She surged forward, blocking a hammer blow with the flat of her dagger. She ducked low, reversed her grip, and rammed the dagger up through the Drogo's jaw, angling for the brain.

The creature gave a wet gasp—and fell.

Ruiha wiped blood from her eyes, shouting above the din.

"The head! Take the head!"

Some heard.

Some did not.

The ones who did began to cut higher, faster, striking not for the heart, not for the lungs—but for the mind that lingered behind dead eyes.

Across the battlefield, Kemp caught her meaning.

She saw the slow nod—the grim understanding. He turned, gathering shadowfire between his hands again, but this time his strikes aimed higher. More precise. More desperate.

Vaelthys howled, a sound that shook the sand itself.

He plunged into the throng, jaws snapping, claws tearing, sending severed heads rolling across the battlefield like broken crowns.

The battle turned—but not easily.

Every blow cost them. Every mistake meant death.

They could win.

But only if they killed every last one.

Silence clung to the battlefield like smoke. Not the stillness of peace. The stillness of exhaustion. Of fear.

The last of the Drogo lay scattered in broken heaps across the bloodied dunes. Heads severed. Eyes blank.

This time, they stayed down.

Ruiha staggered toward the remnants of the Sand Whisperers, her blades heavy in her hands. Around her, wounded men slumped against shattered shields, clutching bleeding wounds, too tired even to curse.

Kemp moved through the survivors, a dark shape limned with the last light of the setting sun, helping where he could. His eyes were hollow, haunted.

Vaelthys landed nearby with a gust of scorched wind, folding his wings tight against his body.

The dragon's scales, once vibrant, now looked more iron than flame.

Ruiha dropped to one knee beside Gundeep, pressing a cloth against the ruin of his shoulder.

He grimaced, baring bloodstained teeth. "You came back," he rasped.

"We were late," Ruiha said, voice rough with dust and grief.

Gundeep laughed once, a broken sound. "Not too late."

A pause, heavy and expectant.

"You killed them?" she asked quietly.

He nodded, the movement sluggish. "Last night. They came under moonlight. We cut them down. Burned some. Buried the rest."

He coughed, blood flecking his lips.

"But at dawn..." His hand shook as he wiped it away.

"They rose again. Same faces. Same wounds. Same fury."

Ruiha's stomach twisted.

She turned, seeking Kemp. He stood a few paces away, listening, his shoulders stiff, every line of him taut as a drawn bowstring.

Vaelthys rumbled low, a sound that seemed to shake the bones beneath her skin.

The dragon lowered his head, golden eyes gone to stormy grey.

"Draugr," Vaelthys said.

The word fell into the sand like a stone into a grave.

For a heartbeat, Ruiha could not breathe.

Walking dead. *Bound souls,* shackled to flesh, denied death itself. The kind of enemy you could kill a thousand times—and lose to once.

Kemp met her gaze across the field.

In that moment, Ruiha felt it fully—the world tilting beneath them, the war they had known slipping through their fingers like grains of sand.

The old battles were over.

What was coming now would be worse.

Much worse.

She swallowed hard, the taste of ash and fear heavy on her tongue.

"The war just changed," she whispered.

Above them, the sky darkened—not with the coming of night, but with the shadow of what refused to die.

Chapter 18

Gunnar

The mist curled around Gunnar's boots, clinging like grasping fingers, as if something unseen wished to hold him in place. There was no ground beneath him—not in any real sense. Just the sensation of weight, of standing on something that wasn't there.

The sky did not exist. No horizon. No moon. No stars. Only an endless expanse of grey, stretching in all directions, swallowing sight, swallowing sound.

He did not know how he had come to be here. He did not remember walking. Did not remember waking. Had he fallen asleep? Had he died?

His last memory was a battlefield. Or was it before that? It unraveled the moment he reached for it, slipping through his mind like sand through his fingers.

Where was he?

The air hung thick and still, pressing against his skin. There was no wind, no movement. And yet—he could hear the whispers.

Not voices, not truly. Just the echoes of something that should not be.

They had no source. They had no language. They seeped into his ears, his bones, a tide of grief pressing inward, suffocating. The weight of it dragged against his ribs, an unseen hand pressing against his chest. His breath came shallow. The whispers weren't calling his name, but they knew him. They knew what he had done, what he had lost, what he had carried.

Then he saw it.

A figure knelt ahead, half-formed in the mist. Clad in the ragged remains of armor, the metal long since dulled and pitted by unseen battles. Their form was thin, frail, hunched forward as if gravity itself had forgotten to let go. The sword at their side was shattered, the blade broken to a jagged stump. Their head was bowed, face hidden.

Alive. But barely.

Gunnar's instincts burned for action. His fingers twitched for a weapon, for something tangible, something to fight. But this was no battle of steel. There was no enemy to cut down, no war cry to answer. Only the figure, and the weight that sat between them.

The voice did not come from them. It did not come from anywhere. It simply arrived.

"Take my pain, or leave me here."

It was not a plea. Not a question. Not even a challenge. Just truth. Cold. Uncompromising.

Gunnar stepped closer, his boots making no sound. The air did not shift. The figure did not move.

"If I leave?" he asked, voice low.

Silence answered him. Silence, and the truth that lay beneath it. Nothing would change. The figure would remain. He would walk forward, unburdened. His path would continue, untouched.

And yet... he knew what it meant to walk forward alone. He had done it before. Left behind the dead, the broken, the lost. Sometimes by choice. Sometimes by force. The burden of a leader was not just to carry his own weight, but to decide which burdens were worth bearing.

His father had once told him that a warrior fights, but a leader carries.

The figure did not ask him to carry. There was no gratitude here, no promise of redemption or justice. Just the truth: Pain does not vanish. It is only moved.

Gunnar exhaled. The cold scraped his lungs. He reached out.

The figure lifted its head.

Once, it had been a man. Now, it was little more than a skeleton—skin stretched thin over bone, its form gaunt, hollowed by time and suffering.

Eyes like empty wells. Deep, but hollow. He saw nothing in them, and yet he saw everything.

He saw them—the man and his children, laughter spilling into the air like birdsong. The man chased them, growling playfully, pretending to be a monster, his hands outstretched as if to snatch them up. The children shrieked, giggling as they ran.

At the edge of it all, a woman stood watching. His wife. Her smile was soft, full of warmth, eyes shining as she drank in the simple joy of the moment.

Then—the scene shifted.

A call to arms. Smoke on the horizon.

The man, now clad in armor, rode away on horseback. A single tear slipped down his face. His wife wept. His children screamed for him, their tiny voices breaking as they called for their father to come back.

He had promised.

Yet here he was.

A tear trickled down Gunnar's cheek and vanished into his beard.

His fingers brushed against the mans shoulder. He would take some of his burden if he could.

The world shattered.

Fire erupted through his bones, raw and merciless. Agony poured into his veins, curling through his nerves, seizing his muscles like iron clamps. His breath caught, strangled by the weight pressing into him—not onto him, but into him.

More memories that were not his flooded his mind. A battlefield lost to time. Blood in the snow. The wrenching sound of steel carving through flesh. Screams. Not the dead—they did not scream. It was the living. The ones left behind. The ones who had to watch, to endure.

He staggered. His teeth clenched against the searing pain.

The figure did not speak. Did not weep. They simply... faded.

But the pain did not fade with him.

Gunnar was alone once more. The mist had thinned. The whispers had stilled. But the pain remained.

He straightened, breathing through the fire still curling through his ribs. His hands trembled. He clenched them into fists.

The path ahead was open.

But now, he carried more than just himself.

Chapter 19

Laoch

The dragon staggered out of the cloud, wings ragged, bleeding. Laoch clung to the saddle, fingers numb, vision blurred. The stone courtyard below reared up to meet them.

Ignara hit hard, claws scraping, wings folding with a shudder. Laoch swung a leg over, dropped from her back. His boots struck the ground and the world tilted, the stone rushing up, his knees buckling.

Get up. Move.

He forced himself upright, gritting his teeth against the fire that ripped through his ribs. Every breath a blade. Every heartbeat an effort.

A hush rippled across the courtyard. Eyes on him. Too many eyes. Soldiers, townsfolk, guards — a thin scattering of survivors, staring as if they couldn't quite believe he was real.

Ash drifted on the wind, soft as snow. Laoch tasted it on his tongue, bitter and dry.

A cry broke the silence. Eira, shoving through the crowd.

He barely had time to brace before she was there, hands clutching at his arms, his face, checking for blood, for broken bones. Her voice broke on his name, half sob, half curse.

"I'm alive," he rasped, voice torn raw. "I'm alive, Eira."

For a heartbeat she pressed her forehead to his chest.

Then she wrenched back, scrubbing tears from her face with the heel of her palm, rough and furious.

He'd missed her. Gods, he'd thought he might never see her again. The sight of her cut deeper than any blade.

But there was no time for this.

No time for anything.

Laoch straightened, muscles screaming, breath ragged. He turned to the crowd, the soldiers still staring.

He made himself loud. Hard.

"Gather the council," he barked, the words tearing his throat. "Now."

Movement exploded, men and women running, boots hammering on stone. The old heartbeat of command thrumming back into life.

He tried to follow and almost fell, the world swaying around him like a storm-tossed ship.

A shape moved beside him—massive, solid.

Ignara's head dipped low, her great eye finding his. She nudged his side with her jaw, rough but steady, like a friend hauling him back from the abyss.

Laoch pressed a hand to her blood-slick scales. Solid. Warm. A heartbeat of strength when he had none left to give.

"I know," he muttered. "I'm still breathing."

He staggered across the courtyard. Slow. Battered. But upright.

The torches guttered. Smoke twisted.

Above, the wind howled like a mourning song.

Tempsford stirred.

So did he.

The council chamber was cold and dim, the air thick with the stink of sweat, steel, and old smoke. Shadows clung to the corners. A fire guttered in the hearth, throwing long arms of light across stone walls.

They were all there, waiting.

Anwyn, sat rigid-backed, her hands clenched in her lap.

Eira, standing a little too close to him, as if afraid he'd vanish.

Karl, arms folded, a scowl carved deep into his face.

Baron Roderic, Draeg, Thraxos, Queen Kathrynne herself, stiff and pale on her seat at the head of the table.

Karl broke the silence first. "What in the hell happened to you?"

The words cracked through the room, rough as a blade drawn across stone.

Laoch shifted his weight, grimaced as pain lanced up his side. He took a breath. Tasted blood.

"They're coming," he said. His voice was a rasp, scraped raw from shouting, from fighting. "An army. Ten days out, maybe less."

A murmur rippled through the council. Roderic leaned forward. Draeg swore under his breath.

Karl jabbed a finger at him. "What army?"

Laoch closed his eyes a heartbeat, steadying himself.

"Draugr," Laoch said. "Ignara called them that. An army of the dead."

A silence fell, heavier than the stone walls around them.

"They're raising the dead," Laoch went on, each word a hammer-blow. "Men. Women. Drogo. Dragons. Doesn't matter. If it falls, they make it rise again."

Anwyn exhaled, the sound brittle. "We knew they were doing it. We just thought we had more time."

Thraxos cursed low. Eira shifted closer to him, just a breath, just enough for him to feel her there.

Queen Kathrynne's voice cracked through the hush, tight and brittle. "How many?"

Laoch shook his head. "I couldn't count them all. Thousands. And it keeps growing. Every death feeds them."

A few heads turned, disbelief scrawled plain across their faces.

"I tried to slow them," Laoch said. "We all did. Ignara, the dragons. We're buying time. Buying Tempsford a chance."

He saw their faces—the flickers of horror, the helpless calculation. Karl's fists clenched so tight his knuckles went white. Roderic just stared at him, stone-faced. Draeg muttered a prayer to his mother.

"And the dragons?" Anwyn asked, voice steady, but her knuckles white where they gripped the table edge.

"They're still fighting," Laoch said. "Still holding the line. But..." He swallowed, throat burning. "Some of them... some of them fell. And rose again."

The room stilled. Not even the fire dared crackle too loud.

"Imagine," Laoch said, voice low, "fighting a beast with wings torn to ribbons, half its skull gone, but still flying, still burning, still killing. It doesn't bleed. It doesn't tire. It just keeps coming."

No one spoke.

The horror hung between them, thick as smoke.

Karl leaned forward, teeth bared. "We can still win this thing. We don't meet them head on. We attack then retreat. We've fortified the city. When they arrive. We're ready for a siege."

"We're not ready," Laoch said, looking around. "Not for this."

"What aren't you telling us?" Thraxos boomed.

Laoch looked at him, and for a heartbeat, he hated what he was about to say.

"They're not all Drogo," he said, voice little more than a whisper. "This army heading for us."

He let the silence stretch, let the weight settle.

"They're human. And Elf too."

It hit like a punch. Anwyn flinched. Roderic sucked in a sharp breath. Draeg shook his head, muttering something under his breath.

"They were ours," Laoch said. "Every soul the Drogo slaughtered on the march. Raised up. Turned against us."

Kathrynne's chair creaked as she sat forward, her face pale, mouth working soundlessly.

"Who's leading them?" she asked, and Laoch heard the hope in her voice, hope already dying.

He looked her in the eye.

"King Luthar."

The words dropped into the room like a thrown stone shattering glass.

Kathrynne stared at him. Shook her head. Once. Twice.

"No," she whispered. "No, no, no—"

She stood too fast, the chair toppling behind her, crashing to the floor. Her hands came up to her face, covering her mouth, her eyes. A sound broke from her—a choked sob, raw and scraping.

She stumbled back, sagging against the cold stone wall, sliding down until she was sitting, hands shaking.

No one moved. No one spoke.

Karl's jaw worked, his fists clenching and unclenching at his sides. Roderic looked away, his face carved from grief. Draeg bowed his head. Thraxos stared at the table like he could smash it apart if he stared hard enough.

Anwyn closed her eyes, a tear slipping free.

Laoch stood in the centre of it all, the messenger of the end, and wished—just for a heartbeat—that he had died out there on the battlefield.

The fire crackled. The world turned.

Tempsford would stand.

Or it would fall.

But it would not fall easily.

Not while Laoch still drew breath.

Chapter 20

Anwyn

The council chamber emptied around her.

Boots scuffed the stone. Cloaks whispered. No words. No plans. Only a heavy, smothering silence.

Anwyn stayed seated, hands clenched in her lap until they ached.

The fire in the hearth burned low, throwing long shadows across the cold walls. Smoke twisted above the broken chair Kathrynne had toppled in her grief.

Dead elves.

Dead men.

Dead dragons.

King Luthar among them.

The world had shifted beneath her feet, but there was no time to fall with it.

She pushed herself upright, muscles stiff with tension, and walked out into the cold.

Tempsford stirred under a grey sky.

Not bustling, not alive—but moving with grim purpose.

Masons braced crumbling walls. Blacksmiths hammered iron struts into the gates. Children hauled buckets of water through the streets, faces pale and pinched.

Every soul here knew the truth now: the dead were coming. And this time, they wore familiar faces.

Anwyn walked through it all, her cloak snapping in the wind, boots crunching over frost-rimed stone.

She found herself at Baron Roderic's mansion.

Or what was left of it.

The once-grand pillars were blackened stumps. The garden was a graveyard of ash and stone.

Here, Gunnar had fought.

Here, he had died, saving her and their children.

She stepped through the broken archway. Rubble shifted underfoot.

No one else had come here. Not since...

Good.

She dropped to one knee, fingers brushing the scorched earth, as if she might feel him still.

As if the blood and ash might carry his voice back to her.

She bowed her head.

Not to the forest. Not now.

To Gunnar.

"If you can hear me," she whispered, the words raw in her throat, "lend me your strength. Your stubbornness. Your fire."

The wind moaned through the ruins.

No answer came.

But when she rose, it was easier to breathe.

Footsteps crunched behind her.

She turned, hand already brushing the hilt of her katana.

Karl.

He looked worn, hair matted from battle, face grim beneath the streaks of dirt. But there was something burning in his eyes.

Purpose.

"Anwyn," he said, voice low. "I want to take a squad out. Hit the Draugr. Delay them. However we can."

She stared at him a long moment. Saw the iron in him. Saw the fear, too—but fear harnessed to duty.

"You're not trying to be a hero?" she asked.

He snorted, a rough sound. "No. Just buying time. Tempsford needs every hour it can get."

Anwyn nodded, slowly. The idea had merit. Risk, yes. But so did standing still and waiting to die.

"Good," she said. "But speak with my father first. He's faced them. He'll tell you how to fight the dead—and how to live through it."

Karl grunted. "Aye. I will."

He hesitated, then gave a sharp nod—a soldier's farewell—and turned, striding back toward the keep.

Anwyn stayed where she was a moment longer, staring back at the blackened bones of where her old life had ended.

"You stood for us, Gunnar," she said. "Now I will stand for them."

The wind tugged at her cloak, cold and sharp.

She turned and followed Karl, her steps steady, her heart hardening like forged steel.

Tempsford would hold, if she had to stitch it together with blood and ash.

She would not break.

Not while her children lived.

Not while Gunnar's memory burned in her chest.

Let the dead come with their hollow eyes and broken bodies.

Tempsford would teach them:

the living were harder to kill.

Karl

The keep's solar stank of old smoke, iron, and worry.

Karl slipped through the heavy oak door, boots thudding on rush-strewn stone. The room was small—thick walls, low-beamed ceiling, a fire guttering in the hearth. Candles guttered in iron sconces, their light casting long shadows across the battered table at the room's heart.

Around it, three figures waited.

Laoch stood at the table's head, his katana sheathed at his hip, the curve of the blade catching faint glimmers of firelight. The elf moved with an ease most only dreamed of—like the weapon was part of him, not carried for show, but as natural as breath.

Dakarai and Kris flanked him, arms folded, grim as carved stone.

A rough map was pinned to the table beneath a rusted dagger, corners weighted with spare hilts and an upturned goblet.

Red wax marked Tempsford's walls. Black strokes spidered over the countryside—roads, rivers, ruins.

The world rendered small and broken.

Karl closed the door behind him with a soft thud.

No guards. No noise.

Just the thick, heavy quiet of people about to gamble their lives.

He made his way to the table, slipping the axe from the loop at his hip and setting it against a bench—within easy reach. No one went unarmed anymore, not even inside stone walls.

"It seems you're handing out invitations to get killed," Karl said. "Save me a good one."

Laoch lifted his head, a brow quirking slightly.

"You're late," he said, voice like cold iron.

Karl shrugged, a tired grin tugging at his mouth. "Had to find my lucky boots."

Kris gave a grunt that might have been a laugh. Dakarai didn't move, a silent mountain.

No one offered him a seat. Fine by him. Karl leaned his knuckles on the table, studying the lines of ink.

"Three squads," Laoch said without preamble. "Three strikes."

He tapped the map—quick, efficient.

A broken bridge. An abandoned village. An old watchtower.

"You'll take the north ridge," Laoch continued. "The Fellwater bridge. Wooden. Rotten. Burn it if you can. If they cross it, Tempsford falls faster than we can hold."

Karl nodded. The Fellwater. Fast, freezing, a death sentence if you stumbled in winter.

"Got it. Make it swim or sink."

A flicker of dry amusement crossed Laoch's face.

He shifted to another mark.

"Dakarai—the flats. Burn the village before they use it for shelter. They're Draugr, but they're being rallied by the living."

Another shift.

"Kris—the old watchtower. Hold the high ground or bring it down."

The hearth crackled behind them, spitting sparks across the stones.

Karl squinted at the map. "Anyone drawing lots for who gets eaten first?"

"If we're lucky," Laoch said, "they'll kill you quick."

Karl grinned wider. "Good thing I've never been lucky."

The wind howled beyond the arrow slits.

Cold slipped through the cracks, gnawing at the back of Karl's neck.

Laoch leaned forward, voice dropping lower.

"When you fight Draugr," he said, "you cut off the head. Or burn them to ash. Anything less is wasted breath."

No room for doubt. No room for second chances.

Karl flexed his fingers against the table's edge. "High and hard. Understood."

Dakarai shifted his weight slightly.

"And if they reach the walls?"

"Draeg and Havoc are laying traps," Laoch said. "Oil trenches. Tar pits. Dragonfire ready to fall from the sky. We'll burn the fields before we burn the city."

Karl liked that. If you couldn't hold the ground, make it bleed instead.

Above them, a heavy shadow swept past the solar's small windows, blocking what little light the morning offered.

Ignara, her wings tattered but proud, circling like a war spirit.

"She'll scout ahead," Laoch said. "Relay what she sees. You'll adapt."

No promises. No easy paths.

DEMIGOD

Karl rolled his shoulders back.

"When do we leave?"

"Now," Laoch said.

They clasped wrists—Karl with Dakarai, with Kris—rough, firm grips.

Laoch clasped Karl's forearm last, his grip strong, steady. No words at first. Just the weight of the fight between them.

Finally, Laoch spoke, quiet but hard.

"Every hour matters."

Karl squeezed back. "We'll buy you all we can."

He turned without another word, the heavy door thudding shut behind him.

Tempsford waited beyond—battered streets, broken houses, soldiers moving like ghosts between barricades.

The forge fires still burned. The walls still stood.

Karl looked up as Ignara passed overhead again, her shadow stretching long across the battered stones.

The dead were coming.

Tempsford was bleeding.

And he? Well, he was still breathing.

For now.

Anwyn

The battlements groaned beneath her boots as she walked them, frost seeping into the cracks of the old stone.

Tempsford shivered under a thin grey sky, smoke curling from shattered chimneys, walls patched with fresh timber and desperation.

Below, soldiers and citizens moved like ghosts through the mist—hammering braces into the gates, stacking barrels of tar and oil at key points, hauling broken carts into makeshift barricades.

No songs. No banners.

Only the sound of cold iron and the will to live a little longer.

Anwyn pulled her cloak tighter against the wind.

Each step burned in her thighs, her back still raw from carrying new life into the world only weeks ago.

But she would not falter.

She could not.

Tempsford would stand, or it would fall.

And she would not break while there was still breath in her body.

She paused near the north tower, eyes sweeping the valley.

Beyond the river, the hills crouched low and dark, hiding the things that marched closer every hour.

The dead were coming.

Anwyn set her jaw and turned away, descending the worn stone stairs into the keep.

The corridors inside were warmer but no less grim.

Soot darkened the beams overhead.

Rushes scattered across the floors hid the bloodstains no one had time to scrub clean.

The keep was alive in the way a wounded beast lives—wary, cornered, snapping at every shadow.

She crossed the great hall—now stripped of its tapestries, every table and chair pushed to the walls to make space for the wounded yet to come—and slipped into the narrow side hall leading deeper into the heart of the fortress.

There, tucked away beyond two thick oak doors, lay her refuge.

Eira was there, her mother's silver hair pulled back tight, sharp eyes watching as Anwyn entered.

Beside her, in a cradle carved hastily from an old chest, slept Owen and Freya.

Anwyn's heart snagged in her chest.

She crossed the room on silent feet, dropping to her knees beside the cradle.

Freya stirred first, her tiny fists punching the air, a soft, helpless sound tumbling from her lips.

Anwyn was there in an instant, brushing trembling fingers across her daughter's brow, desperate to soothe, to shield.

Owen lay still beside her, stubborn even in dreams, his breathing deep and sure.

Something about the tilt of his mouth—the stubborn set of his brow—struck her straight through the heart.

Gunnar.

She sucked in a ragged breath, the ache so fierce it nearly brought her to her knees.

"You're safe," Anwyn whispered, the words thick with all the promises she had left to give. "I'll keep you safe. I swear it."

Even if it shattered her into a thousand pieces.

Even if it cost her her last breath.

She pressed her forehead to the cradle's edge, breathing in the faint scents of milk, smoke, and new life.

She stayed like that a moment longer than she should have.

But not longer than she needed.

Eira cleared her throat softly.

Anwyn rose, masking the ache in her knees with a stiff smile.

"Elara is waiting," her mother said.

Anwyn nodded.

Back to work.

Back to war.

They met in the lower chamber—once a place of song and celebration, of bright banners and new oaths. Now it stank of tallow smoke and fear, its walls hung with rough maps, its tables cluttered with supplies, ledgers, and hastily scribbled plans for a siege no one was certain they would survive.

Elara was already there—the hedgewitch's sleeves rolled to the elbows, face grim and set.

Scrolls and baskets of herbs lay strewn across the table. Parchment lists fluttered under stones.

Anwyn moved to the table, planting her hands against the battered wood.

"We need field stations in the lower courtyard," she said without preamble. "Close enough for the wounded to reach, far enough to stay behind the main lines."

Elara nodded, fingers already dancing across parchment.

"And triage points here," Anwyn added, tapping a rough sketch of the keep's inner levels. "Anyone who can still stand fights. Anyone who can't—they get one chance to heal, or they stay down."

Eira's mouth tightened but she said nothing.

Kindness had to be measured now.

They spent the next hour hammering it out—rough, fast, brutal logistics.

Eira would lead the healers, recruiting anyone too weak to fight who could stitch a wound or mix a poultice.

Elara would manage supply stores—bandages, herbs, clean water.

Runners would be stationed at key points, carrying the fallen back from the walls under shield if necessary.

No heroics.

No waste.

Every hand mattered.

Every breath.

When they were done, Anwyn pulled her cloak close again, nodding once to her mother and Elara.

"Thank you," she said simply.

They would save lives.

Or they would buy the living time to say goodbye.

The Queen was waiting.

Or rather—not waiting.

Just there.

Still broken.

Anwyn found her curled in a high-backed chair before a fire burned low to embers, her body folded small, as if trying to vanish into the wood. Her face was pale, her eyes the colour of old storms—hollow and drifting.

A goblet dangled from one loose hand.

Wine dripped onto the flagstones in slow, dark splashes.

Anwyn dismissed the servant with a nod and crossed the room.

She said nothing at first.

Just pulled a stool close and sat, the silence thick between them.

Minutes passed.

Finally, Kathrynne stirred—a whisper of a woman once clothed in crown and pride.

"He was everything," she rasped.

Her gaze didn't lift. It stayed fixed on the fire, or beyond it. As if she were watching something only she could see.

"I know," Anwyn said, taking the Queen's hand—cold and bird-thin—in both of hers.

She let the silence hold them, the grief thick and settled like dust.

There was no fixing this.

Only surviving it.

Later, after Kathrynne had wept herself empty, Anwyn found Baron Roderic waiting in the antechamber.

She pressed a hand to his chest—firm, steady.

"She needs you more than she needs a sword," she said. "Stay with her. Hold her up, if you can."

Roderic's jaw clenched, but he nodded.

They understood each other without needing more words.

As Anwyn stepped back into the courtyard, the wind had risen and the sky had turned dark.

Somewhere behind her, the wine kept dripping.

Torches flared along the battlements.

The cold bit deeper.

The gates loomed high and black against the starless sky.

Tempsford's defenders huddled against the dark, blades in hand, hearts hammering.

Anwyn tightened her cloak around her shoulders and climbed the nearest wall walk.

She stood there a long time, watching the valley.

The mist.

The waiting.

The dead were coming.

But they would find the living waiting.

Not broken.

Not bowed.

Still breathing.

Still standing.

Still fighting.

Chapter 21

Ruiha

The fires crackled low, casting long, broken shadows over the ruined sands. Smoke hung heavy in the air, the stench of burnt flesh and churned earth clawing at Ruiha's throat.

Kemp tightened the strap on a wounded Sand Whisperer's shoulder, blood darkening the cloth. The man didn't even flinch. No one did. Not anymore.

Gundeep limped toward them, sword dragging a line through the sand. His shoulder was a mess of blood and torn leather, but his spine stayed straight. Pride in every step.

"You're leaving," he said, voice rough as sand on stone.

Kemp rose, dust falling from his cloak. Ruiha shifted beside him, her fingers twitching toward the hilt of her blade out of habit, not threat.

The wind stirred ash across the broken dunes.

"Where will you go?" Ruiha asked.

"Wherever you go," Gundeep said, eyes flicking between Kemp and Vaelthys. "We follow the Elderflame."

Kemp shifted, the firelight glinting against the dark storms in his eyes.

"We need to reach Tempsford," he said. "The war... it's changed. They'll need us."

Gundeep nodded, blood soaking his tunic dark. "Then we follow. The Sand Whisperers, away from the sands." He chuckled, low and rough.

Ruiha studied him, the way a crack ran down his side, red with fresh bleeding. "It's a dangerous road."

"We've survived worse," Gundeep rasped.

Ash hissed against stone. Vaelthys loomed behind them, scales burning green and violet in the firelight, his gaze storm-dark.

Gundeep stepped forward, slammed a fist to his chest. "The Sand Whisperers are yours. By blood and fire. By the oath of the Elderflame."

Kemp flinched. Ruiha saw it—a flicker of old guilt like a knife's edge across his face.

"You don't owe us," Kemp said, voice low.

Gundeep bared bloodstained teeth in a grim smile. "You misunderstand. This is not debt. This is oath."

Around them, the battered survivors rose, one by one, pressing fists to their chests in silent salute.

Kiran limped forward, Nevaeh cradled against her hip, blood slicking her torn forearm.

Ruiha swallowed hard against the lump rising in her throat.

"Then go north," she said, voice rough. "Gather who you can. Fight if you must. But live."

Gundeep bowed his head once, deep and sure. "Then fly," he said. "We'll meet again."

He turned without another word, barking orders.

Swords flashed. Carts rolled. Wounded voices cut sharp against the night.

Kemp brushed her arm. "We should go."

Ruiha nodded, already moving, already reaching for Vaelthys.

Behind them, the Sand Whisperers gathered, a last defiant wall against the darkness.

Above, the first stars bled through a sky bruised with coming war.

Kemp

The dunes bled into the sky, smoke and ash blurring the edge of the world.

Kemp swung up into the saddle behind Ruiha, his muscles burning with the effort. Blood crusted on his tunic, a badge of battles barely survived. Vaelthys shifted beneath them, his scales still slick with old wounds, but the dragon stood strong—massive, breathing slow and steady, a living storm bound in flesh and bone.

Below, the Sand Whisperers gathered. Torn banners snapped in the bitter wind. Wounded men and women pressed fists to bloodied chests, saluting in silence.

Kemp leaned low into Vaelthys' neck.

"Fly," he whispered.

The dragon crouched—a heartbeat, a gathering storm—and then the world lurched, the ground falling away beneath them.

Kemp felt Ruiha's grip tighten around his waist as Vaelthys hurled them skyward.

Ash exploded in their wake. The dunes shrank to dust. The roar of wings beat against the broken sky.

Kemp dared a glance down.

The Sand Whisperers moved like a wounded beast, dragging carts, lifting the fallen, swords flashing like shards of bone in the firelight. They were already dwindling to specks—a last defiant stand against the night.

The stars overhead bled through the smoke, faint and cold. They flew north, the cold slashing against Kemp's face, numbing fingers, biting into the rags of his strength.

Below them, the world was a graveyard.

The first village they passed lay shattered, houses gutted by fire, doors swinging loose on blackened hinges. Crows wheeled above the ruins, their cries thin and sharp.

Further on, a battlefield. A field of bones, churned mud stained black.

No banners flew. No bodies moved.

Only the crows remained.

Kemp tensed his jaw, forcing the sickness down.

His grip tightened as Vaelthys fought the wind—hard, battering gusts that screamed over the broken hills and through shattered woodlands.

They skirted a ruined watchtower, half-collapsed against a crag of stone. Once, it had watched over merchant caravans and travellers. Now it watched over nothing but ruin.

The land here had been alive once—farms, orchards, rivers. Now it was scorched and silent, every mile a wound left to fester.

The horizon darkened.

Kemp shifted, the moonlight glinting off the scars etched deep into his face, the storm behind his eyes unbroken.

Ahead, a smear of smoke bruised the sky.

"Lamos," Ruiha muttered.

Or what was left of it.

From this height, Kemp could see the shattered ring of walls, the spider-thread streets inside, the scars of siege clawed across the fields.

Figures moved below—not soldiers fortifying, but something slower. Heavier.

No horns sounded. No banners flew.

Just the long, slow grind of a city dying.

Vaelthys rumbled low in his chest, the sound vibrating up through the saddle into Kemp's bones.

He smelled it too—the rot, the wrongness.

Kemp twisted to glance back at Ruiha, her eyes fierce.

"We need to do something," she rasped, voice shredded by wind.

Kemp nodded, scanning the ruins.

Gutted houses. Collapsed towers.

No lights. No life.

The Draugr were already there.

Moving like broken marionettes through the wreckage, gathering at the breaches in the wall like ants at a carcass.

The sight gripped his gut and twisted.

"We burn it," Vaelthys said, his voice a low rumble against the wind.

Ruiha nodded once.

No hesitation.

Vaelthys banked, wings flexing with a powerful stroke, tilting them into the wind.

Kemp leaned into the dragon's movement, feeling the raw strength coiled beneath scale and sinew.

Fire welled in Vaelthys' throat—Kemp felt it rising, a growing heat, a heartbeat away from violence.

And then he loosed it.

A river of flame tore through the sky, a living spear of fury.

Below, Draugr caught fire—figures staggering, shrivelling, collapsing into ash and bone. Buildings lit like torches, flame running like spilled blood through the ruined streets.

Kemp tasted smoke and burning flesh on the air, thick and cloying.

No screams.

Only the crackle of fire eating what could not die fast enough.

Vaelthys roared—a sound that tore across the broken city, defiant and wild.

They didn't linger.

No heroics. No pointless deaths.

Vaelthys climbed, wings heaving against the wind, the ruined city falling away beneath them.

Kemp looked back once.

Saw shapes moving through the smoke—not as many as before—but enough.

The Draugr were awake now.

The flight north was a battle of its own.

The land below churned into a wasteland—burned farms, shattered forests, roads blackened by retreat and ruin.

Ash clawed at them, stinging eyes and throat. The wind howled across the broken hills, tearing at cloak and leather.

Vaelthys fought for every wingbeat, his muscles straining against the rising storm.

Ahead, a darker shape cut the horizon.

Tempsford.

The last hope.

The last wall.

Kemp's chest tightened as the city came into view—the battered gates reinforced with iron, the scarred walls crawling with soldiers and masons alike. A city bracing for siege, too proud to fall quietly.

Vaelthys banked sharply, air screaming past, the ground rushing up to meet them.

No celebration at their arrival. Only the hammer of steel on stone, the clatter of barrels being rolled into place, the bark of orders from captains and quartermasters—a living city, digging in for war.

Vaelthys struck the flagstones hard, claws skidding, wings flaring to slow their descent.

Soldiers turned, hands leaping to weapons—then froze, recognising the dragon and riders as allies.

Kemp leapt down, boots slamming into stone. His knees buckled under the jolt, but he straightened, scanning the courtyard.

Ruiha landed beside him, daggers still sheathed, yet eyes sharp, assessing.

Around them, the city moved like a great machine—soldiers laying fire-traps beyond the walls, blacksmiths hammering at broken shields, crossbowmen stationed atop towers like sentinels.

The air was heavy with the scent of oil, smoke, and iron.

No panic. No despair. Only grim, grinding purpose.

Tempsford stood.

And it would not fall easily.

Kemp rested a hand against Vaelthys' heaving side, feeling the pulse of fire still burning beneath scale and scar.

He looked at Ruiha, a bitter taste rising in his mouth.

"We made it," he said, voice rough with smoke and exhaustion.

She nodded once.

"But it's only just beginning."

Above them, the grey clouds churned, and far beyond the horizon, the dead marched closer with every hour.

Ruiha

The wind snapped at Ruiha's cloak as she slid from Vaelthys' back, boots striking stone with a jolt that rattled up her spine.

Vaelthys rumbled low, shuddering from the flight, wings sagging with exhaustion.

But he was alive. Strong.

And they had made it.

Ruiha drew a long, shaking breath, eyes scanning the courtyard.

Soldiers rushed past with bundles of arrows and coils of rope. Blacksmiths hammered bent iron into rough shapes. Tar barrels were rolled into place along the walls.

Everything smelled of smoke and iron and bitter determination.

A living city, not a dying one.

Her gaze flicked higher—and caught.

Across the courtyard, looming near the main gate, a figure she had not dared to hope for.

Ignara.

The great dragon crouched low, her massive body curled protectively around a cluster of soldiers preparing their defences.

Scars laced her hide—fresh ones, savage—but she was whole. Her head lifted, one golden eye fixing on Ruiha across the churned ground.

Ruiha didn't think.

Didn't speak.

She ran.

Mud and ash splattered her boots. She dodged a cart, leapt a length of coiled rope, heart hammering harder than it had during the flight north.

Ignara let out a low, rumbling breath that set the banners fluttering as Ruiha reached her.

Without hesitation, Ruiha threw herself into the warm curve of the dragon's neck, arms flung wide, hands digging into the rough, living scales.

Ignara bent her head, pressing into Ruiha's chest with a sound almost like a sigh.

Tears burned Ruiha's throat. She bit them down.

"Ignara," Ruiha choked out.

Ignara exhaled, a gust of heat that rolled over her like a furnace.

"You live," the dragon rumbled, voice rough as grinding stone.

Ruiha barked a short laugh—bitter, cracked. "Should be saying the same to you."

Ignara snorted, smoke curling from her nostrils.

"I do not fall so easily," she said simply. "Nor do you, it seems."

Ruiha dragged the back of her hand across her mouth, forcing the tremor from it. She turned, stabbing a finger toward Vaelthys sprawled across the courtyard.

"See him?"

She didn't wait for an answer. "His name is Vaelthys. He hatched from the Elderflame. Stronger than anything I've seen."

Ignara's head tilted, her golden eye narrowing, measuring.

A low rumble—approval, deep and raw.

"And Kemp," Ruiha said, jaw tight. "They're bonded. Like we were."

She spoke before the pain could take hold. "One wound. One blade."

Ignara leaned in, until Ruiha could feel the rumble of her breath through her chest.

"They will need to fight too," Ignara murmured. "The real war has not begun."

Before Ruiha could answer, a horn sounded, sharp and final.

The council.

Duty clamped its hand around Ruiha's spine.

She pressed her forehead briefly against Ignara's battered hide.

"I'll come back," she said, voice flat and certain—a promise made of iron, not hope.

Ignara lowered her head, eyes closing.

"I know."

Kemp was there then, his hand brushing lightly against her arm.

"Council's waiting," he said.

Ruiha nodded, the burn in her chest banking down into hard, cold resolve.

One last look—Ignara's steady gaze, unwavering as a mountain.

Then she turned away.

Together, she and Kemp crossed the courtyard, weaving through the frantic heartbeat of a city preparing for its last, hardest fight.

Toward the keep.

Toward war.

Chapter 22

Gunnar

Gunnar stepped forward, his boots striking the obsidian floor with a hollow finality. The sound echoed, swallowed too quickly by the vast emptiness.

Before him, a fortress loomed—black walls rising like jagged fangs, piercing a sky that did not exist. Cold fire flickered in braziers, casting an eerie glow over stone etched with names too worn to be read, each letter cut deep, as if defying the weight of time itself.

The silence pressed in—thick, expectant. No wind. No distant echoes of battle. Only the slow, rhythmic pull of something unseen, a gravity that had nothing to do with the ground beneath his feet.

Gunnar's breath was slow, steady, yet his chest felt tight. His body knew before his mind—this place was not meant for the living. It was a relic of something older than war, something that did not care for kings or warriors, only for those who had been claimed by it.

He stepped forward.

A throne room awaited.

At its heart, the throne.

Iron and bone twisted together in a shape that was neither cruel nor kind, its edges sharp but inviting, its back curving as if to cradle a weary warrior. Shadows clung to it, shifting like breath, like waiting hands. The weight of history settled over Gunnar's shoulders, pressing against his spine like a blade held just above the skin.

The scent of old blood lingered in the air—not fresh, not rotten, but settled.

An offering long accepted.

At last, the voice spoke.

"You have suffered enough, Gunnar."

It did not boom. It did not snarl. It barely even echoed, as if the words had never needed to be spoken aloud to be heard. A voice velvet and measured, the kind a warrior might hear after a long march through frostbitten lands, after standing at the edge of a battlefield where the bodies outnumber the living.

"You have fought. You have bled. You have endured."

Gunnar said nothing.

The weight of his axe felt distant in his hand. His fingers twitched, aching from battles won and lost. He knew the scars that lay beneath the worn leather of his gauntlets, knew the burn of wounds long since healed but never forgotten. His body had been broken and rebuilt a hundred times over. The throne did not offer deception. He saw it for what it was, and that made it worse.

"Sit. Rest. Rule."

A warrior's reward. Not a lie. Not a trick. Just stillness.

He took another step, close enough now that he could see the fine cracks in the bone, the deep grooves where weapons had struck but never broken its form. His hand lifted of its own accord, reaching, fingertips brushing the cool metal of the armrest.

The whispers ceased.

He saw himself seated there. Not a vision, not a dream—just the simple truth of what would be. A figure draped in shadow and steel, no crown, no scepter, but a king nonetheless. No war, no burden, no endless march into the unknown. Just dominion. Just certainty.

He had earned it.

And yet—had he ever wanted it? He'd never sought a crown, never craved the burden of a throne.

Memories surfaced, fractured and uncertain, like glass splintering under pressure. Shapes without faces. Voices without names.

But there was someone.

Waiting for him.

Someone he needed to fight for.

His hand curled into a fist, knuckles white, tension coiling through his arm.

He drew back.

The silence stretched, but now it was empty. He had heard this quiet before. Not in victory, but in surrender. Not in triumph, but in loss.

The throne was not an end to suffering. It was an end to everything.

To sit was to stop. To stop was to fade.

He turned.

The gate stood open, not golden, not shining, not promising. Just open. Just waiting.

"You would have made a great king." The voice was not bitter, not pleading. Just knowing. "But you were never meant to rule."

The fortress trembled. Cracks lanced through the obsidian walls, carving through the forgotten names. The braziers flickered once, then died, smoke curling upward before the dark swallowed it whole. The throne remained, untouched, waiting for another.

Gunnar walked forward. Alone. Unburdened. Unbroken.

The gate closed behind him.

And the fortress fell to dust.

Chapter 23

Anwyn

The council chamber smelled of smoke and old iron. Anwyn stood at the head of the battered table, the weight of every life in Tempsford pressing against her spine. Around her, the others shifted—leather creaked, cloaks dragged against stone—but no one spoke first.

There were no banners here now. No colours but the grey of ash and the red of old blood.

She swept her gaze across them: her father, silent as a drawn blade. Her mother, pale and sharp-eyed. Elara, sleeves pushed back, hands stained with ink and herbs. Roderic, grim and unyielding. Kemp, a storm bottled inside broken flesh. And Kathrynne—once a queen—slumped in her chair, crownless, hollow-eyed.

Anwyn set her hands on the rough wood, feeling the grain bite her palms.

"We need a report," she said, voice low. "Tell us everything."

Ruiha stepped forward. Her cloak was torn, blood dried in dark streaks across the battered fabric. She smelled of smoke and iron and the long, hard miles between life and death.

But her voice was steady. Unbreakable.

"Lamos has fallen," she said. "Nothing remains but bones and ash. The Drogo scour the ruins, gathering strength. And—"

She faltered, just for a heartbeat. A flicker of something deeper than fear crossed her face. "They command an evil now. The undead. Draugr, Vaelthys called them. They rise when struck down. Only fire or severing the head stops them—and even then, not always."

The silence that followed was a heavy thing.

Laoch stepped forward, his katana flashing a sliver of light as he moved. His face was carved from iron. "We know," he said. His voice rang like a hammer against anvil. "They can be stopped. But we must guard our dead, or we will be burying our own swords in friends' hearts before this ends."

A sob broke the stillness—raw, jarring.

Kathrynne.

All eyes turned, just for a breath.

The once-queen sat slumped in her chair, her frame gaunt and hollowed, the lines of her face sharp as old ruin. One skeletal hand gripped the armrest as if the stone itself might carry her away. Her lips moved—soft, near soundless.

Luthar's name, spoken like a prayer. Or a plea.

Anwyn stilled.

She wanted to reach for her. Say something. But grief was a luxury she couldn't afford.

She drew a breath, slow and iron-hard, then turned back to the map.

"The plan stands," Anwyn said, her voice flat as cold steel. "We hold. The walls. The streets. Each other."

No debate. No retreat. No mercy.

Laoch nodded once. Sharp. Certain.

"We still have the dragons," he said. "We still have the Sand Dragons and the Shadow Hawks. We still have hope."

Kemp raised a hand, slow and deliberate.

"And we have Vaelthys," he said. "Born of Elderflame. His power is not just strength—it is old as the mountains, and just as unyielding."

A murmur rippled through the chamber. Half fear, half awe.

Ruiha's voice cut clean across it.

"We should not sit behind these walls and wait to die," she said, fiercer now. "The Elven army is still out there, bleeding. Fighting. We should march to them. Meet this evil before it swallows the world."

Her words hung, bright and terrible, like a sword caught in the sun.

Anwyn's hands tightened on the table's edge.

"No," she said, and her voice was the voice of the battered stones themselves.

"We cannot risk feeding their ranks with our dead. Every soldier lost becomes a blade turned against us. We stand. We make them come to us."

Ruiha's jaw clenched. Her fists did too.

"We cannot simply wait," she said. "Waiting is death too."

For a breath, for a heartbeat, no one spoke.

The fire snapped in the hearth, the only sound in the broken chamber.

Then Laoch stepped forward, his palm flat on the battered table. His voice was low, iron-hard. "Anwyn is right. We hold Tempsford," he said. "We make them bleed for every stone, every street. The Drogo will not find easy ground here."

"No," Ruiha cut in, fire flickering in her eyes. "We can do more than sit behind stone. Vaelthys and Ignara—" she nodded toward the dragons waiting beyond the broken arch "—are not meant to rot behind walls. Let us ride. Strike their heart before they mass."

Kemp said nothing, but his shadowhand clenched, dark flames licking up his arm.

Laoch shook his head, slow and heavy. "You strike too soon, you die," he said. "Dragons are fire. Rage. But they are not endless. You send them out now, you lose them before the worst comes. Ignara and I have fought undead dragons, Ruiha. It is… *difficult*."

"Yet if we wait," Ruiha said, her voice sharp as drawn steel, "we lose the walls. We lose the war."

Eira stirred, her hands knotted at her sides. "Dragons are powerful, but not infinite. They tire. They can be injured. If we lose them," she said, voice tight, "we lose the sky. And the sky is all that will save us if the walls break."

Kemp finally spoke then, voice low, carved from stone. "We do not fly to die." He lifted his gaze, and for a heartbeat, there was something terrible in it. "We fly to break them."

Anwyn closed her eyes, seeing it as clearly as if it had already happened:

Draugr and Drogo surging through broken streets, the wounded rising from the dead to turn against them.

A slaughter.

Or—

A pyre.

She opened her eyes, heavy with the weight of every life in this city. "We hold," she said, slow and certain. "We bleed them against the walls. When the gates splinter, when their heart comes into the open—then we strike."

She let the words settle like iron in the room before adding,

"In the meantime, we do not sit idle. Karl, Kris, and Dakarai are already in the field. Their units move even now—burning supply lines, cutting outriders from the herd, thinning their vanguard. Every hour they bleed is an hour we steal back. Every enemy they fell now is one less draugr we face at the gates later."

A few grim nods answered her.

Anwyn turned to Ruiha.

"Ruiha, you and Kemp will take Ignara and Vaelthys to assist them. But you do not get close. You do not risk them. You strike only when the reward outweighs the cost. You think before every blow. Do you understand?"

Ruiha stiffened. She did not like it. Anwyn saw that.

But slowly, grimly, Ruiha nodded.

"I understand," she said.

Anwyn turned back to the others.

"Go," she said. "Prepare the oil. Ready the streets. Prepare pyres to burn the bodies before they rise. Every hour we live buys another hour of hope."

Elara spoke next, her voice brisk, practical. "Healers are stationed along the second ring. Supplies rationed for a siege."

Eira added, "Field triage is ready. Once the outer wards fall, we fall back and brace for house-to-house."

Anwyn nodded. It was not enough. It would never be enough. But it would have to be. "The enemy comes to bury us," she said. "They will find, instead, a pyre."

Laoch's mouth curled into the ghost of a smile. Eira bowed her head.

Ruiha unsheathed her daggers half an inch—steel singing against steel—and then slid them home. A promise made without words.

Kathrynne did not move. Did not speak. But when Anwyn passed her chair, the Queen's hand brushed her sleeve.

A broken hand. A broken kingdom. But the touch was steady.

Still breathing. Still standing.

Anwyn strode into the cold, where the first horns were already beginning to sound, thin and mournful against the mist.

The dead were coming.

Tempsford would answer.

With steel.

With fire.

With everything they had left.

Chapter 24

Karl

Mist devoured the world. Karl crouched low behind a broken cart, axe slick in his grip. Dakarai tapped twice against his chest—ready.

Ahead, Draugr lumbered through the ash, herded by Drogo cloaked in black, iron staves thudding against the ground with every step.

There was a wrongness to it which scraped against Karl's spirit, a stench beneath the smoke and death.

One deep breath. One heartbeat.

He surged forward anyway.

Steel flashed. Throats parted. Heads rolled. Draugr toppled like felled trees, limbs twitching even after death. Dakarai's small unit moved at his flanks, sure and sharp, blades finding the soft meat of the column.

The stench clung to Karl's skin. The air tasted of old blood and rotten flesh.

The bastards should have let the dead rest.

Instead, the world had turned.

The first Drogo turned, raising his staff, a pulse of magic humming.

Karl's axe split the shaman's skull before the staff could spark.

The nearest Draugr lurched, staggered—untethered. A gap opened in their line.

Karl grunted. "Take the shaman first!" he barked, voice rough against the mist.

His men needed no further urging.

The Drogo handlers fought back—quick, savage, staff strikes snapping through the air—but they were no soldiers. They died hard and fast.

For a heartbeat, Karl thought they had the upper hand.

Until the second wave hit.

From deeper in the mist came more Draugr—faster, hungrier. Their bodies stitched with black iron, mouths torn open wider than any living jaw.

Karl swung into the nearest one.

The Draugr he struck fell, but its spirit clung to him.

It's rotten aura latched onto his axe, snarling and coiling, seeping into the steel like a viper slipping into a nest.

Karl staggered, his own spirit flaring so hard it made his vision blur. He began cycling the aura as Thalirion had taught him in Nexus.

The Draugr's spirit was half-dead, half-burning—*raw*.

His instincts screamed.

Without thinking, Karl pulled.

Magic flared hot across his skin. He wrenched the thing's spirit into the axe, shaping it, forcing it, hammering it with raw will.

The weapon *screamed*—a sound too sharp, too hungry.

Karl grunted, nearly thrown off his feet. The haft vibrated violently against his palms; the axe head pulsed blood-red, veins of light crawling along the steel like living fire.

The Draugr lunged again—mindless, rotted.

Karl swung.

The axe struck bone—and erupted.

A shockwave burst from the impact, searing the mist into sudden clarity. Three Draugr nearby caught the blast head-on, their bodies exploding into ash and burning fragments.

Karl stared, heart hammering against his ribs.

"Draeg's stone balls. What was that?" he muttered to himself.

There was no time to think on it.

More Draugr pressed forward, screeching, staffs cracking the ground behind them as Drogo shaman drove them into the fray.

Karl forced his breathing steady.

Adapt. Forge. Fight.

He tightened his grip on the spirit-bound axe, squared his shoulders, and roared back into the teeth of the dead.

The next Draugr charged him, mouth open in a silent shriek.

Karl swung.

His axe bit—and the Draugr didn't fall. It exploded.

Bone shards whickered past his face. The mist tore open for a heartbeat, and Karl could see the Drogo leader ahead—taller, armour gleaming, black staff crackling with rotted light.

He gritted his teeth, tightened his grip on the howling axe, and charged.

The Drogo shaman lifted his staff, grunted something—but he was too slow.

Karl drove the axe into the shaman's chest. Arcane power bursting from the weapon, the staff snapping like brittle bone. The shaman's scream echoed long after his body hit the ground.

Karl stood panting in the mist, axe dripping black and red.

His men rallied around him, faces pale, weapons slick with gore.

More Draugr howled in the distance—still coming.

Karl bared his teeth.

The wildfire had caught.

And they were far from done.

Ruiha

The clouds tore apart like wet cloth.

Ignara burst through with a scream that shook the heavens, a living storm of scale and flame.

Ruiha pressed low against the dragon's burning spine, hands curled into the iron-hard ridges along Ignara's neck.

The wind ripped the breath from her lungs, searing cold against the heat bleeding from Ignara's body.

Below, the fields spread out in chaos and ruin.

Partially built siege towers clawed at the grey sky—monstrous things of wood and iron, black banners flapping like the wings of carrion crows.

Ruiha's heart hammered.

"Now!" she roared.

Ignara tucked her wings tight, diving like a spear hurled by the gods.

Fire roared from her jaws, pure and endless, a torrent of ancient rage.

The first tower erupted, flames leaping higher than the treetops. Screams rose with the smoke, Drogo soldiers scattering like leaves before a hurricane.

Ruiha laughed, fierce and wild, the sound stolen by the wind.

Another gout of flame. Another tower shattered, its timbers snapping like dry bone.

Beneath her, Ignara's muscles coiled and uncoiled, smooth and terrible. Ruiha could feel the dragon's pulse in the air itself, a thunderous beat beneath the chaos.

Arrows spat upward—screaming iron bolts, black against the firelit sky.

Left!

The thought wasn't words, but instinct—and Ignara answered, rolling without hesitation.

Ruiha faltered, just for a breath.

Their bond—was it back?

No.

It couldn't be.

Just instinct.

That was all.

She gritted her teeth, pushed the thought away as Ignara's wingtip carved a smoking trench along the ground below.

A siege bolt howled past them, close enough for Ruiha to feel the heat scald her cheek.

Still alive. Still flying.

She urged Ignara higher.

They climbed hard, tearing through smoke and mist, the ruined field falling away beneath them.

For a moment, Ruiha saw it all laid bare—the burning wreckage, the broken lines, the jagged scar their fire had carved into the Drogo army.

The land itself seemed to cry out beneath them.

And then the mist cracked open like a wound, the true size of the enemy massing beyond it revealed at last.

Ruiha gritted her teeth, the laughter dying in her throat.

This was only the beginning.

Kemp

The mist pressed in, heavy as a shroud.

Kemp crouched low against Vaelthys's back, feeling the dragon's pulse beat through his scales—slow, deep, ancient.

Below, the battlefield burned.

Fires guttered against the dawn.

Drogo and Draugr staggered through smoke, ranks broken, banners torn to tatters.

Perfect.

Kemp let the breath bleed from his lungs, the cold cutting deeper than the heat.

Dark shadows curled from his hand, thick and seething, eager for release.

Vaelthys growled—a sound too old for living things—and folded his wings.

They fell.

Through smoke. Through fire.

Silent as the grave.

Kemp stretched out his hand—and let go.

Black fire tore from his fingers, roaring across the ruined ground like a tide of ash and broken oaths.

It swallowed Drogo and Draugr alike, leaving scorched bone and shattered steel in its wake.

They rose higher. He pressed his palm flat to Vaelthys's scaled hide, grounding himself in the ancient, thrumming power that lived there.

Time to end this, he thought.

Without a word spoken, they let go.

The world seemed to catch its breath.

For a heartbeat, all was still.

Then—a pulse of magic.

Invisible, but vast.

It tore outward in a silent roar, too great to be seen, too terrible to be heard.

The heart of the Drogo ranks shattered. Soldiers dropped as if cut from their strings—no screams, no last defiance. Just bodies hitting the ground, dust rising in mourning.

Beneath the thunderous silence, only the Draugr remained standing—rotted things, unmoved by death's passing touch.

Kemp's breath scraped his throat raw as he stared.

Vaelthys rumbled beneath him, the sound low and grim, like a mountain grinding its teeth.

For a time, there was only silence.

Then the fallen Drogo began to twitch.

One by one.

Grime streaked hands clawed at the ground. Heads jerked upward. Eyes opened—blank, empty, wrong.

The Drogo rose again. Draugr now. Every last one of them.

Kemp felt his gut clench, a sickness rising in him that tasted of bile and blood.

"Vaelthys," he muttered.

The dragon heard him, needed no command.

They dropped like a blade from the clouds.

Shadowfire poured from Kemp's hand, black and seething. Dragonfire roared from Vaelthys's jaws, pure and terrible.

The front ranks of the risen dead burned and fell, crumbling into ash and cinders.

But for every Draugr that fell, another clawed its way forward, relentless.

They dove again, and again.

Shadowfire and dragonfire raked across the field, burning thousands into ash.

A storm of ruin, black and crimson.

But it was not enough.

The dead kept coming, a tide without end.

Kemp felt the shift first—the subtle sag of Vaelthys's frame, the slow hitch in every breath.

Each wingbeat grew heavier.

Each climb shallower.

The great dragon's sides heaved beneath him, laboured and raw.

Vaelthys rumbled low in his chest—a sound not of fury, but of warning.

Kemp gritted his teeth.

They had thrown everything into the fire.

And still the dead came on.

They would have to fall back.

Or they would fall.

The great dragon rumbled again, this time in warning.

They had broken the living.

But the dead were not so easily defeated.

Ahead, Tempsford's walls loomed—scarred, smoke-blackened, but still standing.

Still defiant.

The dead were coming.

Would they be ready?

Chapter 25

Gunnar

Gunnar stood at the heart of the mountain's ruin. The air carried no dust, no lingering scent of blood or battle… it carried something else. Something older. Something he couldn't quite name.

The cavern stretched wide before him, a scar in the earth, deep and ancient. It was the kind of place that felt untouched.

He looked up and saw jagged pillars which rose on either side, black stone jutting up like the ribs of a dead god.

Beneath him, the rock fell away into nothing. A chasm, deep and gaping, its edges fractured and raw. Gray mist coiled up from below, thick and slow, moving with the steady rhythm of a breath—a breath that belonged to no living thing.

There was no wind. No sound. Only silence pressing against his skin, coiling in his lungs. The kind of silence that came before battle. Before blood. His fingers twitched at his side, reaching for an axe he no longer carried.

Something was here. Not seen, not heard, but felt. A presence woven into the stone, waiting.

Watching.

He had climbed mountains. Waded through rivers of blood. Stood before armies and demons. But here, in the presence of something greater than himself, he felt small. Insignificant.

Then, the mist moved—not with wind, but with intent.

A shadow coalesced in the swirling gray. Then a shape. Then a presence.

Then *her*.

He did not know how he knew her. But he did.

A name surfaced in his mind, not spoken but remembered—as if carved into the marrow of his bones, as if whispered to him through the very stone of the mountains in which he stood.

Dreyna.

She was vast, yet near. A woman and a force, woven from the mountain itself. The weight of the world pressed in her presence, her form shifting like the earth in slow movement. Her eyes burned silver, reflecting the unseen fires of the deep.

Her voice, when it came, was not harsh, nor gentle.

It was enchanting. Like a siren's song, each syllable a thread of gold binding the will of all who heard it.

"You have fought for survival, believing it your only purpose. You were wrong."

Gunnar did not move. His instincts screamed at him to bow his head, to avert his gaze as one would before a storm. But he did not. He would not.

"Then tell me," he said, voice raw. "Why am I here?"

Dreyna took a step forward. The mountain groaned beneath her weight.

"Because you are more than you understand."

The mist thickened, cold against his skin.

"You have not merely endured the torment of the underworld. You have been shaped by it. Every trial, every wound, every battle—it was never meant to break you. It was meant to forge you."

Gunnar's fingers twitched at his side. His axe was gone. No steel would serve him here.

"I don't understand," he admitted.

Dreyna's silver gaze did not waver. "Then listen."

Her words were like distant thunder rolling over stone.

"When you stood against the endless tide, knowing no victory would come, yet you fought anyway—you proved *valour*."

Visions flashed through his mind. A horde that could not be felled. He had fought. He had died. He had risen.

"When you stood by your word, though it cost you everything—you proved *honour*."

He had bled for his oath. Held fast when giving in would have saved him.

"When brute strength failed, and you turned the beast's power against itself—you proved *wisdom*."

The demon. The thing that had matched him blow for blow. He had won not with his axe, but his mind.

"When the abyss sought to break you, and you endured—rising again, and again—you proved *endurance*."

His body had shattered. But his will had not.

"When you held your blade over the helpless, and stayed your hand—you proved *compassion*."

The creature had begged for death. He had not given it.

"When the underworld demanded a price, and you bore another's burden—you proved *sacrifice*."

The warrior. The pain that had dragged him down when he could have saved himself.

"And when the throne of the damned was offered to you, when you could have ruled as more than a mortal, you cast it aside—you proved *dominion*."

Dreyna's silver gaze did not waver. "A god without dominion is no different from a tyrant, a beast that conquers for the sake of power rather than wisdom." Her voice carried the weight of stone, of mountains that had stood long before his kind first raised steel. "To wield power is nothing. To rule oneself—that is dominion."

Gunnar swallowed hard. His breath came slow. Steady.

"Yet I am no god," he said.

For the first time, Dreyna's expression shifted. It was not cruelty. Nor kindness.

"You were a prince. A warrior. A mortal."

The mist curled tighter around his limbs. He felt it then—the pull. Not downward, but upward. The ache in his bones, the fire in his muscles—it was gone.

"But now, you are more."

His heart thundered in his chest.

"How?" His voice barely carried. "How can I be more?"

Dreyna tilted her head. "Because it is within you. Because my son saw to it."

A stillness settled over Gunnar.

"Draeg?"

The name sat heavy on his tongue.

Dreyna inclined her head. "He gave you a part of his essence. You forged a bond."

Gunnar stilled. His breath caught.

"Havoc?"

Dreyna smiled.

It hit him like a hammer to the chest.

Havoc was not just a companion. Not just a creature bound by fate. He was something more.

"You do not walk through the gates of the underworld as a broken soul, nor as a mere survivor."

Dreyna's voice was the weight of mountains, the shifting of stone.

"You walk as one unchained. As one unbowed. As one who has faced darkness and emerged greater."

The mist stirred, wrapping around him like unseen hands. The cavern trembled.

"You are no longer merely a dwarf, Gunnar."

Something inside him cracked open. Something vast. Boundless.

"You are no longer mortal."

A silence settled between them. Deep. Absolute.

Then, Dreyna spoke.

"You are a demigod."

Chapter 26

Ruiha

The wind tugged at Ruiha's cloak as she stood by the broken farmhouse wall, her fingers tracing the edge of a splintered map board. Stone markers littered its surface—some toppled, others stained dark with old blood. Each stone was a four person unti. Each bloodstain, a memory.

"We've given the city days," Karl muttered, crouching beside the fireless hearth. "Maybe a week."

"But not enough," said Dakarai, his shoulder wrapped in soiled linen, the edges browning where the bleeding had slowed but not stopped. "They're still coming."

"They'll be here by dawn." Kris stood by the doorway, blade in hand, steel hissing softly as he ran the whetstone along its edge. "Whatever we bled from them, it wasn't the heart."

Kemp said nothing. He hadn't spoken much since the last raid, when they found the children in the burnt-out chapel. Ruiha glanced at him. The fire was gone from his eyes, replaced by a hollow kind of stillness. She worried for him more than she could say.

Laoch entered, framed by the jagged wooden door, shadows etched across his face. Even weariness bowed to him.

"Report," he said simply.

Karl spoke first—quick bursts, sharp as the knives they'd used. Ruiha filled in the rest: flanking runs, night fires, misdirection and ambushes. Two weeks of shadows and blood. The Drogo were slowed, scattered, but never stopped.

"Any word from Dreynas?" Laoch's voice was low.

"We sent a rider. Two weeks past. Haven't heard a word." Ruiha met his eyes. "Might not've made it through."

The silence hung like smoke.

A sound shattered it.

A deep, sky-rattling roar.

They rushed outside as one. Kris cursed. Kemp drew breath for the first time in what felt like hours. Overhead, the sun vanished behind a vast shape—silver scales glinting in the last light, wings stretched wider than the keep's fallen walls.

A dragon.

Not Ignara. Not Vaelthys.

The silver beast circled once. Then twice. Ignara was first to launch, wings tearing air. Vaelthys followed, a blur of fury. Ruiha's heart leapt into her throat.

"Wait—" Kemp rasped, voice rough from smoke and silence. "That's…"

The sky cracked with wind as the silver dragon banked hard, sun-scorched clouds parting in its wake. Wings stretched wide as sails, its descent was slow, measured—more statement than arrival. Dust billowed as it landed, dry soil spiralling in gritty vortices around its claws. The earth shuddered beneath it.

Ruiha shielded her eyes with a forearm, heart hammering. The ridge of silver scales, the eyes like storm-lit glass—

"Syltharael," she breathed.

The dragon dipped her head. A low hum rippled through the air, deep enough to be felt in the chest more than heard. Behind Ruiha, weapons half-lowered. No one spoke.

"We thought you were in Fenchester," she managed, stepping forward, boots crunching on dry gravel. "We thought—"

She let it hang. Too much had been lost to finish the sentence.

Syltharael's voice rolled like distant thunder. "I bring word from the west."

Wind tugged at Ruiha's braid. She glanced at Laoch. He gave no signal, only watched, stone-faced.

"The Drogo press us," Ruiha said, trying to steady the fire in her voice. "They'll be at the gate by first light."

"You face only part of the tide," Syltharael said. Her neck curled, gaze sweeping over them—Karl, bloodied and defiant; Kris with knuckles white on his hilt; Kemp standing still as a broken statue.

"My kin hold the skies over Fenchester. The elven spears sing in its streets. The enemy breaks there."

No one answered. Even the wind paused.

Laoch's shoulders eased, barely. A breath hissed through his nose.

"Fenchester holds?" he asked, voice low.

A rumble from Syltharael, almost a purr. "They do more than hold. They bleed the darkness."

The words landed like rain on scorched stone. Ruiha felt her ribs tighten, then ease, as though a hand had unclenched from her chest. Hope didn't blaze. It smouldered. But it lived.

Laoch turned, already calling to the nearest scout. "Ride. Find Anwyn. Tell her the fire still burns in Fenchester. That the dragons are not yet fallen."

He moved without a word, vanishing into the tree-line like a shadow made flesh.

Syltharael bowed her vast head, wings folding with a sigh that stirred the grass.

"I will stay," she said. "If I am welcome."

Laoch looked up, the ghost of a smile finding his mouth—sharp and tired. "We've not the luxury to refuse friends. The sky is yours."

Far off, drums beat against the dying light. The sun bled across the hills. But where there had been two dragons, now there were three.

And they were not yet broken.

Anwyn

The wind carried the tang of oil and ash, threading through the battlements like a curse. Tempsford's stone walls, once pale and proud, now bore the bruises of preparation—fresh pockmarks where cauldrons had been mounted, black stains where fires had tested the pitch trenches below.

Anwyn stood beneath the gate tower, hands clasped behind her back, watching the courtyard churn with ordered chaos.

Archers strung bows with cracked fingers. A stable boy hefted saddle harness onto a horse's back, sweat and fear mingling on his brow. Somewhere to the north, a child cried and was swiftly hushed.

Footsteps crunched behind her.

"South wall's reinforced," Ruiha said, voice low. "Sand Dragons and Shadow Hawks are dug in. Kris has the archers. Dakarai's watching the cliffs."

Anwyn nodded once. No need for praise. If Ruiha said it was done, it was done.

They moved together along the parapet. Below them, Karl crouched beside a trench, hands slick with tar, shouting for Draeg to pass the flintsticks. Fire pits lined the approach road like open mouths.

"They'll roast before they breach the gate," Ruiha murmured.

Anwyn's eyes tracked to the main square. Three dragons stood in the field—Vaelthys, Ignara, and now, Syltharael. Their tails twitched in rhythm, reading the coming storm.

Kemp stood beside Vaelthys, one hand resting against the dragon's flank. The creature did not flinch. They moved as one, bonded beyond blood. He hadn't spoken to Anwyn since the they'd returned from the last skirmish.

"We're stretched thin," Ruiha added, eyes on the smoke curling over the rooftops.

"I know."

That was all Anwyn gave. The weight of command didn't permit complaint.

She turned and left her friend without another word, feet taking her through the winding corridors of the keep. Guards stepped aside as she passed. None met her eyes.

Inside the great hall, a low fire crackled, throwing long shadows across old tapestries. Her mother sat near the hearth, hands tight around a half-drunk cup of tea. The shawl about her shoulders had slipped, unnoticed.

"Elara?" Anwyn asked.

"She's not here," her mother said, voice strained. "With Queen Kathrynne."

A long pause followed. The fire popped, casting a brief flare against the stone.

"She hasn't eaten in two days. She... she sees him, Anwyn. In the corners of her chambers. In the firelight."

"Luthar," Anwyn said. Not a question.

Her mother nodded, lips pressed into a hard line. "She says he speaks to her."

Silence settled between them, thick as ash. Anwyn let it linger.

"I'll send the healers," she said at last. "Whatever good it does."

She rose and stepped to the arrow-slit window. Night lay over Tempsford like a shroud—no moon, no stars, only the distant blink of watchfires strung along the walls like dying embers. Smoke curled up from the trench lines. Somewhere, a dog barked once and fell silent.

"One last task," she said, more breath than voice.

She didn't look back as she slipped into the corridor, cloak whispering against stone.

The nursery door gave a soft groan as it opened. Warmth wrapped around her—blankets, breath, the faint scent of lavender and goat's milk. Her twins lay curled beneath woollen throws, nestled like fox kits in a den, unaware of the death inching ever closer to their gates.

She lingered in the doorway, fingers curled white against the frame, as if holding the stone could stop time.

Behind her, wings rustled—soft as falling ash.

Lorellei fluttered in, emerald flight catching firelight in faint gleams. Her mother followed, wrapped in an old fur cloak. Behind them, four guards stood motionless, helms rimed with frost, blades strapped and ready. Black and silver. The colours of farewell.

"They've missed you," Lorellei said, her voice barely a whisper, and for a heartbeat her words trembled.

Anwyn didn't answer. A sob coiled up her throat, sharp and unwelcome. She forced it down like a blade into a sheath.

No softness. Not now.

She crossed the room and knelt beside the bed. Freya's breath tickled her cheek. A single curl clung damp to her brow. Anwyn brushed it back, then did the same for Owen, who stirred but did not wake.

She didn't kiss them. Didn't speak.

Just watched their chests rise and fall and wondered if the world would ever let them stay this small.

Then she rose.

"Take them to Luxyyr," she said. "Take Thraxos and a unit of guards with you."

Her mother nodded. The guards shifted, almost imperceptibly.

Lorellei hesitated. "You don't have to do this alone."

Anwyn looked at her children. At the only part of her that still felt untouched.

"I do," she said. "That's why they go."

Outside, in the tunnel mouth, the horses waited—hooves muffled, breath misting. No one spoke. The guards helped the sleeping bundles into saddlebags lined with fur. One by one, the riders mounted. Then the doors creaked shut behind them, sealing the night.

Anwyn stood at the top of the wall an hour later, wind tugging her braid loose.

And far off, from the dark hills beyond the trees, the first Drogo drumbeats rose.

Slow. Heavy. Certain.

The city would not sleep again for a long time.

But at least her children would.

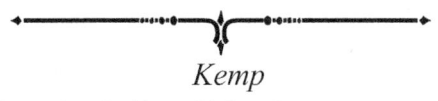

Kemp

The ground stank of oil and blood.

Kemp crouched low behind the firing step, shoulder pressed to the stone, cloak soaked through from last night's rain. Mud clung to his boots, gritty and cold, the hem of his tunic heavy with ash. His hands trembled—not from fear, but from pressure, the kind that built in the bones.

His shadowhand flexed once. Just once. Black flame curled from his knuckles like smoke from a cracked lantern. He clenched his fist to still it. Not now. Not here.

He didn't belong on a wall. Didn't belong on the ground.

Ever since he bonded with Vaelthys, his magic wanted space. The sky. The storm.

But Tempsford needed him here.

The breath in his lungs felt stolen—smoke-thick and sour, the taste of last week's skirmishes still coating his tongue. He hadn't eaten since yesterday. Didn't trust his stomach to hold.

To his left, a soldier whispered a prayer under his breath.

To his right, a boy tried to light a pitch pot with shaking hands. The flint slipped. Sparks died in the wind.

Kemp watched them both. Wondered which would be dead first.

He closed his eyes for a moment, pressing his back to the cold stone. And beneath his ribs, something stirred.

The shadow wanted out.

A low whistle of wind passed overhead—then another. Not arrows. Just the kind of night that made you hear things. To his left, a lad coughed into his cloak. To his right, a grizzled veteran chewed something, eyes locked on the dark beyond the wall.

No one spoke. Not here. Not now.

Drogo and Draugr were already out there—sprawled in the dark like wolves circling a wounded stag. They didn't march. They didn't chant. They just waited. Watching.

Kemp adjusted the strap on his shoulder harness. Not that he needed it. Not yet.

Vaelthys waited in the square behind the tower. He reached for his mind without thinking, skimming the edge of their bond—hot and coiled, sharp with waiting.

Vaethys was ready.

Was he?

He pressed closer to the wall, breath slow, trying not to feel the tremor building in his palm.

The shadowhand twitched. A lick of black flame curled from the knuckle. He clenched his fist. Forced it down.

Then came the sound.

Not horns. Not steel.

Just the wet, meaty thump of a sentry falling from the tower. Then another. Then the gurgle.

Kemp rose slowly, peering over the lip of the battlement. Eyes.

Rows of them. Pale eyes gleaming in dirt-smeared faces. One Drogo rose, raising a hammer thick as a tree limb. He roared. The horde answered.

They surged.

And the oil pits lit.

Flame whooshed into the dark like a dragon's breath. The Draugr front line caught fire mid-sprint. They didn't stop. Didn't scream. They burned, arms flailing, and kept coming.

The archers loosed. A wall of arrows arced into the firelight, cutting shapes from smoke.

He turned as a soldier—a boy, barely more than sixteen—stood frozen beside a crate of pitch pots. The boy's mouth moved. No sound came.

"Move," Kemp barked.

The boy blinked. Kemp slapped him hard across the helmet.

"I said *move*."

Behind them, the wall shuddered.

A low boom, followed by a crunch.

The east flank. Kemp glimpsed them through smoke—siege beasts, crashing against the walls—hulking things, armoured in bone, eyes burning in their sockets. The defenders poured boiling sand from the ramparts, but Kemp could hear it still: the scrape of claws on stone.

Draugr. Climbing.

A scream.

Then two.

Kemp watched as limbs flailed, a body tumbling like butchered meat. A man was dragged from the battlement, boots scraping stone. Another soldier stabbed wildly, again and again, sobbing through a mouth that no longer knew words.

The siege was no longer coming. It was here.

The stink of burning hair.

The slip of blood beneath his boots.

The sound of men dying just out of sight.

Then the horn.

Three bursts. Short. Sharp.

The dragons were summoned.

Kemp moved before thought could root him. His legs carried him, pulled by something older than instinct. He tore down the tower stairs, cloak snapping like a banner in retreat.

Across the square—through smoke and ash and the stink of war—he ran.

And Vaelthys was there.

Wings spread wide as thunderclouds, tail carving gouges in the stone. His scales shimmered with warlight—dark purple edged in shining green, like a blade half-drawn from its sheath. Eyes like storm clouds locked onto Kemp. Not as a master to his mount. As a soul to its shadow.

Kemp didn't speak. He didn't need to.

Vaelthys already knew.

The dragon crouched low. Kemp ran the final steps and leapt—hands gripping the ridge of his spine, fingers biting into the grooves of ancient bone.

Vaelthys surged upward.

The world dropped away.

Wind howled past them, clawing at Kemp's face and hair, tearing breath from his lungs. The walls, the torches, the screams—all fell beneath them, small and flickering.

Tempsford burned.
The Drogo had come.
But now the sky had teeth.
And it had remembered how to bite.

Chapter 27

Gunnar

Gunnar woke with frost in his beard and wind like a knife at his cheek.

The snow fell hard. It slammed into the peaks, hammering them like a smith's fury, relentless and cold.

He drew a breath—sharp, ragged. The cold bit deep, scraping his throat raw.

His hand reached for an axe that wasn't there.

Silence.

Not the hush of sleep. Not the stillness of death.

The kind of silence that *watched*.

He opened his eyes.

White. Blinding. All around him, a world stripped to bone and breath. The wind screamed through the broken stone, and the mountain loomed—high, jagged, ancient.

No tracks. No trail.

No memory of how he had come here.

He rose, boots crunching on hoarfrost. His breath misted before him, slow and sure. He moved without stiffness, without pain.

And that was wrong.

No broken ribs. No torn muscles. His body—unbowed.

Not healed.

Changed.

The snow shifted around his feet, whispering in the hush. The weight of the mountain pressed in—but not as burden. It felt like kinship.

He dropped to one knee. Dragged his glove through the powder and touched the stone beneath.

Grit crumbled beneath his fingers.

And the mountain *answered*.

It wasn't a sound. It wasn't sight. But something stirred in him, deep as old fire.

A breath that wasn't his own. A pulse beneath the stone.

Dreyna's voice came back to him—quiet as snowfall, vast as sky.

"You are no longer mortal."

Her words were the echo of thunder through his bones.

Behind him, snow crunched. A low growl—not threat. Greeting.

Gunnar turned.

A snow wolf stood on the ridge. Ghost—Fellron's steed.

The white wolf had always been strange. Now he was something more. His fur shimmered where no light touched. Eyes like glacier-ice fixed on Gunnar with a knowing that felt… *shared*.

He knelt. Ghost stepped forward.

Gunnar pressed a hand to his thick ruff, and *felt* him.

Not just muscle and sinew.

Fur, stone, wind, blood.

Himself.

He let out a breath and felt the storm ease.

The wind bent around them, no longer cutting—*carrying*.

He rose. Climbed onto Ghost's back.

The wolf took his weight without flinching. As if this had always been coming.

The storm cracked open above them. The sky split.

Below—far below—Gunnar felt battle. Smelled smoke. Heard the cry of a dragon carried on wind from a place too distant to hear.

But he heard it.

Tempsford.

He set his eyes south.

Then he spoke—his voice low, rough as the peaks, steady as rising fire.

"Let the winds carry word," he said—not to Ghost, but to the world itself. "The mountain has risen—and walks among mortals."

Ghost lunged forward.

And the mountain moved with him.

Karl

The gate was bleeding.

Technically, it was the men on the gate who were bleeding—but by now, the wood was doing a decent impression. Bits of soldier. Bits of Draugr. Some bits unidentifiable. If the gate survived the night, Karl made a promise to himself to go up to it and give it a hug. Maybe buy it a pint. They were in this together now.

Karl stood on the parapet, breathing smoke, arms shaking from the kind of fatigue you only earned by surviving long enough to regret it. Below, the world was fire and screaming and far too much gore.

Draugr were on the walls. Not approaching. Not threatening. *On.* One clambered up the south tower like a drunk spider made of meat and malice.

Karl stepped forward, braced, and drove his spear down into its open mouth. The sound it made was somewhere between a crack and a very large fruit being stepped on.

It twitched once, then did the decent thing and fell.

He yanked the spear free and muttered, "South tower's holding."

A pause. Then he added, "Barely."

"Define 'holding,'" Dakarai shouted from the next platform, hacking a Draugr's arm clean off. It didn't scream. Of course it didn't. Draugr never had the good manners to scream. It just kept coming, now slightly more gruesome.

Karl leapt down, plunged his dagger into the thing's neck, and gave it a twist.

The Draugr stilled.

He wiped the blade on his tunic. There wasn't a clean patch left. He was fairly sure his left sleeve was now more blood than fabric.

Somewhere below, a horn blew.

Three short blasts. Wrong rhythm. Wrong tone.

Karl glanced up.

Smoke curled up in greasy tendrils. Arrows hissed through it. Firelight flickered like it was having second thoughts. The air stank of pitch, blood, and spilled bowels.

And then the mist shifted.

Something moved.

Not a horse. Not a dragon.

Something else.

DEMIGOD

Fast. Huge. Pure white. It moved like a boulder rolling down a hill. Unstoppable.

The Draugr saw it. They turned.

They were promptly torn apart.

A white blur slammed through the flank—fur and fang and death incarnate. Something darker rode it, hunched low.

One Draugr leapt and was folded in half mid-air.

Another was flattened into the earth with the structural integrity of mashed turnips.

Karl blinked. His mouth opened.

"What in Draeg's arse crack is *that*?" he breathed.

Beside him, the god Draeg himself, chuckled. A low, rumbling sound that made the stones underfoot *s*hake.

"Something we buried once," he said, eyes flickering like twin forge fires.

He cracked his neck.

"Looks like the bastard clawed his way out. Just in time, too."

Gunnar

The snow melted where he passed.

Not from fire. Not from magic.

From *presence*.

Ghost's paws slammed into the frozen earth, each stride a thunderclap, spraying ice and blood. Draugr scattered before them—too slow, too late. The wolf moved like a storm let loose, white fur streaked with crimson, jaws open in a silent snarl. A Drogo screamed as Ghost leapt, and the sound died beneath splintered ribs and torn throat.

Behind him, astride the beast's back, Gunnar leaned low, cloak streaming like a banner of war. His eyes locked forward—toward the breach, toward the walls of Tempsford rising through smoke.

And in his chest—*the stone called.*

He leapt from the wolf's back.

Ghost didn't stop.

The earth shuddered as Gunnar landed, boots crunching through bone and frost. He dropped to one knee, palm slamming into the ground. Stone split with a deep, groaning *crack*—a sound that was not sound, but *remembrance*. The world knew him.

From the broken ground, the mountain rose.

A shaft of black-veined ore surged upward, runes glowing gold and red-hot in its core. It twisted as it rose—metal and memory entwined—until it formed a hammer: one side flat as a siege wall, the other a crescent hook designed to carve through armoured bone.

Stonecall.

Forged of ancient earth. Named by the gods.

Gunnar's hand closed around the haft—graven with the names of the dead. And the world held its breath.

Then he moved.

The hammer swung low and wide, catching a Draugr mid-charge. Its body folded in two with a wet crunch, armour crumpling like paper. The next fell before it had a chance to scream. And then the next.

Gunnar did not slow.

Did not speak.

He broke them.

Each swing of Stonecall cracked the ground. Drogo fled—but not fast enough. A shaman raised a black-bladed halberd, shouting some guttural prayer—and was silenced as the flat of the hammer drove him into the earth.

Bones shattered. Shadows screamed.

Then the air changed.

Something massive stepped forward.

A golem, ten feet tall at the shoulder, limbs sheathed in spiked iron. A stone club rested across its back—big as a cart axle. Carved runes burned along its chest in crude mockery of Gunnar's own.

It stepped over fallen Draugr and growled low.

Gunnar didn't flinch. His breath steamed from his lips as he stepped forward, Stonecall gripped in both hands.

The golem moved first.

The club came down like falling sky.

Gunnar *caught it*.

One hand. Elbow locked. Muscles braced like columns of mountain-root. The impact shook the ground, split the air. The Drogo watching from behind the beast staggered—some fell.

The golem's eyes widened—too late.

With a grunt, Gunnar *snapped the club in two*.

Stonecall rose.

And fell.

One strike.

The golem's head exploded like a siege boulder hitting a wall.

Its body collapsed, folding into the churned snow.

Gunnar turned.

All around him, the enemy *paused*. Even the brave ones.

A single heartbeat passed.
Then they screamed.
And ran.

The firelight danced off blood-soaked stone.

Above the gate, defenders stood slack-jawed, ash clinging to their skin like a second death. Men who'd fought since first light, hands blistered, armour dented, blades dulled to nothing, now stared out at the field.

And saw *him*.

Walking.

Just walking through the wreckage. Through the Draugr. Through the flames.

"Is that..." a soldier breathed, voice raw with disbelief, "...is that a god?"

No one answered.

Because he didn't stop.

Gunnar moved like the mountain itself—heavy, implacable, made for war. Ash curled from his cloak. Fire licked at his boots and *died*. Draugr flung themselves at him and were swatted aside like flies on a forge bellows. One lunged—he caught it with his shoulder, the crack of bone loud as thunder, and hurled the thing from the rampart.

Arrows fell. He didn't flinch.

Some missed. Others hit—and *ricocheted*, skittering harmlessly away.

A siege beast reared in front of him—twenty feet of plated hide and tusks like spears. It bellowed. Charged.

Gunnar roared back.

He raised Stonecall and drove the hammerhead *into the earth.*

The ground answered.

With a groan like a dying god, the stone split. A jagged chasm opened beneath the beast's feet. It screeched, legs flailing—

Then fell.

Swallowed whole.

The gap sealed behind it with a final crack of earth.

Gunnar kept walking.

On the walls, men broke from their stupor. A few backed away from the merlons, like even looking too long might be dangerous.

Kris stepped forward. His mouth opened. Closed.

Then: "Open the gate."

No one moved.

"He's not… He's not supposed to be alive," someone whispered.

"He's not."

But then Dakarai said it. Quiet. Certain.

"That's Gunnar." His eyes didn't leave the figure below. "Prince Gunnar."

The gate captain hesitated only a moment longer.

Then he nodded. "Open it."

The gears groaned. Chains clanked. The great timber doors shuddered as they were drawn back. Smoke bled through the gap. So did the light.

Gunnar stepped through.

Alone.

Stonecall in one hand, the haft black with ash and still faintly glowing at the rune-lines. His cloak was scorched, his chest plate cracked, blood streaking the curve of his jaw—none of it his own.

Ghost padded beside him, fur matted red, maw flecked with gore, hackles still high.

They walked in like war made flesh.

No one spoke.

Not until a small voice rose from the edge of the crowd.

A child, clutching her mother's leg, eyes wide as moons.

"The mountain walks."

Silence cracked.

Gunnar stopped, turning toward the gathered faces. Men and women who had held the line with blood and fire. Who had burned friends that morning and kept fighting.

He looked at them all.

At the fire. The wall. The ash and blood.

"You held," he said.

His voice was hoarse, deep. Like it had been dragged from the belly of the earth.

He raised Stonecall, just slightly.

"Now let's finish it."

Chapter 28

Anwyn

Anwyn didn't move when she heard the child's voice.

"The mountain walks."

It echoed down the walls like a prophecy. A hush spread. Even the wind paused.

And then the gate opened.

She didn't breathe—not properly. Couldn't.

The smoke parted.

He stepped through.

Alone.

Ash streaked his face. His cloak hung in scorched ribbons. A massive war hammer dragged sparks with each stride. And beside him, a great snow wolf moved like a blade of winter, jaws still red.

But it was him.

Gunnar.

Her Gunnar.

And Anwyn collapsed.

She didn't fall like a soldier struck down. She *crumpled*, knees giving, palms scraping stone. Her breath caught in a dry sob. Not because she saw him—but because *every part of her remembered him*. Her bones knew his name.

No. No, no, no, no…

She had lost him. Held his funeral. Held him with trembling hands. She had whispered his name to the wind and felt no answer. She had *grieved him into her marrow.*

He was dead.

He was dead.

Someone touched her shoulder.

She shoved them away.

Then she stood. Shaking. Uncertain. Moving like a woman haunted.

She stumbled from the wall. Down stone steps. Through the hollow-staring men. Every step was wrong. Every breath was disbelief. Her legs barely obeyed. Her vision blurred.

And when she reached him—when she finally stood before him—she couldn't speak.

He looked at her, quiet, unmoving. As if he didn't dare speak either. As if he was afraid she might vanish.

She reached for him—and stopped short.

"You died."

Her voice cracked like brittle bone.

"I saw you die. Our children—" Her voice broke completely.

"—I told them you were brave."

His eyes—gods, his eyes—were full of silence. And sorrow.

"I tried—"

She drove her fists into his chest. Hard.

The sound cracked like thunder.

Then she threw herself against him and sobbed into his chest. Her fists beat against him. Her cries were low, guttural. She wept like someone being *broken open again*— not with grief, but with everything grief had stolen.

He caught her wrists. Held them gently. Let her scream. Let her shake.

Only when her knees buckled again did he lower them both to the ground.

They sat in the courtyard, the mountain and the mourner, and for the first time in months, she let herself be held.

She ran her fingers along his jaw, trembling.

"You never met them," she said. "You never saw their eyes."

"What did you name them?" he asked softly.

"Owen," she whispered. "And Freya."

His breath caught. She felt it—not in sound, but in the stillness that followed.

He closed his eyes. She watched him break in silence.

"After Dreyna's sister?"

She nodded.

"And Owen?"

"Karl told me of the dwarven warrior. The one the gods blessed."

He gave a quiet nod. Reverent. As if he were hearing their names carved into stone.

"Are they safe?"

"Far from here. With my mother. They're strong. They're… you."

She kissed his forehead—gently, reverently.

"You saved us."

She leaned back. She didn't ask if he was still the dwarf she loved. Didn't ask what death had made him.

She already knew he would have died again, a thousand times, for her and their children. That he *had*.

Some truths are too sacred for questions.

"No, Anwyn," he said. "You saved me."

She took his face in both hands, kissed him, and held him there.

His hand brushed hers—just once—and in that brief touch, the vow was made.

They rose.

Not as they had been. But as they were now.

Worn. Weathered. Woven together by what had broken them.

For a moment, nothing moved. Not the wind. Not the sky. Only them—two ghosts given back to each other by war and fire.

And behind them, carried on the breath of smoke and ash, a low growl stirred the air.

Ghost turned toward the wall.

Toward the gate.

"The gods aren't done with us yet," he said.

She touched his hand. "Then let's finish what they started."

Gunnar

The corridor was quiet.

Not the kind of quiet that comes with peace—but the kind that follows pain. The walls were smoke-worn, heavy with the scent of boiled linen and old blood. A table had been dragged against the wall—its surface dark with dried fluids, a bloodied cloth still clinging to one corner like a forgotten prayer.

They passed a cot left in haste. A snapped arrow lay beneath it.

Someone had tried to clean the floor near the stairwell, but the stain clung stubbornly at the edge.

Gunnar moved through the corridor with slow steps. Anwyn walked beside him, her shoulder brushing his now and then, as if to remind herself he was still there. Still real.

"They're reinforcing the eastern tower," she said softly. "Two archers died in the night. They held it until the last."

He nodded. Didn't speak.

A runner passed them, breathless, carrying a folded bandage roll in one hand and a rusted dagger in the other. Neither of them turned to watch.

Ghost trotted ahead, tail low, ears twitching. The wolf's steps made no sound on the stone. He disappeared around a corner.

"The men are waiting for you to lead," Anwyn added, voice low.

Gunnar gave a faint grunt. "Then let them wait a moment longer."

She said nothing more.

They turned the next corner—and stopped.

Queen Kathrynne stood in the archway, half in shadow, half caught in the light of a dying torch. Her crown was gone. Her hair had come loose from its braids.

Her eyes found him.

And for a moment, she didn't breathe.

Then she stepped forward, hands trembling at her sides, lips parted as if caught mid-prayer.

"It's true," she whispered. "Are you real?"

Gunnar's voice was steady, low. "The mountain goddess called. I answered."

A sound escaped her. Not a sob. Not a laugh. Just breath—as if the weight of silence had cracked in her chest.

She crossed the distance with slow, reverent steps. Her eyes shimmered like a woman beholding a miracle, or something she had begged the gods for and never expected to see again.

Her fingers touched his chestplate. Then rose to his cheek.

"You came back," she breathed. "It's a sign."

Gunnar glanced briefly at Anwyn, who gave a soft smile. Hope, perhaps. Relief. The kind of desperate belief that clings to the return of a hero.

He nodded.

"There is hope yet."

Kathrynne smiled.

It was not the smile of a queen. Not the smile of a mother or widow. It was too soft. Too bright. A smile that didn't belong to the present moment—but to something imagined, something longed for, just beyond reach.

She took his hands in hers.

They were cold.

"Your return brings me hope," she said.

Anwyn stepped forward slightly, her voice gentle.

"It brings us all hope, Kathrynne."

Gunnar watched her carefully now. Her eyes never left him. Her expression did not change. It had become a mask made of belief. Something in him tightened—but he couldn't name the feeling.

He squeezed Anwyn's hand beside him. She looked up at him, calm and steady.

"The dead shape us," he said quietly. "But the living must carry the flame."

Kathrynne's smile didn't falter.

"You've given me what I needed," she said.

Then she turned.

She walked away down the corridor, her gown trailing behind her like smoke.

Gunnar didn't follow.

Ghost reappeared, stepping from the same corridor she had vanished down. His ears were up. The low growl in his throat was soft, almost hesitant.

Gunnar laid a hand on his fur.

"What is it?" he murmured.

Ghost didn't answer. He only stared at the far door.

Gunnar looked back once, but the Queen was gone.

He walked away, never seeing the door that had quietly begun to open behind him.

Queen Kathrynne

The torches had burned low in the corridor.

Their light danced softly against the stone, not bright enough to show the bloodstains, only the shimmer of where they had been. Kathrynne walked with careful steps, hands clasped before her, shoulders drawn tall beneath the weight of memory.

She did not hurry.

This was not a time for haste.

The silence that followed miracles was always sacred.

Her fingers brushed the wall as she passed, tracing old mortar lines, the same path she had walked the night Luthar was crowned. He had been younger then. Full of fire. The same fire that now smoked in the ruins behind her.

"You always said you'd come back to me," she murmured. "The gods have returned one husband—why not the other?"

A breeze stirred down the hall. It should not have—there were no windows here. But it touched her skin, light as breath. It carried something with it. The faintest scent of him.

She smiled.

At the base of the inner gate, the iron bar sat across its latches. No one had posted a guard. Another sign.

The gods did not send symbols without purpose.

She knelt—not from age or weakness, but from reverence. Her hand rested on the cold steel.

"You waited," she whispered. "I knew you would."

She thought of Gunnar's face. The soot on his cheek. The silence in his eyes.

He had come back. And in doing so, he had reminded the world that the dead were not gone—they were only waiting to be called.

Luthar was waiting.

She rose.

Lifted the bar.

It came free without resistance, settling into her arms like it had been meant for her all along.

The lock groaned once. Then fell still.

She placed the bar aside. Brushed her palms together. Straightened her back.

Outside the gate, the wind was cold.

But she didn't feel it.

"I'm here, my love," she said.
And she opened the door.

Chapter 29

Karl

The corridor felt... *wrong.*

It wasn't just the blood—though there was plenty of it. No, this was something colder. Quieter. Like the silence before a spear breaks the shieldwall.

Karl squinted through the smoke. The torches were still lit, though they burned like they were tired of trying. Men moved like shadows. A few whispered. No one shouted.

Then he saw her.

Queen Kathrynne.

Walking.

Alone.

She walked like someone half-remembered from a story—back straight, eyes glazed, draped in a gown that trailed like smoke. The kind of walk you saw on the field sometimes. After the blast. When men wandered, guts in their hands, too stunned to know they were dying.

Karl stepped forward. "Kathrynne?"

No answer. Not even the twitch of an eyelid. Just the steady clack of her heels on stone, as if death were something she could walk into politely.

The gate loomed ahead—ironbound, blood-slicked, still holding. Still sacred.

Until she touched it.

She rested her hand on the bar like a lover's cheek. Bowed her head. Whispered something soft—words eaten by the distance.

Then she lifted it.

The gate groaned like a thing betrayed. Steel screamed.

And the world changed.

The wind surged in—knife-cold, ash-heavy, thick with the rot of a thousand burning prayers.

Then came the shapes.

Smoke peeled back like skin, and the Drogo stepped forward.

Tall. Pale. Silent.

Karl froze.

Kathrynne stepped across the threshold like a queen into her coronation. Arms outstretched. Eyes bright. The wind caught her hair. For a heartbeat, the Drogo paused.

And then—

The first one took her leg clean at the knee.

The second cracked her jaw open with a rusted blade.

She folded without a sound. No cry. No struggle. Just blood—and then more blood, and then she was gone beneath a tide of limbs and hunger.

Karl tried to speak. But the words never came.

His throat tasted like blood and bile.

There were no words for this.

Just the wet sounds of tearing, and the thud of her head skittering across stone.

Then the horde looked up.

And charged.

Kemp

Smoke veiled the world.

From the spire's edge, Kemp watched the gate bleed.

The bodies were already piling—blackened shapes writhing and torn, the courtyard coated in gore thick enough to drown. Screams rang like bells cracked in the heat. Below, Karl stood alone.

One dwarf. One hammer.

Holding nothing.

The Drogo were pouring in now—bone-masked, skin pale as death, blades lifted high. The Draugr followed, stumbling corpses stitched from skin and bone. They came like hunger made flesh. They came like the end.

And Karl stood in their path. Hammer high. Eyes unblinking.

Vaelthys growled beneath him—wings shifting, hot wind curling around claw and scale.

"He's not holding them," Kemp said. "He's bleeding loud enough to buy us some time."

And then they dove.

The world tilted. Smoke peeled back. Kemp drew breath that burned his lungs. And Vaelthys roared.

Fire leapt.

It spilled across the courtyard in a wave—incinerating the front lines, Drogo stumbling, Draugr wailing as flame devoured sinew. The horde faltered, momentum broken. In that moment, the fire held back the world.

Karl muttered something—could've been a prayer, could've been a joke. He grinned like someone with nothing left to bet, then strolled into the fire like he was late to his own execution. *Mad bastard.*

Vaelthys banked hard, sweeping wide. Kemp leapt free—landed on the edge of a half-collapsed tower, his boots striking stone slick with gore.

He raised his arm—and the shadow answered.

Smoke peeled back, his fingers splayed wide, crackling with violet-black fire.

He thrust his hand forward.

The street below ruptured.

Shadowfire screamed from his palm—ravenous, searing. It tore through the front rank of Drogo, disintegrating flesh from bone, slamming the rest backwards like leaves before a storm. Limbs shattered. Spines bent. The ground cracked beneath them.

Silence followed—brief, awful.

Below, Dakarai was shouting—gathering the scattered, dragging them back to the keep. Kris and Laoch hauled wounded over blood-slick timbers behind an overturned cart, building a barricade of bone and breath.

The wall would fall. But not yet.

"Again!" Kemp shouted.

Vaelthys obeyed.

Fire split the night, carving a line through flesh and steel. Bodies burned. Blades melted. The Drogo shrieked—but still they came.

Kemp saw the shimmer of the ballista too late.

A shadow in the smoke. A glint of black steel. A streak—

Vaelthys roared as the bolt tore across his flank.

A searing line of agony lanced through his own side, sharp and sudden, as if the bolt had torn through them both. His vision blurred. His breath caught.

Blood fountained from the dragon's wound, catching the firelight as Vaelthys banked hard—wings faltering, flight stuttering.

Kemp dropped.

He didn't jump—he *fell*, spine arched in a spasm not his own. Pain bloomed across his ribs. He slammed onto the rooftop below, his shoulder wrenching sideways with a pop that stole the world from under him.

Something tore. Maybe bone. Maybe muscle.

Didn't matter.

The pain was still there—and it wasn't all his.

He managed to rise.

His shoulder screamed. His ribs shifted with every breath. But his shadow hand was steady.

It flexed once.

And then it burned.

Shadowfire ripped through the front line—Drogo hurled backwards, armour curling, flesh unmade. The air turned black and violet and ruinous.

Through the haze, Kemp saw Karl stumble.

His knees gave. Blood poured from his leg. His hammer dropped.

"Get him," Kemp rasped.

Vaelthys roared from the sky—and dropped like vengeance.

He tore through the horde in a cyclone of claw and flame, clearing the street with one bone-shaking sweep. Then he scooped them both—Karl in one talon, Kemp in the other—lifting from the blood-slick stone like they weighed nothing at all.

They rose.

Through fire and smoke, through ruin and ash. A dragon, a mage, and a broken warrior. Ghosts of a story not yet ended.

They landed hard by the barricade.

Stone split. The air cracked.

Dakarai was already shouting. Kris knelt beside Karl, hands bloodied.

Kemp rolled from Vaelthys's grip, coughing. His shoulder hung low, wrong. Blood tickled the back of his throat. But his shadowhand twitched—*still burning, still ready*.

The fight wasn't over.

Not yet.

The Drogo screamed their fury and charged the breach.

And then—

The sky sang.

A roar split the heavens.

Ignara.

And behind her, like the breath of winter itself—Sylthareal, wings silver, eyes bright as stars long buried.

Ruiha rode the fire.

Flame cascaded. The horde shattered.

Two dragons descended—red and silver, heat and light. The Drogo faltered. The Draugr shrieked.

And for a moment—just a breath, just a heartbeat—Kemp believed the gods were watching.

And waiting.

Chapter 30

Ruiha

Smoke coiled around Ruiha's face, stinging her eyes despite the wind whipping at her. The sky rippled with heat. Flame danced over rooftops like a dirge, and the cries of the dying rose higher than the spires. Below, the gates were open—but still the line held. The Drogo pressed forward like a tide straining against stone, their numbers swelling at the breach, searching for a crack to widen.

Ignara's wings beat once—twice—and the world surged. They rose.

The air thinned. Cold bit deep, but fire still licked the edges of her sight. Ruiha tightened her grip with knees gone numb. No whispers passed between them now. No shared breath. That thread was cut—clean as a killing blow.

Ignara banked west on a gust, wings carving the smoke. Below, a silver flash—Laoch's blade cutting clean through the dark.

Ruiha reached out with her mind, out of habit more than hope.

Nothing.

No flicker. No pull in her chest. Just wind. Just fire.

She opened her eyes. Tightened her grip.

Ignara flew on, unshaken.

Ruiha sat still, her hands clenched white against Ignara's scales.

Ignara plunged.

Flame poured from her jaws, flooding the breach with fire. Drogo shrieked. Draugr withered. Steel curled in the heat. The street became a furnace—and still, the horde came.

Below, through smoke and ruin, Ruiha saw him.

Kemp.

His cloak torn, blood running from his side. Shadow coiled along his arm like a serpent in mourning. He stood atop a ruined tower, casting ruin with a raised hand. Fire and darkness bent to him now. Not the boy she met in Lamos. Not the mage she'd fallen for.

Now he was a man made by war and darkness.

A stranger, in some ways.

And still—the man she loved.

It broke her. The silence where Ignara once was, the hollow in her chest—it broke her. And still, she would trade it all again. The bond. The fire. Her very breath. If it meant he lived.

She gave no command. Only leaned forward, teeth gritted, fingers white.

Ignara answered not with thought, but with thunder.

They dove.

The wind screamed past her ears, tore at her hair, and lashed her cloak into a banner behind her. Flame licked her boots as Ignara plunged toward the keep—where Vaelthys dragged Kemp and a blood-slicked shape toward the wall. Karl. Gods. Still breathing. Barely.

The Drogo converged, blades raised, teeth bared.

Ruiha screamed—and the sky caught fire.

Ignara tore through the front lines in a wash of crimson. Drogo burned. Stone shattered. She reared back, wings cracking open with a sound like heaven breaking.

And then—

A shadow behind her. A song in her bones.

Silver wings. Sylthareal.

She felt the cold before she saw her—winter on the wind, stillness before the storm.

Sylthareal swept in, tail slicing the air, silver gleaming.

Not a charge.

A reckoning.

The Drogo screamed as two dragons fell upon them. Fire and fury. Tooth and claw. *Vengeance given form.*

Let the gods watch, Ruiha thought, eyes burning. *Let them see what rises when you try to break us.*

Gunnar

Gunnar had stopped counting kills when his arm went numb. His hammer was slick with blood and worse.

The southern gate was lost—but the eastern breach still held.

The ground trembled beneath his boots. Not from dragons. From the sheer weight of bodies—Drogo and human alike—scraping, screaming, slipping in their own ruin. Gunnar spat, ducked a blade, and drove Stonecall into the bastard's chest hard enough to split rib from spine.

"Hold the line!" he roared, voice raw.

The breach yawned just fifty paces ahead. They couldn't let the Drogo spill further into Tempsford. Couldn't give an inch. Not one.

Kris fought to his left, blade flashing through the air, a gash above his eye pouring blood like tears. To his right, Laoch dragged a boy—no more than fifteen—screaming, leg twisted the wrong way, half his face burned.

Someone grabbed Gunnar's shoulder. He nodded once. The kind of nod you gave when you weren't sure if you'd see each other again. Then he turned and ran back into the crush.

A Drogo lunged. Gunnar caught it with the hammer's edge. Bone cracked. Blood sprayed hot. The thing shrieked—then went still.

Another scream cut through the noise. Familiar.

Gunnar looked up and saw her—Anwyn. Cutting down two Drogo, her katana a blur, body low, precise.

Dakarai was behind her. On the ground. Bleeding out.

Their eyes met. Just for a breath.

She moved first.

A flicker, then flame—Anwyn surged into the Drogo like a storm loosed from flesh. Her katana caught the light as she spun through two Drogo warriors. One head rolled. The second fell with its chest split open, ribs curling back like snapped fingers.

Dakarai was on the ground, bleeding hard, teeth red. Anwyn didn't pause. Her free hand lit with fire—she hurled it like a spear, punching a hole clean through a Draugr's chest as it reached for him.

"With me!" she shouted, voice raw, blade raised.

Gunnar started forward—and the world exploded.

A wall of Drogo smashed into him, shield to chest. He stumbled, slipped in gore, then roared. Stonecall rose—and came down like the wrath of mountain gods.

The first Drogo crumpled. The second went flying, ribs crushed in. The third—he never saw the third. Stonecall caught it mid-charge and split it in half.

"We need the gate!" Kris bellowed beside him, carving through a howling Draugr. "If they take it, we lose everything!"

Gunnar knew. Of course he knew.

Anwyn was fire in the dark now—darting, striking, shielding Dakarai with her own body. A Drogo tried to flank her. She spun, swept low, and severed its leg clean at the hip. It howled. She silenced it with a thrust through the throat.

Beyond the breach, the battlefield shifted.

Draeg arrived.

Not walking—*wading*. The dwarven god of strode through the crush of Drogo like a mountain tearing loose. One massive hand seized a screaming warrior by the throat and flung him *skyward*. The Drogo flew—and did not come down whole.

Draeg's foot came down—*and the ground cracked open.*

From beneath, something darted. A blur.

Havoc.

The little stonesprite zipped through ankles and gore, cackling as he drove his fists into the earth. Fissures exploded. Drogo and Draugr slipped screaming into the dark—before the earth closed over them like a mouth.

Stone spears burst upward, skewering a dozen more.

Gunnar watched them fall—and then lost sight of Anwyn.

A surge of panic rose.

But there was no time.

The gate buckled. He turned back. Raised Stonecall. Roared like the ancestors were watching.

His hammer struck a Drogo with such force the thing ceased to exist—just blood, mist, and memory. He kicked another in the chest and sent it crashing through a barricade of timber and corpses.

Kris fell. Gunnar caught him with one hand, yanked him to his feet, and shield-bashed a Draugr into paste.

Then—dragons.

The sky cracked open. A scream of flame. Two shapes swept over them—one red, one silver. Fire and ruin and vengeance made wings. The Drogo faltered. Some ran. Others froze.

Gunnar looked across the battlefield—he saw her.

Anwyn.

Dragging Dakarai, blood-soaked and breathless, toward the gate. Towards a semblence of safety

A Drogo rose behind her.

She didn't look. Just flicked her hand. A whip of fire snapped backward—took the creature's head clean off.

Then she was gone.

Into the smoke.

Dakarai limp in her arms.

The screams didn't fade.

But now—they had names.

Chapter 31

Anwyn

The world narrowed to pain and purpose. Anwyn gritted her teeth and drove magic into her legs, felt it surge through tired muscles like fire in cracked stone. Dakarai hung heavy across her back, his blood soaking into her, warm and constant.

Too much blood.

Her boots slid on broken stone. Her knee buckled. She hit the ground hard—gasped, nearly lost him.

No.

She hauled herself up. One hand planted. One breath taken.

"Almost there," she whispered. "Just hold on, Dakarai. Just hold on."

His head lolled. Lips parted. A wheeze escaped.

"You're fine," she lied. "You're still here."

The chamber yawned ahead, burning with torchlight. Stone walls dripped with sweat and smoke. The air stank of blood and herbs, of scorched bandage and rotting cloth.

She ducked through the archway.

Someone sobbed. Someone else whispered prayers in a language she didn't understand.

She pushed through.

Elara turned at once.

Saw him.

The sound she made wasn't a scream, not at first. It was smaller than that. A question, a plea, a breaking.

"Help me," Anwyn rasped. "Please."

Elara ran forward. Together, they laid him on the nearest cot. One of the healers was already moving—hands bloodied, calm. Compress. Thread. Cloth.

Elara wiped his face with her sleeve. "Stay with me," she whispered. "Dakarai. You stay. You hear me?"

His eyelids fluttered. A flicker.

"It's me," she said, pressing her forehead to his. "Come back. Come back to me."

He didn't look at her.

He looked past her.

And smiled.

"They're here," he breathed.

Elara stilled. "What?"

"Melagai," he said. "Drakamor… they're laughing. They're happy to see me."

A tear traced down his cheek.

Not pain.

Joy.

And then—

No last breath. Just a stillness.

His chest did not rise again.

Elara placed her hand over his heart, as if she could catch what was already gone.

"He was just speaking," she said. "He was—"

Her voice broke.

Then she did.

A cry left her that had no shape. It wasn't rage. It wasn't grief. It was what happens when both find the same body and burn.

The healer stepped back.

Anwyn did not cry.

She turned, walked from the chamber.

The door closed behind her like a curtain pulled over light.

She walked into the bloodied dawn.

Her fists clenched. She didn't feel them.

And she didn't look back.

Chapter 32

Magnus

He'd received the message a week ago.

A human courier—thin, bruised, more blood than man—had stumbled into Dreynas under heavy escort. Fair play to him. Magnus had seen war-hardened dwarves lose their minds in the tunnels of Hornbaek. Yet this one had come alone, on foot, all the way from the Fenmark—through Draugr-infested lands and Drogo scouting patrols.

Then through the mountain's throat itself.

He'd never have made it without the dwarven scouts who'd found him.

The old tunnels of Dreynas were dangerous still—home to predators and worse—but Magnus had posted his best to keep them clean.

Dreynas had bled.

It wouldn't bleed again.

The Drogo had all but ruined it. Blackened halls. Collapsed chambers. Statues torn from their roots and hurled into firepits.

But dwarves were not so easily broken.

They'd rebuilt.

Not fully—not yet. Some of the great arches still lay half-crumbled. The forgehalls hadn't sung in full chorus since the siege. But it was rising again. Stone by stone. Rune by rune.

Magnus had watched it take shape.

And every time he walked those halls—every time he looked up at the great hall that once held council meetings led by his father—he thought of Gunnar.

They'd heard. Of course they had.

The mountains had echoed with grief.

Gunnar, Prince of Dreynas.

Slain at Tempsford.

The people had wept for him. Called on the gods. Lit fires that hadn't burned since the war.

But none had grieved like Magnus.

His brother.

First his father. Then Gunnar.

And the truth he never spoke was that some days, he wished it had been him instead.

Now it was down to him.

Not by crown. Not by choice.

But by blood.

Until the council gathered. Until the mountain steadied.

He bore the weight of Dreynas.

And so, when the message came—delivered by bloodied hands, the name scrawled in a clipped, decisive hand—*Anwyn*—he hadn't hesitated.

A week later, he led five thousand dwarves through Fenmark.

The marshes stretched around them, stinking and grey. Pools of stagnant water. Trees with rot-black bark. Fen-fog rose in curtains, heavy and still.

They'd fought Drogo twice already—quick, brutal ambushes in the mist.

They'd taken prisoners.

From those prisoners, they learned the truth:
Fenchester was under siege.
So they marched.
Steel on mud. Cloaks sodden. Shields crusted with bog grit.
Five thousand strong.
Every one of them ready to die with a hammer in hand.
Call it what you want. Vengeance. Honor. Anger.
Magnus knew the truth.
It was all for Gunnar.

The fen thinned.
Ahead, the trees grew sparse. The ground rose, dryer now, packed hard with gravel and ash. A battered watchtower loomed crooked on the horizon—half-collapsed, roof scorched black. The iron sign of Fenchester swung on rusted chains, creaking.
Magnus pulled his cloak tighter. The wind had changed.
It wasn't just cold now.
It *smelled* of war.
Char and blood. Singed hair. Burned pitch.
He lifted a gauntleted fist.
The column behind him halted—five thousand dwarves falling still, not a word spoken. The wind carried distant thunder. Not from the sky. From steel. From dragons.
Magnus climbed the ridge alone.
One step. Then another. His boots sank into the mud, then struck stone. The ground shuddered—once, faintly, as if the bones of the earth themselves had flinched.
He reached the crest.

And saw it.

Fenchester.

Or what remained of it.

Siege engines lay cracked and burning, their great arms split like broken fingers. The walls—once white stone—were blackened, pitted, crumbling in places. The eastern gate was gone entirely, reduced to a maw of wreckage and flame.

Shapes moved in the smoke. Thousands. Fighting in the breach. Some in crimson cloaks, some skeletal and wrong, all locked in the dance of war.

And above it all—

Dragons.

Not one. Not two.

Dozens.

Wings tore through the smoke—some copper, some deep green, one pale as pearl. They moved like weather given shape, wheeling above the burning city like hawks circling prey.

One broke low over the western tower—its roar was thunder wrapped in iron, flame licking from its jaws as it swept the Drogo lines.

They were fighting for Fenchester.

Alongside them, he saw the shimmer of steel—twin katanas flashing, cloaks slicing through ash. And human soldiers—no more than a few hundred—held the gate with a desperation he knew too well.

The siege was breaking.

But not broken.

Not yet.

A red-scaled beast dived from the clouds, jaws open, flame pouring like a river—and struck a siege tower with full force. The blast snapped the structure in half. Timber screamed. Ash bloomed.

Magnus felt the heat even here, miles out.

He turned, heart steady.

Then to the ranks behind him:

"Sound the horn. Dreynas stands with Fenchester."

The horn cried out across the fen.

And somewhere beyond the smoke, the gods were listening.

Chapter 33

Gunnar

The gate groaned.
Gunnar braced his boot on broken stone, shoulder to shoulder with Kris and Laoch. Blood steamed on his gauntlets. A Drogo corpse twitched at his feet.

"That was the last of the push," Kris gasped, blinking sweat from his eyes.

"No," Gunnar said. "They're waiting for something."

He was right.

A ripple passed through the horde. Not fear. Not fury.

Reverence.

Five figures stepped through the smoke—tall, cloaked, faces hidden beneath bone-stitched veils. Their staffs struck the ground in unison.

Thud.

Thud.

Thud.

"What the hell are those?" Kris muttered.

"Shamans," Gunnar said, low.

The air thickened. A scent like burnt hair and rot crawled into his throat.

Then the bodies moved.

Behind them—within their own lines—the dead rose.

Gunnar's heart punched once, hard.

A man, split down the chest—sat up with twitching fingers. A boy from Tempsford dragged himself upright, spine visibly broken, jaw hanging loose.

"They're ours," Kris whispered.

"No," Gunnar said. "Not anymore."

The shamans raised their staffs again.

And the dead *charged.*

"They've turned them!" Laoch shouted, blades drawn. "Draugr from our own bloody fallen—!"

"Form up!" Gunnar roared. "Shield wall! Don't let them through!"

A Draugr slammed into Kris. He blocked it with his forearm, stumbled, then drove his sword into its gut. It didn't flinch.

"Go for the head!" Gunnar bellowed. *"Take their heads!"*

Stonecall swung wide, cracking through bone. The Draugr dropped. Another took its place.

"By all the damned—*they don't stop!*" Laoch dropped low, blade slicing through bone. The Draugr crashed down, still crawling, still clawing.

Kris parried a sword stroke—then froze.

"Thalric?" he breathed.

The man—or what was left—lunged. Kris blocked once, twice, then screamed and hacked downward with everything he had.

Thalric's head hit the ground.

Kris turned away, bile in his throat.

"We're going to lose the line," Laoch rasped.

"Then we die holding it," Gunnar growled.

The shamans raised their staffs again.

The ground pulsed.

And then—

Flame.

It roared past them, searing heat driving back the Draugr like a scythe through grain.

Anwyn stormed into the breach, blade alight, eyes wild. Her katana carved a burning arc through three undead. Her off-hand flared—flame leapt from her palm and caught a Draugr mid-run, folding it into ash.

She didn't speak.

Didn't blink.

Only burned.

"Anwyn!" Gunnar roared.

She didn't hear him.

Or she didn't care.

Another Draugr lunged—she twisted, ducked, severed its legs, then buried her blade in its brain and twisted. It screamed, finally, and went still.

Gunnar turned. "With her!"

The dwarves rallied.

A howl split the sky. Havoc shot past, driving his fists into the earth. Fissures cracked wide, swallowing Drogo whole. Stone spears burst upward—one impaled a shaman through the chest. Its chant stopped mid-breath.

The others faltered.

"Now!" Gunnar shouted.

He and Laoch surged into the fray. Kris followed, eyes burning. Shield met shield, steel kissed bone. The breach rocked with the force of their charge.

A shadow passed overhead.

They looked up.

Draeg.

The mountain god strode through the enemy like a storm on two legs. A Drogo warbeast charged him—he caught it in both hands and *ripped it in half.* Blood fountained. The ground trembled.

The remaining shamans screamed something guttural and fled.

Too late.

The dragons arrived.

A scream split the clouds—Ignara, wings aflame, dove in a spiral of fire. Sylthareal followed, silver slicing the sky.

Gunnar saw the Drogo hesitate.

One of them dropped his weapon.

Another turned and ran.

"Press!" Gunnar bellowed.

They did.

Dwarves surged. Flame rained. Anwyn spun, eyes wild, mouth open in a cry he couldn't hear but *felt*. Kris rammed his sword into a Draugr's throat, gritted his teeth, and screamed something Gunnar couldn't understand.

And then—

It ended.

The breach was theirs.

Smoke rose. Ash settled.

Gunnar stood, breath ragged, hammer slick and heavy in his grip.

Beside him, Anwyn dropped to one knee. Her blade clattered beside her. Blood soaked her boots—not her own.

She didn't cry.

Not now.

But her hands shook.

Gunnar looked up at the sky. The dragons circled. The sun broke through the cloud just long enough to touch the broken stones in gold.

He let out a long, silent breath.

Kris leaned on his sword. "What now?"

Gunnar didn't answer at first.

Then he turned toward the smoke where the Drogo had fled.

"We finish it."

Ruiha

"I see it," Kemp said. His voice was hoarse, barely audible above the wind. Blood streaked his jaw. His arm hung limp at the shoulder. But his eyes—they burned.

Below, the Drogo scattered—most of them. But a knot held fast on the south flank, blades raised, dying loud. One siege engine still stood: jagged against the red-glow sky, arming again.

Ruiha pressed her knees tighter to Ignara's ribs, one hand against warm scales.

"They fire that again, they'll take out the gate."

Ignara snarled, thunder low in her chest.

"Dive," Ruiha said.

They dropped.

Air screamed past her ears, tore at her cloak, drove tears from her eyes. Kemp crouched on Vaelthys's back, one arm braced, the other limp. His shadowhand twitched, trailing black smoke.

The siege engine shifted. A Drogo crewman pulled a lever. The bolt rose—black steel, barbed, enormous.

Ignara screamed—a raw, guttural thing that didn't sound like victory.

Syltahreal answered above, her cry sharper—a knife flung skyward.

Flame poured from Ignara's jaws, brilliant and bright.

But it fell short.

The bolt was already in flight.

Kemp raised his hand.

Shadowfire shrieked from his palm—no, from *Vaelthys*, as if the dragon's very lungs exhaled it through Kemp. It fell like a comet, struck the platform below, and turned it to splinters.

But the bolt still tore through the sky.

Ruiha turned—too late.

The bolt punched through Syltahreal's wing.

She didn't cry out. Just twisted, bled, and fell.

"No—" Ruiha's breath vanished.

Syltahreal spiralled earthward, wings dragging, smoke trailing behind her like torn silk.

"Go!" Kemp rasped.

Ignara banked hard, clawing sky.

Ruiha didn't hesitate. She leaned forward, gripping the ridge of Ignara's spine, and urged her downward. The dragon dove toward the falling shape, talons wide.

Closer.

Closer.

With a final beat of her wings, Ignara caught Syltahreal's shoulders. Ruiha slid low along Ignara's neck, grabbed a spur of scale slick with blood, and helped brace the wounded dragon.

Syltahreal groaned. Her eyes fluttered. But she was alive.

Above them, the sky rippled. Ruiha looked back—

And saw Kemp and Vaelthys, rising alone.

High above the battlefield. Alone against the dark.

Vaelthys's body shimmered—not red like Ignara's flame, but dark with an inner storm, as if something ancient raged beneath his hide. Kemp stood on his back now, braced, both hands raised. One flesh. One shadow.

They weren't two anymore.

Not dragon and rider.

They were *one*.

Shadow coiled from Kemp's fingers like smoke from a furnace.

Then Ruiha felt it—

Not heat. Not cold.

Absence.

The shaman below had raised his staff. The Drogo and Draugr rallied beneath him, forming their last stand in the square. A circle of blades. A breath held.

Kemp didn't wait.

He pointed. Vaelthys folded his wings.

They fell.

Dragonfire and shadowfire streamed from them—not side by side, but *entwined*. Red and black. Heat and void. Fury and silence.

Kemp screamed—but not in pain.

In fury.

In defiance.

The blast struck like a star collapsing.

The shaman's voice died mid-chant, torn from his throat.

The Drogo didn't fall. They crumbled—flesh to ash, steel to smoke.

The Draugr were unmade, as if they had never been.

The world went silent.

When the smoke cleared, only charred bone fragments remained. The last banner snapped once—and fell.

Ignara glided low, wings shuddering with exhaustion. They guided Syltahreal gently to the courtyard, where guards rushed to meet them.

She slid down Ignara's flank, boots striking stone. Her legs shook. She glanced back.

Kemp and Vaelthys landed farther off—away from the others. Kemp slumped along the dragon's spine, his posture cracked and unguarded, smoke still curling from his hand.

He looked... *hollowed out.*

Ruiha stood still, watching. Her heart thudded. She had seen it. All of it.

The power. The rage. The bond.

The way they'd burned—*together.*

Kemp raised his head. Their eyes met.

Storm met storm.

He opened his mouth as if to speak—but no words came.

Ruiha rested her hand on Ignara's shoulder, fingers trembling.

Then, soft—but certain:

"It's over," she whispered.

Kemp smiled, a crooked thing. Then collapsed.

Chapter 34

Anwyn

The firelight danced along the stone walls, casting wavering shadows that looked too much like things they'd killed.

The war table—splintered at one corner, blood-stained at another—still stood. Somehow. Like the city. Like them.

Anwyn's hand hovered over the scorched edge of the map as if it might burn her. The silence in the chamber wasn't peace. It was the kind of quiet that came after screaming. After dying.

The kind that knew it would be broken again.

They were all there, or what remained of them.

Gunnar stood at her left, arms folded. He hadn't said much since the battle ended—just enough to hold them together. Just enough to make them believe he could.

Ruiha sat near the end of the table, half in shadow, her shoulders hunched not from weakness but from grief worn heavy. Kemp lingered beside her, silent, gaze distant. His left arm trembled slightly. The magic coursing through him had taken more than flesh.

Kris leaned on the hilt of his sword, armour scratched and bent. Laoch was stone still, arms crossed, staring at nothing.

Baron Roderic had found clean robes. He looked the part again: noble, measured, hopeful. "The Drogo remnants are being hunted through the lower quarter," he said, voice too smooth for the room. "Scouts report no resistance beyond what stragglers remain. It seems... the siege has broken."

No one replied.

Roderic looked around, expecting nods. Approval. Something. "The pyres are lit. The bodies will not rise again. And the gates—they hold once more."

Anwyn studied the map. The edge closest to her was scorched. Kemp's fire, she thought. Or Vaelthys's. Or both. It didn't matter.

"We've done what no one believed we could," Roderic pressed on. "Tempsford stands. Let us say it, at least once—we have won."

Gunnar moved.

He didn't raise his voice. Didn't need to.

"No."

Just that.

Roderic blinked. "My lord?"

Gunnar's gaze cut across the table, slow and sure. "The siege is broken. That's true."

He stepped forward, resting a hand—scarred, calloused, still flecked with blood—on the map's centre.

"But the war isn't over."

The room cooled.

"Nergai still waits," Gunnar said. "We've fought his army. Not him. Not the thing behind his eyes."

Laoch grunted. "The darkness hasn't gone."

"It never does," Kemp added, quietly. His voice was hoarse, like it had been scraped raw by smoke and silence.

Ruiha looked at him, then at the door. As if she already knew where they'd go next.

Roderic cleared his throat. "But the people... they need rest. A breath. We've lost so many."

Anwyn looked up.

"So have they," she said.

No one answered her. No one needed to.

A breeze moved through the broken window, rustling ash from the stone sill.

Gunnar stepped back from the map. His eyes met Anwyn's for a heartbeat. She saw the exhaustion in him, deeper than bone. He wouldn't show it. Not here. But it was there.

"What now?" Kris asked, not to anyone in particular.

Gunnar didn't answer. He turned and walked toward the door.

When he reached it, he paused.

Then, without looking back:

"We finish what we started."

And he was gone.

One by one, the others followed.

Anwyn stayed a moment longer, watching the map.

It was scarred. Burned. But still whole.

Like the city.

Like her.

For now.

Ruiha

The corridor was cold. Not from winter. From what had been lost.

The council chamber's murmur had vanished behind her. Steps echoed soft against stone, every footfall a weight she

DEMIGOD

couldn't shake. The city slept, or tried to. Pyres cracked in the distance, low and steady, like they were breathing.

Ruiha found her by the arch. She was staring at the square.

It used to be a garden. Now it was a grave made of ash.

She didn't speak at first. Just stood beside her. Close, but not touching.

"He died well," Anwyn said, softly.

Ruiha closed her eyes.

"I know," she murmured. "I just… I wanted to hear it."

A beat passed. The wind shifted.

Anwyn turned to her, her face tired but kind.

"He was smiling," she said. "He said his wife's name. Then his son's. And then he was gone."

Ruiha's throat caught.

She nodded once, then again. Too quickly.

And then she broke.

It wasn't loud. It wasn't wild.

It was quieter than breath.

Her shoulders trembled once, and then the tears came—hot, unrelenting, shameful in their suddenness. Her fingers curled against her own arms like she might hold herself together that way.

"I told him we'd make it," she whispered. "Out of that pit. Out of the sands. I said we'd see the sky and never go back."

Anwyn didn't answer.

She stepped closer. Put an arm around Ruiha's shoulders—not tight, not firm. Just enough. Just present.

They stood like that for a while.

Two women who had fought gods, and wars, and men who called themselves warriors—reduced now to what all soldiers become when the fighting stops.

Numb.

"He followed you," Anwyn said, finally. "Because you gave him something no one else did."

Ruiha looked up.

"Hope?"

Anwyn shook her head.

"Fire."

Ruiha gave a soft, broken laugh. It didn't last.

The wind stirred again.

When Ruiha pulled back, her face was streaked but calm.

"We've got work to do," she said.

Anwyn nodded.

They didn't speak again as they walked away.

The pyres still burned.

Gunnar

The infirmary was quiet.

Too quiet for a room filled with breathing.

Most of the wounded were asleep or drugged to the point of it. A few moaned softly. A healer moved between cots, muttering to herself, bandages red-stained and hands shaking.

Gunnar walked past her without a word.

Karl lay at the far end, beneath a narrow window where light filtered down like ash.

His chest rose slow. Shallow. The blanket over him was soaked through, and not with sweat. His skin had gone pale beneath the beard. Older somehow.

He looked like someone who'd been halfway dragged to the underworld and hadn't made up his mind about returning.

Gunnar stood there a moment before saying anything.

"You stupid, stubborn bastard."

Karl blinked.

Then smiled.

"Was hoping I'd hallucinated you," he rasped.

Gunnar pulled a chair up beside the bed. It groaned beneath his weight.

"Sorry to disappoint."

Karl winced as he shifted. "Tried to hold the line. Worked, didn't it?"

Gunnar looked at him.

"You went at the Drogo army with one axe, two bad knees, and no plan."

Karl chuckled. It turned into a cough. Blood flecked his lip.

"Made a dent though."

"Aye," Gunnar said softly. "You did."

Karl turned his head slightly. "You're really back?"

"I walked the underworld. Faced what was left of me in the dark. The mountain goddess took me in. Turned me into something… not from this world."

Karl stared at him a moment longer.

"Should've known," he muttered. "Only a demigod could pull off that much brooding."

They sat in silence.

The kind of silence that doesn't ask for anything. The kind that comes only between brothers who've seen each other break and still stood beside them.

Gunnar looked down.

"Thank you," he said. "For staying. For watching over Anwyn. The twins."

Karl shrugged—then regretted it. His jaw clenched.

"I didn't do it for you."

"No," Gunnar said. "But you did it."

Karl's eyes drifted half-closed.

"You owe me a drink. And a week's sleep."

"I'll bring the drink," Gunnar said, rising. "You worry about the sleep."

As he turned to go, Karl's voice stopped him.

"Hey."

Gunnar looked back.

Karl's face was drawn, but there was still that flicker of mischief behind the pain.

"If you see Dreyna again," he said, "tell her I'm not impressed."

Gunnar smiled.

"I'll let her know."

And then he left, the door closing softly behind him, the weight in his chest somehow heavier than the mountain he carried.

Kemp

The ash still fell, soft as snow.

Kemp watched it drift between the blackened towers and scorched walls, each flake a ghost of something burned. The sky above Tempsford had cleared, but the air still carried memory—smoke, old blood, the fading scent of dragonfire.

Ruiha walked beside him, silent. Her stride was slower now, heavy in a way it hadn't been before. Not from wounds. From something else. Laoch followed a few paces behind, arms folded, the haft of his katana rising over one shoulder like a banner he hadn't lowered yet.

They moved together across the outer field, to where the dragons waited.

Sylthareal stood tall but tense, her torn wing folded close. Ignara lay curled beside her, eyes half-lidded, one flank twitching in sleep or pain. Vaelthys paced alone at the far edge of the clearing, wreathed in coils of dusk-smoke, wings restless. Something in him hadn't settled.

Neither had Kemp.

The wound on his side throbbed beneath the bandage. But it wasn't the pain that unsettled him—it was the *pulse*. Something moved in him still, just beneath the flesh. Not magic, not anymore. Not fully.

Something left behind.

He flexed his fingers and felt it in the bones.

"Gunnars right," he said quietly, eyes on the dragons. "The siege is over. But the war isn't."

Ruiha didn't look at him. "The siege was just the beginning."

Laoch snorted. "We broke the teeth. But the thing behind them's still breathing. Nergai's watching. Waiting."

Kemp nodded. "Fenchester's still under siege. If they've fallen—"

"They haven't," Ruiha said, too fast. Too sharp.

The words rang out like a blade thrown in a room gone quiet. Kemp turned to her, saw the tension in her jaw, the way her gaze didn't quite meet his.

He said nothing. Just let the silence settle.

It wasn't the kind of quiet that brought peace. It was the kind that knew what loss felt like. The kind that had seen too many friends laid on pyres.

She was pulling the walls back up. He could see it.

And maybe she needed them. Maybe they all did.

He shifted slightly, the wound at his side still raw and deep. Something beneath the bandage pulsed—not pain exactly. A reminder of the bond he shared with Vaelthys.

Laoch cleared his throat behind them.

"We should fly out. See it for ourselves."

Kemp nodded, grateful for the change in air.

He stepped to Vaelthys, laid a hand against his leg. The warmth steadied him, but only just.

"I'll take Vaelthys," he said. "He's strong. Fast."

Ruiha stepped closer. "I should come."

Kemp looked at her, really looked.

The same woman who had screamed against the Drogo charge. The one who had led from the sky. The one who had wept for Dakarai, quietly, where no one else could see.

"You can't," he said. "Not this time."

She stiffened, but he held her gaze.

"Syltharael is still grounded. And the city still needs a dragon. The people here trust you more than it trusts shadow. Stay."

She didn't reply. Her hand resting against Ignara's warm scales.

Kemp nodded toward Ignara, steam rising off her scarred flanks.

"They see hope when they look at you. When they look at me and Vaelthys... they see something they don't understand."

He didn't say more. He didn't need to.

Ruiha's hand found Ignara's neck. She didn't speak. But after a moment, she gave him a single, quiet nod.

Kemp stepped back toward Vaelthys, who lowered his head with a grunt that almost sounded like protest. Kemp touched his neck and felt it again—that *thrum* beneath the skin. The bond between them was changed.

Tighter. Stranger. As if something had fused that shouldn't have.

The fire had answered him. So had the shadow. But neither had fully let go.

He didn't know what that meant.

Not yet.

"Fenchester," he said. "We'll scout it. If they're still holding, we reinforce."

Ruiha met his gaze. "And if the gates are already gone?"

He mounted Vaelthys in a single, clean motion.

"Then we light another fire."

The dragon roared once, a sound that shook the broken stones.

Wings cut the air. The ash scattered in whirlwinds.

And they were gone—rising into the sky, toward a city still choking on fire.

CHAPTER 35

Anwyn

The wind had stilled.

Tempsford had not known quiet in weeks. Only the groan of the dying, the grind of blades, the creeping dread of what would come—and the weight of those they had lost.

Now, for the first time, there was nothing but breath, and the crackle of the hearth in the room she once called hers.

She sat by the fire, fingers resting on the arm of the chair, though she didn't remember sitting down. The light caught the lines of her palms, the ones life had carved, and grief had deepened.

Behind her, the door opened.

She knew it was him by the weight of the pause.

Gunnar stepped into the room without speaking. Closed the door with a care that undid her.

He wore no armour now.

Only a wool cloak, threadbare at the shoulders, smelling faintly of smoke, steel, and stone.

There was always earth in him—somewhere beneath the skin.

As if the mountain goddess had not merely spared him, but laid claim.

He sat across from her, saying nothing.

"I thought you were a dream," she said at last.

His eyes—*gods, those blue eyes*—met hers with a silence that held more apology than any words could carry.

"It felt like a nightmare," he said, voice low. Rough-edged. Honest.

She looked at him—really looked. Not at the warrior. Not at the ghost reborn.

But at the dwarf who had once carved his way through Vellhor to save her.

He had walked through death and come back—not untouched, but *true*.

The face was the same. The lines deeper. The voice quieter. The presence heavier.

He was changed. Scarred.

But the soul she loved still sat behind his eyes.

"You died," she said, softly. Not blame. Just truth, still tender on her tongue.

He nodded once, as if she'd named the only thing he still knew for certain.

"You saved us," she said. "All of us. I was on the floor, bleeding. The twins—"

"I remember," he said, and his voice broke on it like a blade snapping under strain.

He looked down, as if the words weighed more than armour.

"But I forgot you. After I died... I wandered. Faced things no living soul should see. And in that place—without memory, without name—there was still a voice inside me. Small. Stubborn."

He looked up again.

"It told me to stand. To choose right. And now I know why. Even in death, I hadn't let go of you."

Anwyn didn't move. Couldn't.

"Dreyna gave me power. More than I understand. But I see it now—I was never meant to carry this alone."

He stepped forward.

"I need you. The one who held the line when the world broke. The one who stood when gods took me away."

She moved closer. Her body remembered him before her mind dared to. The way he stood. The way the earth seemed quieter around him.

"You're a god, then?" she whispered.

He shook his head—slow, certain. "Not quite. Just someone given another chance to protect the people he loves."

She reached for his hand. His scarred fingers trembled before closing around hers.

"I don't know how to do this," she said, voice breaking. "You were gone. And now you're here. You missed their first breath. Their first cry."

"I know," he said again. This time quieter.

"You gave everything for us."

He looked at her, and the grief in his eyes was not for his death—it was for *what he'd missed*.

"I'd give it again," he said. "A thousand times. I just… hoped I'd get to see them. To see you."

"You will," she said.

Their foreheads touched.

And in that silence, they held not just each other—but the months of absence. The cries he never heard. The nights she held their children and whispered his name into their skin.

He had died for them.

And now, for a while, he lived again.

DEMIGOD

Magnus

The western ridge carried the scent of blood.

Magnus stood alone atop the broken parapet, his hands clasped around the haft of his warhammer, blade to stone, head bowed—not in prayer, but in memory.

Below him, Fenchester smoked. Not the roaring fires of battle, but the slower, curling kind—the aftermath. The kind that lingers in cloaks and lungs for days, maybe weeks. The kind that remembers.

The city had held.

They had come too late to save the gates—those were gone, splintered beneath Drogo fury. The walls bore the scars of battle, stone cracked where elven steel met scaled flesh.

But the dwarves had helped finish it. Had made the killing count.

Blood filled the spaces between cobblestones, pooling around broken arrows and torn banners.

And still, the city stood.

That was something.

A dwarf walked past below, dragging a cart of the fallen—elven and human bodies alike, stacked gently, wrapped in cloth where they could. Their faces were soot-streaked, some still open-eyed. No one spoke. Words didn't belong in moments like this.

Above, dragons circled low. Only ten remained—some limping in flight, others scorched along the wing—but alive, still.

The rest had not risen.

Magnus had watched one fall—its body pierced by a forest of spears, fire pouring from its throat until the roar became silence.

He had never thought he'd witness such a thing.

And he would never forget that sound.

He looked down to the square where the pyres were being built. Elves moved among the stones, their grief quieter than men's. A man knelt beside a child, too small for armour, and removed his helm with shaking hands. There was a wail then. A single, sharp sound that cut across the ruins like a blade.

Magnus closed his eyes.

He felt every name. Every loss.

They had won. Gods, they had. But some victories were hollow as the drums that called them to war.

Boots scraped behind him.

Brenn approached, blood still crusted on his neck. He was one of the few left from the Snow Wolves. Fewer still from the march through Fenmark.

Brenn stood beside him, leaning on his axe like a crutch. Blood had dried on his gauntlets. He hadn't spoken since the fighting stopped.

"The city held," he said at last.

Magnus nodded, eyes still on the city below.

"Aye. But it cost us."

Brenn looked toward the pyres. "Always does."

The silence that followed was not empty. It was full—of names, of brothers, of flames that still burned in both memory and air.

A raven circled overhead. Not an omen. Just a witness.

And from beyond the hills, the wind shifted.

Not smoke.

Something colder.

Kemp

The sky bled amber as they crossed the ridge.

Kemp shifted slightly in the saddle, his shadowhand resting against Vaelthys' scaled neck. The dragon's wingbeats were steady—powerful as a war drum—but below them, the land bore scars of fire and rot.

The darkness had left him. Yet he felt it in the tremble of his hand still. In the way fire sometimes curled beneath his ribs when no flame was lit. In the cold that no dragonfire could quite banish.

What if I'm still its vessel?

He hadn't said it aloud. Not even to Ruiha. But it lived beneath the surface now—just beneath the skin.

Vaelthys turned his head slightly, one gold eye catching him in profile.

"You are not."

The voice filled his thoughts like wind fills sails—not soft, not cruel. Certain.

"It took me once," Kemp murmured aloud. "It used me."

"Then. Not now."

A pause.

"You were weak then. But no longer. Our bond protects you."

Kemp didn't answer. Just let the wind bite into him as they flew lower. The city unfurled beneath them, broken and bloodstained—but standing.

Fenchester had held.

He could see the remnants of the battle: collapsed walls, scorched stone, mangled Drogo bodies heaped in trenches. Smoke curled from pyres.

They landed in what was left of the northern square.

Magnus was already there—his hammer slung across his back, shoulders stiff as stone. Beside him stood an elven commander with silvered braids and sharp, tired eyes. A human officer—broad-chested and bandaged at the brow—saluted as Kemp dismounted.

None of them spoke at first.

Magnus offered a slow nod. "You look like death," he said.

Kemp gave a ghost of a smile. "You don't look any better."

A moment passed.

Then the elven commander stepped forward. His cloak was singed at the hem, his braid streaked with soot. In his hand, a scrap of bloodstained parchment.

"I am Emrys, Commander of the Elven Host," he said, voice like riverstone. "This came an hour past. From a scout. South of the River Alghari."

Kemp took the page. Torn. Ash-smeared. But the words were enough.

"Alghari?" he said, too sharp. "He's heading east?"

Emrys nodded once.

Magnus stepped forward. "Do you know it?"

Kemp nodded, slow. "I studied at Lakeview. It was more than an academy. It was the last place I knew peace."

Magnus grunted. "Then we'll make sure there's something left of it."

But Emrys did not smile.

"They will not stop at the lake," he said. "Nergai will march for Vaeloria."

Silence.

"Why?" Magnus asked, though something in his voice already knew.

Emrys met his gaze.

"Because the Sacred Tree still stands. And if he destroys it—as he did millennia ago—he ends all this. He ends everything."

Kemp's hand clenched around the parchment.

The human commander swore under his breath.

Magnus's jaw tightened, fingers curling through his beard.

The wind shifted around them.

Vaelthys growled low.

And in that growl, Kemp heard it—not rage. Not pain.

A warning.

They were running out of time.

Chapter 36

Gunnar

The sky held its breath. The scent of rain on stone lingered like memory, and not even the wind dared disturb it.

Gunnar stood bare of his armour, sweat and silence clinging to the linen of his tunic. Beyond him, two soldiers worked without words, lifting stone to patch the breach—hands slow, faces hollow with exhaustion. The wall would not hold. Not truly. But they built it still.

Anwyn stepped beside him, her golden hair pulled back, though strands had already escaped—like threads of sunlight unraveling in the wind.

Her eyes, rimmed with sleeplessness, searched the sky—not the wall, not the men. She had seen it before: how the darkness swallowed light, how the storm had nearly torn the world apart. She knew where it would return.

Then they saw him.

Vaelthys.

Moving like a scar across the heavens. A shadow too large to be cloud, wingbeats silent, as if even the air parted willingly before him. His descent was not swift, but final—like dusk overtaking the day.

Kemp rode low on the dragon's spine, cloaked in the dark that clung to both man and beast. He did not speak when he dismounted. Dust scattered around his boots. The stones seemed to recoil.

Gunnar stepped forward. He saw the change in him—older by more than time. A day, perhaps two, had passed. But Kemp had crossed a threshold from which none returned whole.

"You're back early," Gunnar said.

Kemp said nothing. He held out a folded parchment. Creased, smudged, bloodied at one corner.

Gunnar took it with care, as if it might burn.

"Nergai's gone east," Kemp said. "He's regrouping."

The letter crackled as Gunnar opened it. Anwyn stepped nearer, and for a moment, they read in silence—three souls leaning toward something they could no longer stop.

"Luxyyr?" Gunnar asked, voice low.

Kemp nodded. "The elven commander believes he marches for the Sacred Tree. He means to end what he started."

Anwyn's fingers reached out, resting on the edge of the parchment. Her voice was a whisper, but it cut deeper than any blade.

"My children are in Luxyyr."

Kemp didn't speak. Gunnar hadn't expected him to. What was there to say?

The silence that followed wasn't hollow. It pressed in—tight, heavy, real. Not the quiet of calm, but the kind that settled after something breaks.

Gunnar felt it gather behind his ribs, cold as stone, certain as death.

"You're certain?" he asked.

"He's not hiding," Kemp said. "He moves with intent. Fast. Draugr and Drogo at his heels. Every straggler is made into something worse. Every village he passes turned. His army grows by the day."

The parchment curled in Gunnar's hands, its edge lifting in the wind that had finally returned.

He passed it to Anwyn, eyes never leaving Kemp's face.

"Then we go," Gunnar said.

Kemp's voice was flat. "To war?"

Gunnar stared at the horizon. The light was failing there, bleeding out behind the trees. He clenched his jaw. "Aye," he said. "But not for glory. Not for vengeance." He looked back at Kemp. "We go because if we don't, there'll be nothing left to go back to."

Behind them, Vaelthys let out a low growl, the kind that spoke of fire waiting. His head turned north, to where the forest lay under shadow.

Ruiha

Ruiha stood in the courtyard as Kemp approached, the dust of flight still clinging to his boots. His expression conveyed urgency before he spoke.

"We move for Luxyyr," he said. "We'll meet Nergai in the open. Intercept him before he reaches the Sacred Tree."

Her jaw tightened. "How long?"

"Three days, maybe less. Gunnar and Anwyn are in council with Laoch, Draeg, and Kris now. They're debating how many to take."

"They're debating who to leave behind," she corrected. "Because if we strip Tempsford bare—"

"It'll fall," Kemp said, blunt. "And if we don't move fast, Luxyyr will burn."

Her hands clenched. Fingernails dug into her palms.

Ignara landed behind them with a sound like a rockslide, wings folding tight as she slunk into the courtyard. Vaelthys stood nearby, still and watchful—a shadow made solid.

"They're going," Ruiha said. It wasn't a question.

Kemp nodded. "They've already decided."

Sylthareal limped into view, her wing still half-bound in leather and linen. The ancient weight in her eyes met Ruiha's without flinching.

"I'll stay," Sylthareal said quietly. "Tempsford needs fire and claw."

Ruiha turned to her, words rising—and failed. There was too much in her throat. Too much that hadn't been said in days of dust and ash and waking to the weight of loss.

She met Sylthareal's eyes. That was enough.

Then the horns sounded.

Not once.

Again.

A third time.

The sky did not move, but something inside her did.

Every muscle in her body tensed.

Kemp turned without a word and vaulted onto Vaelthys.

Ruiha didn't hesitate. She swung onto Ignara's back as the dragon snarled and launched skyward, chasing thunder into the clouds.

Let it be returning scouts, she thought. Let it be anything but another battle. It was too soon. They weren't ready.

Minutes passed like held breath.

Then a roar split the sky—not of fury, but signal. A cry flung wide across the valley.

Ruiha leaned forward, every nerve drawn tight.

Vaelthys banked hard, wings flaring wide, and came down fast. Kemp leapt off before his dragon touched stone, hit the ground running.

He was grinning.

Ruiha blinked, and something broke loose in her chest. Not relief. Not yet. But the sharp crack of it made her breath catch.

"They're alive," he said, breathless. "Gundeep. The Sand Whisperers. What's left of them."

Behind him, the dust parted as riders emerged from the trees—line after line of weather-beaten faces, cloaks of ochre and crimson, banners torn but still lifted high. Two thousand strong. Some wounded. All worn. But still standing.

At first, the gate guards didn't move.

Dust rolled in waves. More emerged—riders in loose formation, cloaks torn, faces shadowed by sun and grime. Banners hung limp, unrecognisable in the haze.

One guard stepped forward, hand on his hilt. Another raised a crossbow, hesitated.

Then Ruiha strode toward the wall, Kemp beside her. The dragons flanked them, wings folding tight, eyes burning like coals.

Recognition came slowly—like dawn over smoke.

One guard lowered his weapon. Another followed. Then a clenched fist rose.

The rest followed, one by one.

Ruiha didn't pause. Her voice was clear. Steady.

"Open the gates," she said. "Let them in. Prepare the square."

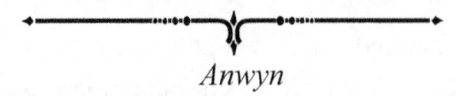

Anwyn

The council was in motion.

They had been arguing—not shouting, but close. Draeg stood with his palms braced against the table, voice like gravel over stone. Laoch paced. Kris said nothing, but his silence had a weight of its own.

Nergai marched for Luxyyr.

They all knew it. The scouts had brought the truth in blood and ash: twenty thousand strong, and most of them Draugr. Undead. Remorseless. Some still wearing the armour of men who had fallen at Fenchester.

The map was marked, the distance drawn. If they moved by morning, they would reach Luxyyr in time.

But they would leave Tempsford vulnerable. Again.

Gunnar had said it first, voice low but ironbound. "We made that mistake once."

No one had challenged him.

They had five hundred guards in Tempsford. Seven thousand soldiers between Fenmark's battalions, the Sand Dragons, and the Shadow Hawks. And now, the numbers didn't matter.

Nergai's force outmatched them nearly three to one.

And then there were the dragons.

Two of them. Undead.

The reports were fragmentary—scrawled in haste on a torn scrap of parchment, edges blackened by fire. Ink blurred. Names missing.

But the words were there. Crude. Shaking.

One dragon, black as pitch, ribs visible beneath rotted flesh, wings stretched like cracked leather. The other—gold—but dulled, twisted, its scales fused with bone. Chains across its throat. Eyes without flame.

Not even the scouts could say for certain what they'd seen.

Only that they'd run.

Still, no one doubted.

Anwyn listened. Contributed where she could. She kept her voice calm, her thoughts ordered. She was Seishinmori. She was supposed to lead, to weigh lives, to command.

But her children were in Luxyyr.

Every breath she took was a controlled decision. Every heartbeat, a delay. The part of her that wanted to scream was buried under a thousand moments of discipline. She folded her hands to hide the tremble in her fingers.

Gunnar spoke again, standing still now. "We split the force, Tempsford survives. But we will not succeed in Luxyyr. If we ride with everything, we risk both."

A silence fell. Heavy. Steady.

Then the horns sounded.

Once.

Twice.

A third time.

Anwyn didn't wait for the signal. She crossed the chamber in three strides and threw open the high window.

Gunnar joined her a breath later, his hand tightening on the stone sill.

Too far to see clearly. But they both knew those shapes in the sky.

Ignara, burning crimson, circled overhead.

And then—Vaelthys. Banking low, shadow-wreathed, wings beating like war drums. He dove hard, disappearing from sight behind the outer wall.

Minutes passed like held breath.

Then the gates opened.

Anwyn stared as dust rolled up from the plain, banners half-torn, faces sun-blackened and bloodied. Two thousand riders marched through the gate—battered, ragged, and alive. The Sand Whisperers. Survivors.

At their head rode their leader, one arm bound in sling and cloth, his helm dangling from the horn of his saddle.

The council moved as one toward the steps, the chamber forgotten.

Gunnar did not speak for a moment. He only watched. Then:

"Well," he said, voice rough. "This helps things somewhat."

Anwyn didn't look at him. Her eyes were still on the gate. On the people coming through it.

Two thousand blades. Against twenty thousand dead. And two dragons raised from death.

She swallowed, hard.

"Somewhat," she said. "But not nearly enough."

Chapter 37

Ruiha

The city square still pulsed with dust and weariness when Ruiha caught Gundeep's eye. His armour was cracked, one arm bound in cloth and linen, but his spine held straight, his gaze unbroken. She gave a single nod. He fell in beside her without a word.

Kemp walked ahead, boots striking hard against stone.

The silence between them wasn't empty. It was full—of fire and ash, of choices made and lives buried beneath them. There was no need to speak until the walls closed in again.

As they turned into one of Tempsford's inner corridors, Ruiha broke it. Her voice was low, clipped by fatigue.

"We held the wall. Barely. They came in waves—Drogo, Draugr, siege beasts, towers taller than the gates. We held... but Dak—" She paused, breath catching. "We won. But it cost us."

Gundeep's brow furrowed. "We saw the smoke from miles away. We didn't know what we'd find when we got here."

Ruiha didn't smile. "Death."

They passed beneath the high arches where the last light of day angled through narrow windows, casting long shadows like scars across the floor.

"Nergai's not done," Ruiha said. "He's marching on Luxyyr. Twenty thousand strong. Draugr. Drogo. And worse."

Gundeep gave her a sidelong glance. "Worse?"

Her jaw tightened. "Undead dragons."

He stopped walking. Just for a heartbeat. Shock flickered across his face, chased by something deeper. Fear. Rage. Maybe both.

"Gods," he muttered. "What's he after?"

Ruiha looked straight ahead. "The Sacred Tree."

Silence stretched between them, heavy as chain.

"To end it," she said. "Burn it to ash."

Gundeep's jaw tightened. He didn't answer, but his knuckles whitened around the scimitar at his side.

They reached the council chamber doors. Kemp didn't pause—he pushed them open with one hand and stepped through.

Inside, the air bristled. A map of the Vellhor was unfurled across the war table like a wound, red-marked with threat and consequence. No one sat. This wasn't a council of debate. This was the edge of a blade.

Gunnar stood at the head of the table, shoulders square, eyes sharp. Anwyn, Laoch, Draeg, and Kris flanked him, all turning as Ruiha entered with Kemp and Gundeep at her side.

"Kemp," Gunnar said, giving a nod. "Ruiha."

Ruiha stepped forward, her voice steady. "This is Gundeep. He leads the Sand Whisperers. He's with us."

Gundeep stepped up, grime still fresh on his face, sling tight around his shoulder. He gave a short bow.

"Two thousand riders at your call," Gundeep said. His voice was steady.

He offered the ghost of a smile. "Not our finest hour. Some can't stand straight. None have seen a bed in a month. A few are held together more by stubbornness than stitching."

He looked each of them in the eye.

"But we're here. And we'll fight. For as long as it takes."

Gunnar's expression didn't shift, but something eased behind his eyes. A breath not quite taken.

Anwyn spoke next, her voice even. "We need to leave at dawn."

"Then we'll be ready," Gundeep replied.

Draeg cleared his throat, stepping in. "We still haven't settled the defence of Tempsford. If we leave it bare…"

"It won't be bare," Kris said quietly.

The room stilled. All eyes turned to him.

"I'll stay," he continued, arms crossed. "A thousand Shadow Hawks. Five hundred city guards. It's thin, but with Sylthareal's help, we can hold. So long as it's not a full assault."

Laoch frowned. "That's barely enough to cover the gates."

"It's not about winning," Kris said. "It's about buying time. Making them think we're still strong. If we end this at Luxyyr, they won't get the chance to test us here."

"Then it's decided," Gunnar said. "Kris will stay. Syl255haereal and fifteen hundred to hold the city. Everyone else rides to meet Nergai."

The silence that followed wasn't filled with fear. Nor hope.

Only resolve.

A final, quiet agreement among those who had nothing left to give but everything.

Ruiha looked around the chamber—at faces etched with loss, at hands curled into fists not from anger, but necessity. She felt the hours shrinking around them.

She turned to Gundeep. "Rest what you can. Tomorrow, the real war begins."

He gave a slow nod.

And the war council ended—not with command or decree.

But with silence.

The kind that came before fire.

Gunnar

Tempsford held its breath.

Gunnar walked through the lower levels of the keep, boots echoing off stone, the chill of pre-dawn air pressing against the back of his neck. Lamps burned low in iron sconces. The scent of smoke and boiled herbs clung to the corridors. Somewhere above, a dragon stirred, a deep rumble of breath rolling through the tower walls like distant thunder.

Outside, the streets were quiet. Not the peaceful kind. The kind that felt like the air had thickened, waiting for the sound of hoofbeats and horns. Soldiers lay where they'd dropped—against doorways, under awnings, wrapped in cloaks. A few priests walked among them, offering quiet blessings or sharing water. Blacksmiths worked in silence, finishing last repairs with red-rimmed eyes and blistered hands.

The city wasn't sleeping. It was *enduring*.

He made his way into the infirmary—an old chapel once, now stripped of its icons and lined with cots and bloodstained linens. The smell hit him first—iron, ash, and the sharp sting of poultice.

Karl was propped against a stack of furs, his left arm bound in a splint, thick bandages wrapped tight around his middle. One look told Gunnar he shouldn't be sitting up at all, but Karl straightened the moment he saw him.

"I'm coming," he said, voice hoarse but certain, before Gunnar could even open his mouth.

Gunnar let the door swing shut behind him. "You're not even breathing without wincing. What exactly are you going to do—glare the Drogo to death?"

Karl grinned. "If it comes to that."

Gunnar frowned, arms crossing. "You'll slow us. Maybe die halfway there for no good reason."

"There's always a good reason," Karl said. "And besides, I've got Draeg muttering to his mother and Anwyn waving her hands. I'll be right as rain by the time we reach Luxyyr. And it's better that than lying here while the rest of you bleed."

Gunnar didn't answer straight away. He just looked at him—really looked. The lines of pain behind the grin. The sheen of sweat along his collarbone. The bruises turning yellow around the ribs. But the eyes? Still sharp. Still stubborn.

Karl leaned down and pulled something from beneath the cot.

It was a tankard.

But not just any tankard.

Silver-chased, wide-mouthed, engraved with intricate patterns and forgotten runes. The metal gleamed despite the low light, its handle carved in the shape of a stag, details worn smooth by time and use.

Karl held it out with both hands, like a blade being offered in ceremony.

"The Vessel," he said.

Gunnar gave a low chuckle. "Gods. Only you would turn Vellhor's salvation into your personal drinking cup."

Karl let out a slow grin. "Blasphemy."

Gunnar took it, surprised again by its balance. "Are you sure you want me to take it? Now that you're coming with us…"

"You've carried me off enough battlefields to qualify," Karl said, pressing it into his hand. "Just don't let Draeg fill it with some god-blessed goat's milk or whatever he's into."

"No promises," Gunnar muttered. "It might see stew yet."

Karl snorted. "If you pour stew in that, I'll rise from the dead and murder you myself."

Gunnar gave a quiet huff. Almost a laugh. He turned to go, fingers tightening around the tankard.

"Send Draeg in when you pass him," Karl called after him. "He's been pacing outside like a monk with a guilty conscience."

Gunnar paused in the doorway. "If you're not at the gate come dawn, I'll assume you've found some sense."

"Then don't hold your breath," Karl muttered.

Gunnar didn't.

Outside, the sky had begun to pale. A single star still clung to the west, stubborn and slow to fade.

The first horn hadn't sounded.

But it would.

And when it did, they'd ride.

Kemp

The sky hadn't yet made up its mind.

Dawn lingered behind the hills, caught in that trembling hour between ash and gold. Tempsford held its breath beneath it, a hush like the pause before a blade falls.

Kemp stood beside Vaelthys in the yard. Mist rose from the dragon's flanks like smoke from coals. The bond between them was quiet now. No shadows. No murmurs. Just breath and presence. Just him and the dragon, still and certain.

The ground still remembered the night's dew, though the air was dry. A lone rider passed—cloak tight, gaze lowered. No greeting. Just motion.

Vaelthys shifted, wings half-furled. Not unsettled. Ready.

Across the square, Ruiha ran her hands along the horns at Ignara's withers, every motion precise. She didn't look up. She didn't need to. Kemp knew the rhythm of her now—the set of her shoulders, the pause before her final check for hold and balance.

He crossed the yard in silence.

They met between the dragons.

"I leave for Fenchester," he said.

She nodded. "We'll head out before dawn fully breaks. Gunnar rides point."

Kemp glanced to the open gates. The first ranks had begun to form—banners still furled, voices low, hooves muffled on earth not yet stirred.

He looked back. Her eyes met his—she looked like hell, but held his gaze.

No salutes. No ceremony. Just work between them now—tested, reliable.

He lingered a moment longer than he should have.

"If I'm delayed," he said, quiet but deliberate, "don't wait on me. Move when the window opens."

She gave a small nod, almost a smirk.

"Then don't be delayed."

Not hope. A decision.

He nodded, turned, mounted.

Vaelthys surged upward—two beats, then air. The yard dropped away. Wind peeled the weight from his shoulders. Tempsford receded—light, shadow, motion. Sunlight licked the helms of the army below: silver, crimson, steel. A river drawn taut.

The sky opened before them—clear, cold, and vast. No drag. Just speed. Just purpose.

He didn't look back.

The horizon rose like a blade.

The darkness inside him—the one that once coiled and whispered—was gone. Burned out, maybe. Or buried deep. It didn't matter.

What remained was clarity.

He thought of Ruiha once. Not with ache. As anchor. She would hold. He would fly beyond her line.

A gust kicked sideways. Vaelthys adjusted mid-air, instinct catching balance. It snapped Kemp into the moment.

He scanned the sky. Nothing.

Still, he touched the bond. Vaelthys answered.

They dropped lower.

Fenchester rose as the sun crested the ridge. The outer walls bore scars—patched stone, blackened burns, new dwarven steel. But they stood. The banners flew low now—practical, not ceremonial—catching the morning like old vows remembered.

Two dragons circled above. One limped on a torn wing. They flared as Vaelthys approached, then drifted into formation.

Vaelthys landed hard. Dust rose. Stone shifted.

At the base of the keep, Emrys waited—silver braid still streaked with ash. Magnus stood beside him, arms crossed, a wall of storm-worn stone.

Kemp dismounted.

"Tempsford marches," he said. "Eight thousand. Fifteen hundred stay to hold the city."

Emrys hissed something unintelligible. Magnus's jaw flexed.

"How many here?" Kemp asked.

"Four thousand elves. Five thousand dwarves. A thousand human. Ten dragons," Emrys replied. "We keep the humans here—no time to rotate."

Kemp nodded. "Twelve dragons. Fifteen thousand bodies."

Magnus's voice was flat. "Against what?"

"Over twenty thousand Draugr and Drogo. Two corrupted dragons. Nergai leads them. He's coming."

Silence fell. Not doubt—just the weight of knowing.

Then—a young elf tore through the gate, breathless. No bow. No words. Just a scroll, thrust into Emrys's hand.

He read.

Then again.

"Nergai camps at the Great Elven Forest," he said, voice low. "He has summoned a dark storm."

Magnus turned east. The clouds there churned—too thick, too still. The color of dying steel. "The darkness returns. We move tonight," he said.

Emrys didn't argue. "Kemp, take half of our dragons. Speed matters."

Kemp said nothing.

He turned. Vaelthys watched him, storm clouds churning in his eyes.

Kemp mounted.

They rose.

He looked east.

The darkness was already moving.

But so were they.

And this time, light would strike first.

Chapter 38

Ruiha

The column stretched beneath her like a scar across the land.

Dust rose in low spirals from iron-shod hooves and the steady tramp of boots, curling between the trees that lined the old trade road north of Tempsford. It was a march stripped of ceremony. No banners lifted. No horns. Just the heavy rhythm of men and women who had fought too long and bled too much—and were still moving forward.

Ruiha circled once, Ignara banking into the wind. The sky above them was open, washed in thin light. The clouds were high and sharp-edged, like teeth.

And then she saw them.

A formation, tight and deliberate—six dragons, spearheading from the north. The lead was unmistakable. Broad wings. Darker scales. The controlled descent of a creature that once raged like wildfire and now moved like stone.

Vaelthys.

And Kemp, just behind the horns. He didn't raise a hand. Didn't wave. He didn't need to. She felt the shift in her chest the moment she saw him. Not ache. Not fear. Just... steady ground. The click of something in place.

Five more dragons followed behind—ragged but flying true. One with a broken horn, another with fresh scarring across its flank. Survivors.

Ruiha pulled Ignara into a matching arc, descending. Wind cut beneath her as she dropped toward the column, feeling the shift of the army's eyes lifting skyward.

They were watching hope fall from the sky.

She landed first in a swirl of dust and wingbeat. Vaelthys followed. The others came in hard behind—landings not elegant, but sure. Dragons returning from the edge of ruin.

Kemp dismounted, his movements clean, economical. He hadn't changed. But he had. She could see it in the way he stood—not tense, not guarded. Centred.

She dismounted without flourish, boots sinking slightly into the churned loam. Kemp turned as she approached. He looked tired. No surprise. But the lines around his mouth had hardened into something more than weariness. Purpose, maybe.

Vaelthys stood behind him, in front of the five other dragons.

Their eyes met.

Kemp didn't speak at first. He didn't need to.

"Nergai?" Ruiha asked.

He nodded. "Camped outside Luxyyr. He's summoned the storm again."

She exhaled slowly through her nose. Not fear. Not surprise. Just confirmation of what they'd already begun to feel in their bones. The wind had shifted. Even Ignara had grown restless in flight—flicking her head toward the north like she could smell the rot on it.

Behind them, the command group approached—Gunnar at the front, Stonecall strapped to his back, Anwyn beside him, silent and flame-eyed. Laoch followed with his usual careful tread, cloak pinned high against the wind. Kemp watched them come, said nothing more.

"We go to Vaeloria," Ruiha said when they were gathered. "They must act. Nergai's at their border. The Sacred Tree won't survive hesitation."

Gunnar said nothing. Kemp folded his arms.

Anwyn looked at her father, brow furrowed, a flicker of something unreadable in her eyes.

Her voice, when it came, was quiet. Almost regretful.

"They won't listen. Not if it comes from humans."

She paused, then added—

"The council moves slow—even when the storm is on their doorstep. But they would hear me. They have to."

Ruiha felt the truth of it. She had been bonded to a dragon, yes. She had led in fire and battle. But she was still human. Still young. The Elders would hear her words and nod politely and do nothing until it was already too late.

"Anwyn is right," Laoch said. His voice was quiet, but sure. "But Anwyn must stay here. She must lead the attack. Alongside Gunnar."

He stepped forward, wind tugging at his dark hair.

"But they'll listen to me. I've stood in those chambers. I know their fears. I know the words that will move them."

Ruiha turned to him. "You'd go?"

"I should've gone days ago," he said. "Now is better than not at all."

Kemp looked to Ruiha. "Vaelthys and I can take him. We'll leave the other dragons."

Ruiha hesitated, then nodded. "Six dragons with us. That will help when the sky breaks."

Laoch offered a short, shallow bow. "Then we leave now."

Anwyn stepped forward. Her fingers tightened at her side.

"When you reach Vaeloria," she said to her father, "you and Mother—watch over Owen and Freya. Protect them. For as long as you can."

Laoch inclined his head.

"By the roots of the forest," he said. "I will."

Ruiha saw it then—just for a heartbeat.

A flicker in Anwyn's eyes. Not fear of battle, nor death. But of leaving her children in a world about to burn.

Then it was gone—replaced by the calm she'd worn so long it might have been carved into her.

Fire beneath stone.

Kemp mounted. Vaelthys rose behind him, wings unfurling like a banner. Laoch climbed with elven grace. The dragon didn't wait.

They launched.

No roar. No flame. Just air and motion and vanishing scale against sky.

Ruiha watched them go until they were gone.

The wind shifted again—this time from the north.

She turned to it. The clouds there were no longer clouds.

They were waiting.

And they were coming.

Anwyn

They crested a low ridge, and the Forest came into view—at first only as a deepening of the green, a shift in the texture of the horizon. Then the edges became real: twisted branches, ageless trunks, the faint shimmer of ward-lights woven into the highest boughs.

Anwyn reined her mount to a slower pace. Gunnar did the same beside her, saying nothing. He rarely did, in these moments. Not because he lacked words, but because he understood the ones that mattered were not always meant to be spoken aloud.

She felt it before she saw it.

A subtle heat. A pulling in her chest, as if something long-abandoned were stirring within her spirit. The Sacred Tree. Still distant, but not beyond reach. It hummed faintly in the air, in the rhythm of hoofbeats against stone, in the breath she hadn't realised she'd been holding.

Her palms tingled against the reins. A soft thrum moved through her shoulders, up the back of her neck.

She inhaled, and it was there. The magic.

It was her magic, but more than hers.

It belonged to the Forest. to the Sacred Tree. And it remembered.

The wind stirred once. Then again, harder. It was not cold, but neither was it warm. It carried a weight. A knowing.

Anwyn blinked.

The shimmer of the Forest's aura—once a steady, golden pulse—was flickering. Not absent. But strained. As if something lay draped over it, something heavy, pulling it into the earth.

She looked up.

The storm churned above the Forest, black with veins of violet lightning, slow and coiled like a serpent in slumber. It did not move with the wind. It was the wind. And it watched.

Something in her dimmed.

Only slightly. But she felt it. Like a thin veil pulled over the flame within. A quieting. Not extinguished—but challenged.

She narrowed her eyes, reaching. The wind pushed back, then rushed forward again, stronger. Leaves rose in spirals around them. Her horse stamped once. Lightning flared high in the clouds.

There.

A voice—or something like it. Not words, not sound. But she heard it all the same. Just outside understanding. Just outside time.

Gunnar shifted in beside her, eyes narrowing toward the Forest. He'd felt it too.

She closed her eyes and reached inward. To her spirit. She was breathing in the way Thalirion had taught her. Using the aura around her.

"Not yet," she whispered.

The trees creaked before them.

Another flash lit the sky—sharper this time. Closer.

She opened her eyes, turned to Gunnar, and took his hand without asking.

His fingers closed around hers—solid, steady.

Together, they turned toward the growing cluster of banners ahead, where the command group waited, half-shielded behind a rise of stone and broken root.

"It's time," she said.

Gunnar crested the hill at a slow trot, hoarfrost crackling beneath Ghost's paws. The ground was rimed where it shouldn't be—beneath a spring sun, the grass smoked like breath in winter. A mile ahead, the edge of the forest swayed in unnatural silence, its leaves already blackened at the tips. Above, the storm churned without sound, a vast bruised wound stitched across the sky.

He passed the outer sentries without a word. Elves with hoods drawn. Dwarves shoulder to shoulder, hammering runed stakes into the earth. A young soldier kissed a sealed letter, then fed it to flame. His eyes didn't blink as it turned to ash.

This was no longer a war camp.

It was a pyre waiting for fire.

He dismounted Ghost and stepped into the heart of it.

The war tent pulsed with heat and quiet fury. Magnus was hunched over the map table, hands planted like he meant to split the wood. Emrys stood beside him, steel-trimmed robes drawn tight against fatigue. Anwyn watched from the side, arms crossed, silent and taut as a bowstring. Draeg paced the perimeter, each step a low thud of weight and war-readiness. Ruiha stood near the rear, silent and still, the scent of smoke still clinging faintly to her cloak.

Magnus didn't look up when Gunnar entered.

"They're coming," he said, matter-of-fact.

There was no shock in his voice. Gunnar had witnessed that earlier, when Magnus had stared at the brother he'd thought dead, yet standing alive with eyes that remembered. He had embraced Gunnar not in joy, but in the desperation of someone anchoring himself to a world that no longer made sense.

Gunnar stepped to the table. The map was blackened at the corners, bleeding ink from too many redrawings.

"How close?"

"Scouts place them less than ten miles out," Emrys rasped. "The storm moves with them. Faster. And hungrier."

"The trees are dying where they stand," Anwyn murmured, eyes far away. "As if even in death, they're too proud to fall."

"We have dragonfire," Ruiha said. "It clears a path. Briefly."

"Like sunlight through smoke," Draeg muttered. "Then the dark surges in."

Gunnar's hand settled on the haft of Stonecall, the runemarks pulsing faintly.

"The dragons are no longer our vanguard," he said. "We wield them as knives, not hammers."

Silence folded in. Even the tent canvas seemed to still.

Draeg broke it.

"So what's the plan?"

Gunnar drew a sharp breath.

"We draw Nergai into the Forest."

A ripple passed through the tent.

"He expects a wall," Gunnar continued. "He'll get a thousand blades in the dark."

Anwyn nodded, already seeing the shape of it.

"We don't face him on open ground. We unmake that ground. Step by step, we draw him in—until he's buried in it."

"The forest will slow him," Emrys added. "Break his formation. The storm can't stretch as wide beneath the canopy."

"It feeds on openness," Gunnar said. "But under the boughs, it folds. We scatter his lines. Shatter the dark into pieces."

Draeg crossed his arms.

"We've got the elves for paths, the dwarves for traps, and dragons to cut corridors when we strike."

"We give him targets," Anwyn added. "Routed units. Wounded scouts. A young dragon too eager, flying alone. Let them think we're panicked."

Magnus grunted, rough approval. "And the deeper he chases, the worse it gets."

"Exactly," Gunnar said. "He follows a scent of blood and glory—and when he's in deep enough, we cut off the exits."

Emrys looked at the map, tracing fingers over root-lines and glades long buried in memory. "Three zones—east, west, and centre. Each collapses in turn. We time it right, we break them one by one."

Gunnar nodded. "Let him drag his darkness through every sacred path we know. And when he thinks he's won—when he believes the forest itself is dying under his feet—we close the cage."

Anwyn stepped forward, her voice low.

"And then we end him."

Draeg spoke next, rough as stone. "What of the dragons?"

Ruiha stepped forward then, her voice level, her presence quiet but commanding.

"We have six," she said. "Three hold for the final strike—low, cloaked, waiting at Gwydir. One guards the Sacred

Tree. One flies decoy—young, a little reckless. She'll look wounded, peel off, draw the Drogo deeper. That leaves one to fly with our mobile units—dwarven sappers, elven scouts, fast infantry. No drawn-out fights. Hit hard, vanish."

"And the rest?" Draeg asked.

Ruiha shook her head once. "That's it. The rest are gone. Dead. Grounded. Kemp brought five. Add Ignara—six total."

Draeg's jaw tightened. No surprise. Just the weight of what they'd lost.

"Wards will need to track their movement," Emrys said. "We can arc them across ley-points. Give them windows."

Gunnar looked to Laoch. "And Vaeloria?"

"They'll be too late for the kill-box," Laoch replied, his tone flat. "But they'll hold the Tree. And when the sky flares—they'll come."

Gunnar met Ruiha's gaze.

"Will the dragons agree to this?"

Her mouth tightened.

"They're not here for survival, Gunnar. They're here for the end."

Draeg grunted.

"Good," he said. "Then we cut this bastard up one fireline at a time."

Kemp

They landed in silence.

No horns greeted them. No guards at the ready. Only the whisper of wind through high branches, and the creak of root and bark beneath Vaelthys's talons as he touched down atop the moss-veined stone.

The roots of Vaeloria spread wide beneath them, vast and gnarled like the hands of something ancient and enduring—a god who had once shaped the world and now chose only to watch it unravel. The trees here were older than kingdoms. Their canopies stretched far above Vaelthys's head, heavy with gold-edged leaves that caught what little sun the storm had not yet stolen. Even in shadow, they held light.

And then there was the Tree.

Kemp had heard of it, of course.

In tavern songs and dusty texts, in the guarded reverence of elven whispers. But no tale, no scholar's ink, had ever come close to this.

It rose not like a tower, but like a truth—an unbroken line from soil to sky, its bark silver and white as frost-lit bone, spiraling in whorls like written scripture. The branches reached outward in slow arcs, each one tipped with leaves the colour of fire before the fall. A low hum pulsed from it—not sound, but something deeper. A resonance in the chest. A memory in the blood.

Laoch bowed his head the moment they saw it. Not out of ritual. Out of reverence.

Kemp dismounted before Vaelthys's claws had fully settled. The dragon exhaled behind him, steam rising in tendrils between the roots.

Laoch stepped down with a fluid grace, adjusting his cloak with the quiet precision of someone returning to a place that had once belonged to him. He didn't speak. He didn't need to.

DEMIGOD

They entered the Great Hall without flourish. Without preamble.

Not with ceremony. Not with command. Because there was no time left for either.

Kemp had expected resistance. Suspicion, perhaps. Fear, even—of the news they carried.

But the faces that turned toward them were not shaped by fear. They were carved by memory, weathered by centuries. Watching. Waiting.

Not unkind, but.. *unwelcoming*.

Seven Elders.

Three seated upon thrones shaped from living root, their posture as still as the stone that had no place here.

Four stood behind them, robes ink-dark and threaded with leaf-gold, ceremonial and simple all at once.

Light fell through the high canopy and found their hair, silvering it further.

None bowed.

None spoke.

Kemp's boots sounded louder than they should have—like punctuation in a place that did not favour speech. But he did not falter.

At the centre sat a woman whose presence gathered the room around her.

Her braids were storm-grey, wrapped in a circlet of branch-steel that caught the light like frost on winter bark.

Her eyes were riverstone: calm, cold, and older than questions.

She inclined her head—just enough. Polite, but precise. No more.

"You have come far from Tempsford, shadowmage," she said.

Her voice was not cruel.

But it was cold—the kind of cold that lives in deep water, beneath the places where sunlight fades and names are forgotten.

Kemp flinched, but only within.

He knew he had earned the name.

Carried it. Endured it.

But even now, after something like redemption, it still struck bone.

He said nothing.

Laoch stepped forward, his cloak barely moving, but the air shifted around him all the same.

"Lady Siara. Councillors. We bring grave news."

She spoke, measured. "Tell us."

Kemp did.

"Nergai camps less than five days from here. Twenty thousand Draugr and Drogo. Two corrupted dragons. A storm that tears the sky and births the dead."

They did not flinch. But something changed. A breath held. A silence thickened.

"You are certain?" asked one of the robed elders.

"We've seen it with our own eyes," Laoch said.

Another—tall, silver-eyed—frowned. "And why has he come to us?"

Kemp folded his arms. "Because of the Sacred Tree. He means to destroy it. And if he does… what comes next won't stop at Vaeloria."

Laoch stepped forward again.

He did not raise his voice.

"I have stood in this hall when words still carried weight. I have seen the roots tremble beneath prophecy. I know you feel it now."

No one answered. So he pressed.

"You know me. You know my daughter. You know the road I walked away from here. And you know I would not return without grave cause."

His gaze moved across them, deliberate and slow.

"If you let the storm reach the Tree, nothing will survive."

A long pause followed.

Then Lady Siara spoke. "What do you ask of us? We will confer."

Laoch's voice cut clean across the room.

"There is no time for deliberation. I do not come to ask. I speak now with the full weight of the Seishinmori. This is no longer a request."

The council stirred. One turned away, another winced. A third touched Siara's arm.

Still, her gaze did not lower. But whatever resistance lingered in her eyes, it did not reach her voice.

"Tell us what you need," she said. "You will have it."

Kemp stepped forward.

"Those willing to fight," he said. "And those willing to believe. That will be enough."

The Elders whispered—hands like script, glances sharp as bladepoints. Then Siara raised her hand, and the hall stilled once more.

"We will prepare," she said.

Laoch offered a shallow bow. Not of gratitude. Of finality.

"If you need me," he said, "I will be with my wife. And my grandchildren."

Then he turned and left the hall, his steps neither hurried nor slow.

Kemp followed.

CHAPTER 39

Ruiha

The last trees of the border passed beneath her.

Open grassland lay behind—broken only by the churned lines of the army's passage. Ahead, the forest rose like breath held too long. Tall and quiet. Watching.

They had crossed into the Great Elven Forest at first light. Not in triumph. Not with banners.

They had entered like ghosts.

Ruiha sat low on Ignara's neck, eyes narrowed against the wind. Below, the grove darkened. Gwydir. The heart of the trap. It didn't look like a battlefield. It looked like a cluster of trees that remembered too much.

She scanned the edges—fast. One blink too long and she'd miss it. Decoy units had already peeled back, feigning disarray.

Sand Whisperers vanished into the trees like dust beneath desert wind—silent, certain, gone.

Elven scouts moved soundlessly between shadows.

And above them—

Dragons.

Six in formation. Two circling higher. Their wingbeats slow, careful. One dipped too low, its right wing stitched where it should've been whole. Wounded, but flying.

They needed to hold.

Below her, the enemy swarmed—Draugr and Drogo in tangled waves, pressing through broken underbrush, blades drawn, teeth bared. Nergai's dead things moved without fear, without sound. His storm had no voice.

Just pressure.

Just the sense of the world bending toward something wrong.

And then, lightning.

Violet streaks ripped the sky, crooked and violent. Wherever they touched, trees died on their feet—splitting, blackening, falling with no fire and no scream. The storm wasn't striking at soldiers. It was peeling back the forest. Trying to see. Trying to open it up.

Ruiha watched. Waited.

A dragon broke formation.

Ignara rumbled beneath her, sensing the shift before Ruiha did. She veered right, wings tilting too wide—chasing a cluster of Drogo slipping through the trees.

A bolt caught her.

Not a killing blow, but close—slicing the membrane of her left wing.

She dropped fast. Spiraled once.

Then, by instinct or grace, her wings flared—catching air just before the forest floor rose to meet her.

Ruiha ground her jaw. Close. Too close.

She was a planned decoy—but she wasn't meant to fall.

They needed every dragon in the sky—no room for error. Not now.

Her fingers curled tight around Ignara's horn. The wind cut sharper here. Carried the scent of iron and bark, of something burning where it shouldn't.

"Steady," she murmured.

The flare hadn't come yet.

She swept her gaze across the ridgelines. West. Then South.

There.

A streak of red fire arced into the sky—curving above the treetops, casting sparks like blood.

The signal.

The kill box was ready.

She was the first of the final three. The signal flare had marked their moment—and now flame would follow.

Ignara surged before she gave the command. Ruiha leaned low, eyes locked forward, wind screaming now.

The sky was breaking.

And she would be the first into the fire.

Draeg

The flare split the sky.

A crimson arc above the trees, burning like war made visible. For a moment it hovered, trailing sparks through the stormlit canopy—and then it was gone.

The silence after it was worse than the waiting.

Draeg watched from below, crouched in a hollowed root trench, hand pressed against the earth. The dirt was wet. Not from rain. From breath. From sweat. From the grove itself holding still.

He looked to his left. Karl nodded. Torch in hand, his other gripping a hammer etched with runes. There was blood on his cheek and soot in his beard. Both of them had knelt in this same spot three hours earlier, marking fuse lines with powdered chalk.

Now it was time.

"Light it," Draeg said.

Karl did. Flame touched rune. The line hissed—then crawled.

Above them, the world rumbled.

The Drogo had entered the kill zone. You could feel it. The tremble of boots not meant to touch sacred soil. The breathless hush of trees waiting to scream.

Draeg looked up. Just enough to see a corrupted dragon pass overhead—wings tattered, ribs showing between scale-plates. Its cry wasn't a roar.

It was a memory. Of something that had once been noble, now dragged into a godless shape.

Karl grunted.

"They'll see us soon."

"No," Draeg said. "They'll see fire."

The root-wall to their right shook.

Something was coming—not Drogo. Too big. Too quiet. Draeg felt the wrongness before he saw it. Like it was dragging shadow through the soil, leaving rot in its wake.

Then came the sound.

A wet scrape. A low hum. Like a song sung too deep for the living.

And then it burst through.

A thing of limbs, blackened and glistening. No eyes. Just mouths. Twisting, biting, breathing wrong.

Karl turned with his hammer.

Almost too slow.

The thing lunged.

Karl staggered back, swung hard. Steel met flesh. The creature reeled.

Draeg stepped in. No weapon. Just a clenched fist like a falling stone.

He hit it once. Twice.

Didn't stop until bone cracked and black ichor sprayed the roots like spilled ink.

Then silence.

Draeg stood, chest heaving. The stink of the thing clung to him like smoke.

He turned. The fuse line was nearly gone.

It had reached the main charge.

Fire ripped through the trenches. Explosions rolled under the grove like thunder with no sky. Roots split. Soil bucked. Drogo above screamed as the earth opened beneath them.

Draeg fell back, arm over his face. Heat tore at his skin. Debris rained down like ash.

When it ended, the trench was dust.

He stood, blood on his face, eyes scanning. Karl was on his arse, armor blackened, legs kicking like a beetle on its back.

Draeg barked a laugh.

"Get up, you lazy bastard. No time for a nap—we've got more Drogo to kill."

Karl grunted, swung to his feet, growled something Draeg didn't catch.

Didn't matter.

There was more work to do.

The eastern kill zone down.

Two to go.

Anwyn

The forest was burning.

Not in flame. Not yet.

But in pressure. In silence.

The kind that presses behind your teeth and into your bones. That makes the world feel thinner, like breath held too long.

Anwyn stood in the centre of the grove, Anwyn stood in the centre of the grove, hands braced on her knees, breathing slow. Beside her, Emrys was murmuring a spell—runes pulsed faintly beneath their feet. This was the heart—the central kill zone. And they both knew it.

Above them, the storm boiled like a living thing. Lightning forked in violet lines. The clouds didn't move—they waited.

"Here they come," Emrys said.

He didn't need to.

Anwyn could feel them. Could feel the Tree flinch.

Drogo. Draugr. Creatures twisted from the dead and dreaming. They poured into the grove like a tide, teeth bared, voices gone. And then—

The dragon.

It came low through the trees, shoulders wide enough to snap branches in passing. Its scales were dull, its eyes wrong. The beat of its wings was heavy. Corrupted. It had once been bright.

Anwyn stepped forward, the wind tugging gently at her cloak.

"Hold the perimeter," she said.

Emrys gave a single nod and stepped back, the words already on his lips—old magic, spoken like a prayer only the wind could hear.

Around the Grove, a thousand stood in silence.

Dwarves with crossbows cradled tight. Elven warriors, their katanas dull in the low light. Grim-eyed humans wrapped in weather-worn cloaks, blades drawn.

They stood shoulder to shoulder.

No one spoke.

They didn't need to.

Anwyn raised her hand.

The flame came freely.

It rose in her palm, a soft pulse at first, then curled up her forearm in warm arcs—familiar, measured, steady. Not a weapon. A promise.

It felt like the forest's voice.

Like memory, half-buried but never lost.

Like home.

But when she reached for more, she felt it.

The Forest was weakening.

Its light—always so steady—flickered. Not absence. Not yet. But darkness pressed against it. Like rot under bark.

Anwyn tightened her stance. Closed her eyes for half a breath.

Not yet.

The corrupted dragon saw her. Roared. A black sound, empty and echoing.

She raised her hand again. Called the flame deeper. Let it thread through the ground. Through the root. Through her spine.

When it opened its jaws, she met it with fire.

Two waves clashed—flame and void.

The blast shook branches loose. Leaves burned in the air. The ground split beneath them. And still, she stood.

Then came the voice.

Not from the dragon.

Not from Emrys.

From the storm.

Not words, exactly.

She felt it like a hand at her throat. Gentle. Curious. Wrong.

Her knees buckled. Just slightly.

She looked up—and saw him.

Nergai.

Standing at the far edge of the grove. Cloaked in shadow. Watching her.

Not attacking. Not commanding. Just watching.

Anwyn gritted her teeth. Focused. Called the flame again. The Tree pulsed once, weak but true. Her hand steadied.

She didn't speak.

She didn't need to.

She raised a ward of fire, and Nergai vanished from view.

Behind her, Emrys whispered, "You saw him?"

She nodded once.

"We hold," she said.

And she turned to face the next wave.

Gunnar

The flare went up. Then the world began to close.

Gunnar stood at the center of the western kill zone, boots sunk into soft earth. Around him, the grove groaned beneath the storm's weight. Roots curled like fists above the ground, bark split with the sound of too many footfalls pressing into sacred soil.

"They're fully committed," Magnus growled beside him, peering down the slope. "No formations. Just fury."

"They smell blood," Gunnar said. "They think we're retreating." He watched the enemy come.

Drogo and Draugr surged between the trees. Half-armored. Scarred. Snarling. Some holes where eyes used to be. Some had missing limbs. Yet they climbed over the broken ground, heedless of the burning traps still smouldering at the grove's edges.

Laoch stepped in beside them, his katana strapped across his back, eyes like stone.

"They're in position," he said.

Gunnar turned. "Your ward lines?"

"In place. Bound to the Tree's rootpaths. The moment you give the word—we close the net."

Gunnar nodded once. Looked down into the Grove.

"Now," he said.

No cry. No flourish.

Just a word. A command. A judgment.

The dragons moved.

From the tree line, three shapes dropped like falling stars. The largest at the front—scars along his flank, flame already curling at his throat. The others flanked him, fire trailing from wings, light bouncing from steel and scale.

They hit the enemy line like thunder given breath.

Flame. Screams. Impact.

Draugr scattered like leaves in fire. Drogo screamed as flame found flesh. The storm struck back—violet arcs ripping down through gaps in the canopy. But it was too late.

Behind him, Laoch raised both hands. Light snapped from his palms, a spiderweb of glyphs spilling outward.

Laoch's voice followed—a chant in Elven. The kind of chant that had once bound trees to stand and rivers to bend.

The grove answered.

Wards snapped into place. Lines earlier by dwarven hands flared gold, then green, then white.

And the cage began to close.

Gunnar stepped forward.

Stonecall pulsed at his back. A deep vibration. Not magic. Not memory.

Permission.

The grove had opened. The grove had burned.

Now it would become a tomb.

He raised his voice—not loud, but final.

"Let him come."

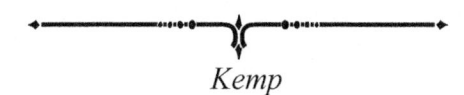

Kemp

The storm howled like a thing in mourning.

Kemp rode Vaelthys through the high arcs of the canopy, the dragon's wings carving air that had no business holding weight. Smoke curled in pockets. Ash swirled where leaves should've been. And above them, the storm pulsed—not lightning now, but *holes*. Rents in the sky that breathed shadow.

"There," Kemp said, pointing.

Below, the Drogo were breaking. Dragons had struck. Wards were rising. The kill-box was folding shut.

Vaelthys banked hard, wings slicing the smoke. Kemp scanned the treetops below.

Nergai's guard still held the inner ring—three thousand strong, shields locked, unmoved by flame.

And there—between two broken trees—Kemp caught a glimpse of black cloak trailing behind twisted armor.

Nergai.

Still moving. Still alive.

Vaelthys snarled low in his throat.

"Not yet," Kemp said, voice steady.

Suddenly, a corrupted dragon rose through the smoke ahead.

Black as tar, broader than Vaelthys, its body rippled with old scars and fresh rot. One wing was torn—half-missing, flapping loose like a broken sail.

But it still flew.

Its eyes were wrong. Hollow.

It saw them. And it dove.

Vaelthys banked hard. The air screamed past them, and Kemp's shoulder slammed into the dragons ridge. He grit his teeth, fought to stay upright.

The two dragons twisted in the sky—claws scraping, wings folding, fire flaring too close to treetops.

"Higher," Kemp snapped.

Vaelthys obeyed.

They soared through a break in the storm.

Up here, the air was cold and strangely still. Silent. Below, the grove burned. Ahead, the corrupted dragon wheeled, ready for a second pass.

Kemp closed his eyes.
And felt it.
Shadowfire.
It stirred beneath his ribs. Always there. Always waiting.
It offered him speed. Strength. Fury.
But not control.
Not unless he took it.
His breath slowed.
He did not fight it.
He *held it*.
Shaped it.
The fire bent.
It obeyed.
His eyes opened. The storm inside them swirled frantically.
"Now," he whispered.
Vaelthys dropped into a dive.
The corrupted dragon rose to meet them.
Shadowfire coiled around his fingers—no longer a storm, but a blade.
Below him, Vaelthys roared. Fire poured from his throat—bright, pure, searing.
The flames met.
Shadow and light. Dark and gold. Twisting, merging.
Not clashing—becoming.
Together, they became destruction.
They dove.
Through smoke. Through storm.
Through the corrupted dragon.
It didn't fall.
It came apart.

Wings sheared to ash. Bone unmade.
The roar it tried to loose never reached the air.
The wind took what remained.
Below, Nergai's guard faltered.
Kemp raised both hands, fire arcing from each palm, cleaving through the ranks.
A corridor of flame opened beneath him.
The grove lit up.
The path to Nergai was opening.

Chapter 40

Gunnar

The ground shook with the weight of the charge. Gunnar ran at the front, Stonecall in hand, the roots of the forest heaving beneath his boots.

The world was noise and blood. Steel clanged and screamed, blades sheared through bark and bone, warriors shouted, wept, died. Somewhere close, a voice cried for help—cut short. Another rose in a ragged war-cry. All of it crashing together, thick as mud in his ears.

Behind him, the line surged forward—elves with katanas raised and eyes hard, dwarves shouting over the clash as they heaved hammers and axes into skull and shield. Magnus fought a pace behind, blood streaking his face, one gauntlet dented where it had punched through a Drogo's helm. Gunnar barely registered it. His focus was forward—on the thinning line of Nergai's guard.

The storm still broiled overhead, but it had no bite. Not now. Not yet.

A cry rose above the treetops, sharp and trailing smoke. Ignara dove low over the battlefield, her wings snapping through the shattered canopy, a streak of gold fire trailing from her mouth. Drogo scattered, screaming as the flames took them.

"Hold the push!" Gunnar bellowed, voice hoarse from too many hours of command. "Don't let them regroup!"

He drove Stonecall into the chest of a Draugr rising from the muck, the runes flaring white as they met corrupted flesh. The creature folded, mouth open in a soundless scream as it collapsed into ash.

Beside him, Laoch limped into the fray. His cloak was gone, one arm pressed tight to his ribs, but his katana moved like a serpent, slicing through the reanimated dead with ruthless precision. A step faltered—his leg. Still broken. But he gritted his teeth and kept going.

"The bastard's retreating!" Magnus shouted, swinging wide as he cleaved a spear-wielder in half. "We break them here!"

Gunnar looked past the front line.

And saw it.

Nergai stood at the edge of the grove. Alone. Watching.

His army was folding. The trap had worked. The kill zones had collapsed. Fire and steel had done their work.

The defenders pressed harder.

To Gunnar's left, a wedge of dwarves charged in behind a dragon's flame, roaring as one. To his right, Anwyn strode through burning roots, her hands alight with fire and purpose, her face streaked with sweat and blood.

Even the forest, broken and wounded, seemed to breathe again.

For the first time in weeks, Gunnar felt it.

Hope.

Stonecall pulsed in his hand—deep, steady, certain.

"We end this," he growled, voice low.

And he charged.

Anwyn

They were winning.

She could feel it—not just in the battle's rhythm, but in the wind itself. The Sacred Tree pulsed through her with a weak but steady light, its roots humming beneath her boots like a heartbeat struggling but alive.

Anwyn stood at the edge of the grove, flame dancing along her palms, eyes fixed on the battlefield. Beyond the smoke, shapes surged—dwarves and elves and men, pushing the Drogo back through mud and root, their cries fierce and full of living fire. Dragons passed above like shadows cast by gods.

Her father limped into view, blood pouring down his side, but his blade was high.

It almost felt like something had shifted.

As if the Forest had drawn a breath.

And then—

The breath became a scream.

She felt it before she saw it: the pulse. A wrongness beneath the soil. A shudder in the bones of the world. Her flame dimmed.

Across the grove, Nergai lifted his hands.

The sky answered.

A column of darkness, coiled like a serpent, slammed down through the canopy. Not lightning. Not rain.

The storm.

It wasn't a thing above them now. It was here. Among them. It crashed through branches, splitting age-old trunks like snapped arrows. It tore wards apart like paper. It devoured light.

Anwyn barely raised her hands in time. Flame surged, met shadow, broke apart.

Beside her, Emrys stood firm.

He didn't falter. Not once.

Not until the sky opened and took him.

One blink, and he was there—

The next, he was gone.

No scream. No fire. Just ash.

Anwyn staggered, heat clawing her face, the air turning to knives. She dropped to one knee, pain blooming in her ribs where the ward backlash had struck her.

She saw her father fall, thrown like a child's doll across scorched earth. He didn't move.

"No," she gasped. "No, not yet."

The Sacred Tree behind was pulsing erratically now, a flickering heartbeat. Her flame guttered.

She reached into the ground, desperate, calling the magic.

A hand touched her shoulder—Ruiha, ash-streaked and bloodied, her dragon just touching down.

"Hold the circle," Ruiha said, voice like flint. "The storm isn't done."

Anwyn nodded, teeth clenched.

The wind howled.

Then she looked out—and saw them.

Bodies. Dozens. Hundreds.

They were rising

Karl

The first thing Karl noticed was the smell.

Not the blood or the burning—those were old friends by now—but the sharp, coppery stink of *wrongness*. Like someone had struck a match in a tomb and stirred up all the things best left sleeping.

The second thing he noticed was the headless elf trying to eat Draeg.

"Not today, you bastard," Karl muttered, and brought his hammer down like he meant it.

Bone cracked. The body spasmed once, twice, and finally stopped chewing on Draeg's shoulder.

Draeg, pinned beneath a broken root and half a corpse, blinked up at him.

"You took your time," he grunted.

Karl offered him a hand. "Had to finish my ale. Don't want it going warm mid-rescue."

He yanked Draeg up with a grunt and shoved the corpse off with the heel of his boot.

They were surrounded.

The grove was crawling—no, *shambling*—with bodies. Some burned. Some pierced clean through. One still had a sword in its chest, dragging it along like a forgotten accessory. Friend and foe alike, all with that glass-eyed stare and twitching limbs.

"Is it just me," Karl said, "or are they getting uglier every bloody time?"

"Less talking, more killing," Draeg growled, swinging his fist into something that had once been a dwarf and now smelled like wet fungus and spite.

Karl obliged.

The first thing he hit used to be a Sand Whisperer. Still had the silk wrappings, but the elegance was gone—now it moved like a drunk spider. Karl didn't hesitate. The hammer came down, rune-glow flaring, and the thing folded like bad scaffolding.

He turned. Draeg was holding his own.

A blade flashed from the side—

Instinct took over.

Karl stepped into the blow, shoulder raised, hammer sweeping wide.

Steel met wood. Met ribcage. Met something that **screamed without sound**.

The dead dwarf staggered back, now **armless and still moving**. Karl didn't wait. He lunged, roared, and brought the hammer down with both hands. Once. Twice. A third time—until the forest floor cracked and black ichor sprayed like **spit from a poisoned lung**.

Draeg stared at him, chest heaving.

"What?"

"You saved my life."

Karl shrugged, breath ragged. "I don't fancy explaining to Dreyna why you died getting chewed on by a former drinking buddy."

A pause.

"And anyway—you're a god? Can you even die?"

Draeg barked a laugh. "You're an arse."

Karl grinned through the blood and smoke. "Wouldn't have it any other way."

A scream rose behind them—human, alive.

More defenders were falling. The dead just kept rising. Karl looked around and saw nothing but smoke, ash, and moving corpses. The storm was still here, not above, but *within* the grove, in the roots and the rot and the air that refused to stay still.

And somewhere beyond that—

He saw Nergai.

Standing like a shadow sewn to the centre of the world.

"Tell me you've got a plan," Draeg said.

Karl's knuckles tightened around the haft of his hammer. The runes were flickering now, not steady. Dying.

"No," he said. "But I've got enough rage to fake one."

They stepped forward, side by side.

And the dead came to meet them.

Ruiha

The air above the grove was smoke and shrapnel.

Ruiha leaned into Ignara's neck, her fingers wrapped tight around horns, eyes narrowed to slits against the wind and ash. Below, the battlefield was chaos—shifting like a wounded animal, snapping and shuddering as the dead refused to stay down.

The first kill-box had done its job but was now was quickly turning into a graveyard.

"Lower," she whispered.

Ignara obeyed, banking left, wings slicing through a curtain of blackened leaves. One caught her shoulder, and Ruiha smelled the scorched leather—something else too, deeper. The scent of magic curdled and turned.

Beneath them, figures moved: some clumped and lurching, some fast and jagged. None of them right.

She spotted Karl and Draeg near a split in the grove floor, backs together, hammer and fist rising and falling in rhythm. Draeg looked small from up here. Mortal. She hated that.

A scream rose from the other side of the tree-line—someone young. Human. Then cut short.

Ruiha gritted her teeth. "Ignara—arc west. Burn the line."

The dragon turned with a snarl, her wings rolling in hard.

A moment later, flame followed.

Ignara's breath was white-gold, a line of fire that traced the grove's edge in a perfect crescent, lighting the blackness like a second sun. The undead caught in it flailed, collapsed, curled in on themselves.

Some kept coming anyway.

They didn't scream. They just burned.

Ruiha's stomach twisted.

A blur split the smoke to her right—Vaelthys, wings slicing wide.

Kemp rode low along the dragon's spine, arm raised, shadowfire coiled around his fingers like venom ready to strike.

He loosed it in a tight arc—surgical, silent—carving a clean path for a battered line of defenders below.

Ruiha raised her hand in salute. He didn't see her.

No time for it.

She looked past the smoke, to the center of the grove.

There he was.

Nergai.

Standing alone. Again.

The defenders were pushing toward him, slow but steady—Gunnar, bloodied but upright; Anwyn, her hair alight, flame pouring from her hands. Even Laoch was moving again, dragging his injured leg like he could bully the pain into obedience.

But Ruiha knew war. She knew rhythm. And something here—was wrong.

Nergai wasn't fleeing.

He wasn't fighting.

He was waiting.

And the air around him—no, the ground—was beginning to hum.

"Ignara, pull up. Now."

The dragon surged upward just as the hum became a thrum, then a pulse.

A ripple moved through the grove—through stone and root and corpse.

It wasn't magic.

It was something older.

Ruiha looked down. Her breath caught.

Nergai had dropped to his knees. Hands open. Blood pouring from his forearms like ink drawn from deep wells.

Around him, the air folded.

No chants. No screams.

Just a stillness that tasted like the moment before lightning. Like a breath too long held.

Ruiha went to scream a warning, but her voice was snatched by the wind, ripped away before it left her throat.

She didn't know what she meant to say.

Didn't know what, exactly, was happening down there.

But whatever Nergai was calling—

It wasn't power.

It was sacrifice.

Whatever came of it… would change everything.

Kemp

The grove was burning.

Not with fire—though there was fire enough—but with motion, noise, pressure. The kind of burning that came from blood in the mouth and breath torn raw from the throat. The kind that came from refusing to break.

Kemp dropped from Vaelthys's back and hit the ground running.

The acrid tang of scorched iron lingered on every breath, chased by the low, sulfurous reek of brimstone—like the forest had opened a door into something older and crueler than flame.

Screams rose around him. A knot of dwarves fought to his left, surrounded by corpses that wouldn't stay down. To his right, Anwyn stood over Laoch's half-crumpled form, casting arcs of flame into a swarm of dead that had once worn their colors.

Kemp didn't hesitate.

Shadowfire coiled in his palm before he even summoned it—drawn, eager. He narrowed it, forced it thinner, tighter. It became a blade. Not a storm. Not this time.

He swept his hand in a flat arc and the fire surged forward, slicing through three of the risen before they could turn. Another reached for him with scorched fingers, and he drove a lance of black flame straight through its chest. It crumpled like wet parchment.

He turned, sought the next break.

Found it—at the center.

Nergai.

He stood beneath the ruined arch of a once-living tree, blood running down his forearms, soaking the earth. He wasn't chanting. Wasn't laughing or screaming. Just still. Silent.

Waiting.

The defenders were pushing toward him, step by ragged step. Gunnar limped forward at the point of the wedge, his cloak torn and soaked in blood, Stonecall gripped in both hands. Behind him, Draeg and Karl carved their way forward, side by side. Ruiha wheeled overhead. Vaelthys banked low behind her, flames trailing from his jaws like banners made of light.

The momentum was theirs.

They were winning.

And Kemp hated it.

Because it felt wrong.

Too clean. Too easy.

Not the cost—but the lack of it. Nergai had lost control of the field. And yet he hadn't run. He hadn't broken. He hadn't moved.

Kemp moved to flank Gunnar's line, carving down two more corpses, then breaking into the open space before the Tree. His boots struck roots, blackened and steaming.

He stopped.

Something pulsed beneath the earth.

A deep, slow rhythm.

He looked at Nergai again, and this time, he saw it.

The Drogo was weeping.

Blood poured from his eyes. His hands were trembling. The magic around him wasn't gathering—it was *leaving*. Or being *torn* from him.

Sacrifice.

Kemp's breath caught.

Nergai was giving everything.

The earth shivered.

The wind vanished.

The defenders hesitated, just for a moment, watching the shadow rise around Nergai like smoke rising from the bones of gods.

And Kemp understood.

Whatever came next… would not be death.

It would be a rebirth.

Anwyn

There were moments, she had been told once, when time turned inward.

Not stopped, not frozen—but drawn in, like breath held too long. As if the world itself was waiting to exhale.

This was one of them.

Anwyn stood beside her father, her hands lowered now, the fire along her arms guttering into embers. The wards had fallen hours ago—or minutes, or seconds. Time no longer moved cleanly here. She could feel the Sacred Tree's pulse within her still, uneven, frightened. But not dead.

Before her, across the torn earth of the grove, Nergai knelt in silence.

Blood seeped from his arms, his eyes. Not as a wound, but as if something deeper inside him—older than bone—had begun to unravel.

The defenders had stilled. All of them.

Gunnar stood with Stonecall resting against the ground. Kemp, a dark silhouette beside the roots. Ruiha circled once overhead, then held, Ignara's wings stretched wide and unmoving.

No one spoke.

Not even the dead.

The storm no longer howled. It waited.

Shadow gathered around Nergai, not like smoke, but like memory—thick, curling, reluctant. It did not rush to him. It clung. As if it knew this shape would be its last.

Anwyn did not raise her flame.

There was no spell to cast for this.

She watched as he bowed his head.

Not in surrender. Not in peace.

In cost.

A noise began. Low, mournful, like stone cracking beneath water.

And then—

He rose.

Not all at once. Not like someone standing from prayer. But in fragments. In pieces.

The darkness took him. Folded him inward. His cloak became wings. His skin, a shell of ash and void. His arms broke and reshaped. His face—what had once been a face—vanished in a column of smoke, replaced by something with no eyes, no mouth, just presence.

Wings spread. Enormous, ragged, black as forgotten sky. The ground shuddered.

One heartbeat.

Two.

Then the forest remembered it could scream.

The Sacred Tree wailed—a sound without sound, a pulling of light from the earth. Roots buckled beneath her feet. The flame along her spine flared, then died.

He did not roar.

He did not need to.

He simply was.

And they all understood what had happened.

Nergai had not summoned a monster.

He had become one.

Chapter 41

Gunnar

The ground shook with every beat of its wings. Gunnar braced against the trunk of a half-burned tree, Stonecall heavy in his hands. Blood ran from a cut at his temple, seeping down into the edges of his beard. The wound wasn't deep, but it wouldn't stop bleeding. None of them would. He was leaking from a dozen places, each a whispered reminder that this body—strong as it had once been—was wearing thin.

He looked up.

The sky had broken.

Where once there had been branches and banners and the pale shimmer of magic, now there was only wings—vast and black and wrong. Nergai, reborn in the shape of a dragon, moved like a storm given form. His wings didn't beat; they ripped the air apart. Every breath from his maw seared the ground, left craters glowing and steaming.

Not fire. Not shadow. Something in between.

Something meant to unmake.

"Form up!" Gunnar roared, voice raw from smoke and shouting. "Hold the left flank!"

Only a few turned. Fewer still obeyed.

Most were already dead. Or dying.

A band of dwarves clustered near the ruins of a tree, hammers raised, faces set. Beside them, Karl and Draeg stood side by side, not moving, just breathing hard, watching the sky like they'd both already decided what they'd die protecting.

It wasn't enough.

A dragon—he couldn't tell which—fell from the sky, struck mid-arc by a lash of darkness from Nergai's jaws. It crashed into the grove with a sound like the sky splitting open, ripping through bark and stone in a trail of ruin that scarred the heart of the forest.

Gunnar turned back to the front. His hand tightened on Stonecall.

A Drogo came at him—faster than expected. It screamed, blade flashing.

He stepped aside, ducked low, and drove his shoulder into its ribs. The Drogo staggered. Gunnar brought his warhammer down, cracking skull and spine in one wet crunch.

He didn't stop moving. Couldn't. Not now.

He saw Magnus ahead—blood running from a gash across his back, eyes wild. His brother was still swinging, still holding. Somewhere to his right, Anwyn's flames rose and fell like a heartbeat struggling to stay steady.

They were giving everything.

And it still wasn't enough.

Not against *this*.

Not against him.

Gunnar slammed his back against a fallen log, sucked in a breath that tasted of iron, and looked to the sky.

Nergai passed overhead, his wings blotting out the sun.

"We cannot kill what has become myth," someone whispered near him.

And for the first time in this war, Gunnar had no answer.

Anwyn

There was a silence beneath the battle.

Not absence—never that, not here—but a stillness older than war. A quiet that lived beneath noise, beneath fire and screams and the iron ring of blades. It ran through the roots of the forest like water beneath stone.

Anwyn felt it now. She stood at the edge of a broken glade, her hands open at her sides, her flame flickering low but steady. The wards were gone. The wind had stilled. She could feel the air thickening with magic—but not hers.

Not the forest's.

Something else.

She knelt and pressed her hand to the ground.

The soil was warm.

Too warm.

She inhaled, and the scent came with it—brimstone, and something stranger: sap turned sour, bark burned before it fell.

This is where it begins, she thought.

But she was wrong.

It had already begun.

The Sacred Tree in Vaeloria was far from here. A day's ride. But distance didn't matter.

The Sacred Tree wasn't a place.

It was a *presence*.

Its roots, unseen by any eye, ran beneath the forest like threads sewn by gods who had once believed in binding things together.

And now—they were being pulled apart.

She felt the tug, sudden and sharp, like a child's cry in the dark. The ley-lines writhed under her touch, skittering away as if her hands burned them. Her magic, once so certain, flared and faded in fits—no longer fed by the Tree's rhythm.

She whispered words to steady them, to call the roots back into rhythm.

They faltered in her mouth.

The ground did not answer with light.

It answered with heat.

She closed her eyes.

And a vision came—*not summoned*, but *given*.

She was walking here again. The same grove. But gentler, greener. Owen's laughter rising like birdsong through the trees. Freya darting ahead, small feet sure between roots that seemed to bend out of her way.

The vision was soft. Sharp. Whole.

And Anwyn, in that moment, could not tell if it was something she was hoping for—or saying goodbye to.

The thought broke something in her.

Tears slid down her face, unbidden.

Then the tremor came.

It moved through the grove like a heartbeat struck out of rhythm.

She staggered.

And the forest—so old, so proud—shuddered with her.

Above her, the wind did not stir—but leaves fell anyway, as if the forest was shaking off its skin.

Anwyn looked to the heart of the battlefield. Nergai stood there, not moving. His wings were wide, vast enough to darken half the glade. But his eyes—

His eyes were not looking at her. Not at the flame she still held.

They were looking down.

To the earth.

To the roots.

He wasn't trying to kill them.

He was trying to sever the world.

A sob rose in her throat—dry and useless. She swallowed it and dropped to her knees. Her fingers curled into the soil. She reached—not for flame, not for power, but for connection.

Please, she thought. Not a cry. Not a spell.

Just one word, sent into the roots.

Help.

The forest heard her. She felt it—a pulse like a heartbeat half-lost. Distant. Weak. Still there.

For now.

Anwyn looked up.

Nergai was watching her now.

And the ground beneath her feet had begun to smoke.

Kemp

The sky was on fire.

Not in the poetic sense. Not some battlefield flourish to be remembered in songs. This was fire that blinded. That seared the lungs. That made the world above the trees feel more like a forge than a sky.

Kemp held low against Vaelthys's spine, knees clenched tight, one arm gripped around his horn. The other crackled with Shadowfire—contained, controlled, barely.

Below them, the grove burned. The earth had split open in places, roots torn from their beds. Magic surged through the ground like veins about to burst. Nergai was somewhere in that ruin—wings wide, body black as scorched bone, his roar a sound that made the wind itself shudder.

"Left," Kemp murmured. Vaelthys banked hard without hesitation, even wounded.

A spear of dark magic tore through the space they'd just vacated.

They dove.

Another dragon streaked past below them—he couldn't tell which. Its flank was torn open. The dragon hit the ground a moment later, skidding through smoke and ash.

Kemp didn't watch it fall.

There was no time left for mourning.

They leveled out above the treetops. The air was thicker here—more resistance, less risk. Kemp scanned the battlefield.

Too many fires.

Too few friends left.

Vaelthys grunted beneath him, a low sound of fatigue and fury. Blood dripped from his right wing where a bolt had grazed him earlier. He was slowing.

Kemp exhaled through clenched teeth, pulled his body tighter to the dragon's frame. Shadowfire gathered in his palm—sharp and narrow now. A blade, not a storm.

He pointed. Vaelthys dove.

They cut across the grove's northern edge, flanked the line where Draeg and Karl still held. Kemp lashed out with the flame—controlled bursts, surgical. Not beautiful. Not showy. Just death, where it was needed.

Then he saw her.

Ignara.

She was climbing. Fast.

Too fast.

She was rising like a star that didn't plan to come back down.

Kemp could see it even from here. The angle she was climbing. Something was wrong.

He said nothing.

Did nothing.

There was nothing to do.

Vaelthys kept flying, steady under him, but Kemp felt his dragon's body change—tension bleeding into the wingbeats, the ache of shared grief rising between them.

He pressed a hand to the warm scales. Just for a moment.

"I know," he murmured. "I know."

He didn't look back at Ignara.

Couldn't.

But he felt it—the pressure in the air. The pull of something immense.

Magic was building.

Not Nergai's.

Hers.

And every living thing still left in that ruined sky was about to feel it.

Ruiha

Ignara was climbing too fast.

Ruiha knew it the moment she felt her wingbeats shift—deeper, broader, unnatural for this low a pass. There was no banking, no tactical arc. Just a straight ascent through ash and smoke, pushing higher into what was left of the sky.

She leaned forward along the ridge of Ignara's spine, hands gripping the fire-slicked scales, breath caught in her throat.

"What are you doing?"

No answer.

Just heat, and the steady rise of muscle beneath her.

"Ignara," she said again, louder this time.

The dragon kept climbing.

Ruiha shifted her weight, a silent command. Pull back. Circle wide. Return.

Ignara didn't respond.

Not with her body. Not with her voice.

Not until something—somewhere—opened.

The bond snapped back into place like a blade drawn from a wound. One moment, Ruiha was alone in the climb. The next, she was inside it—inside her.

Heat. Pain. Memory.

They were flying through fire and the years at once.

A hundred shared flights. Wind underwing. The rhythm of breath. Blood and storm. The long silence after the valley.

And something else.

Goodbye.

"No," Ruiha said aloud. Not a command. A plea. "Not like this."

Ignara turned her head slightly—not enough to break the climb, just enough for Ruiha to see her eye.

She was not afraid.

She was resolute.

"It has to be me."

Below, the black dragon reared. Nergai, reborn, terrible. He opened his jaws and a scream of magic tore through the air like cloth catching fire.

But Ignara didn't turn.

She flared her wings wide, and for one still breath, she hung there—balanced between sun and shadow.

Ruiha held tight to Ignara's back as they dove, her arms locked, her breath torn from her throat by speed and fire.

The bond between them blazed—every thought, every memory surging between them like a storm refusing to break.

"If you do this," Ruiha whispered, "I do it with you."

Ignara didn't answer with words.

She roared.

A deep, shuddering sound that rattled the sky—and carried a name.

"Vaelthys."

Below them, green-purple wings spread—Vaelthys banking hard, trying to turn, to follow, too late to stop what was coming.

But Ignara was faster.

She twisted mid-dive—a single, fluid movement, a flare of her wings and the wrench of her neck—and Ruiha felt it before it happened.

A shift. A surge. A targeted burst of magic—not heat, not flame. Force. Direction. Purpose.

Ruiha was thrown.

She didn't scream. Her voice was already breaking inside her. She reached for Ignara—not to pull her back, just to feel her, one last time.

But the air took her, and the moment was gone.

She arced outward from Ignara's spine—sailing through smoke and speed—and dropped straight toward Vaelthys's open back.

He caught her.

She landed hard, bones jarring, but alive. Kemp reached out and grasped her as the great dragon grunted and corrected for her weight.

Below, Ignara kept diving.

Faster now.

The bond still blazed between them, for one final second.

Then it broke.

The light changed.

Not fire.

Not shadow.

Something between.

And she knew—Ignara had held on as long as she could. Not for the grove. For her.

Grief came not as a scream, but as a silence so deep it felt like sleep.

Ignara met Nergai in mid-air, body blazing with every ounce of magic she'd ever held back.

There was no scream. No roar.
Just a rupture in the sky.
The world collapsed inward.
A soundless detonation. A pulling, not a blast. Like a star dying quietly.
The grove vanished.
Light folded.
And then—nothing.
The bond was gone.
No pain. No burning.
Just absence.
Not like before. Not severed.
Empty.
The smoke hung like a veil over the grove, thick with ash and silence.
The wind did not return.
There was no breath left in the world.
Nergai was gone.
But the darkness—
The darkness remained.
Not shape, not voice.
Just a presence, coiled in the air, pulsing slow as a god's last breath.
It clung to the edges of the sky, staining the clouds, leeching the light from them.
It did not strike.
It did not flee.
It simply waited.

Chapter 42

Anwyn

They reached Vaeloria in silence. Not because there was nothing to say—but because there were too many things that could not be spoken aloud. Not yet. Perhaps not ever.

The Sacred Tree stood as it always had.

Tall. Ancient. Listening.

Its roots sprawled across the clearing like the arms of something sleeping, or wounded. Sunlight filtered through its upper canopy in long, pale shafts, turning the moss silver and the dust into floating stars.

But the air around the Tree was wrong.

Something lingered there—low and waiting. It pulsed not in rhythm, but in defiance.

A residue of what had not been truly defeated.

The darkness.

Not Nergai—not anymore.

What remained was the wound of him, still bleeding quietly into the world.

Anwyn stepped forward, slowly, her bare feet brushing over blackened grass that had not yet regrown. She could feel the echo of the rupture in her bones. It had sunk deep—too deep to burn away entirely.

Behind her, Gunnar approached. In his hands, he held the vessel.

Karl's tankard.

The runes beneath its base pulsed gently. The heat inside it felt like a forge awaiting metal.

Anwyn knelt before the Tree, grounding her hands in the roots.

The Tree did not resist.

It knew what she had come to do.

She called the darkness.

Not with words, but with memory.

With everything Nergai had broken—every death, every tree felled, every dream devoured.

It came slowly.

A coil of shadow, rising from the soil like smoke. No shape. No voice.

Just presence.

It circled her.

She kept her hands steady.

She did not flinch.

The darkness drifted toward the tankard—drawn not by force, but by intention. The vessel hummed. Runes glowed. The darkness resisted.

Then faltered.

Then flowed.

"You will not be forgotten," Anwyn whispered. "But you will not be free again."

With a low sound like wind across hollow stone, the last of it slipped into the tankard.

The lid sealed with a click that echoed deeper than it should have.

Then there was silence.

True silence.

Anwyn exhaled.

Gunnar stepped forward. His face was pale with awe, or exhaustion, or both.

"Is it done?" he asked.

"No," she said. "Not yet."

She picked up the tankard. It was heavier now—not in weight, but in meaning.

She turned to the Tree and knelt again at its base.

Together, she and Gunnar placed the tankard between two vast roots. The Tree shifted—*in acceptance*. Bark curled inward, slow and sacred. The roots wrapped around the vessel.

And began to take it in.

When it was gone, Anwyn remained kneeling.

She laid one palm flat on the bark, the other on the ground.

"It's yours now," she said.

The Tree said nothing.

But she felt it—a faint, low pulse, like a wound turning toward healing.

Gunnar

He had held many things in his hands.

Swords. Shields. The dying breath of comrades. The broken helm of his father. The weight of Stonecall, etched with runes that had sung in his blood since the moment he took it up.

But never this.

Never them.

Gunnar stood at the edge of the clearing, where the light fell softest and the Sacred Tree's roots made gentle shelves of the earth.

Anwyn was already there, half-shaded by the low curve of a branch. In her arms, wrapped in simple green cloth, were two children.

A boy. And a girl.

Twins.

They looked like her.

But there was something in the set of the boy's brow. The small, restless curl of the girl's fingers.

Something of him.

He had died for them.

Come back for them.

Fought gods, and monsters, and the black wind of memory for a chance to see them.

Now that he could, Gunnar found himself unable to move.

The world had grown too large.

Or he had grown too small.

Anwyn stepped forward, slowly. No fire in her gait. Only root and soil and the stillness of trees.

She didn't explain.

She simply said:

"These are your children."

Nothing of war or resurrection or legend.

Just that.

Your children.

She placed Freya into his arms first.

Gunnar's hands shook. Not from fear, not quite. Just from the weight of her.

She was warm.

Heavy in the way only the living are.

Her breath fluttered gently against his chest.

Then Anwyn passed him Owen, and the second weight made it real.

He held them both.

One against each shoulder, their heads nestled into the groove of his collarbone, as if they had been carved to fit there all along.

His war-worn hands had crushed bones. Broken shields. Dragged men out of fire.

Now they held two lives.

And he couldn't stop staring.

Anwyn knelt beside him.

"They've waited," she said quietly. "So have you."

He didn't speak.

There was nothing he could say that wouldn't break him.

So he lowered his head, pressed his lips to the downy warmth of their hair—

And wept.

Not with sound. Not with anguish.

Just tears, steady and silent.

Like rain in a place that had been dry too long.

Ruiha

The ash still clung to her cloak.

No matter how many times she brushed it off, it settled again. In folds, in seams. A fine grey dust from wings burned too bright.

Ruiha sat beneath a pale-limbed whitebark tree at the edge of the Vaelorian courtyard. The wind here was gentler than in the grove, and it smelled faintly of sap and clean moss.

But she could still taste smoke in the back of her throat.

Ignara had died days ago.

The world had not.

That was the part she couldn't quite seem to reconcile.

The sky still opened every morning. Birds still called from the high branches. Children laughed near the pools.

And Ruiha sat alone, with ash on her shoulders.

Kemp didn't announce himself.

He simply lowered himself beside her, one hand braced against his knee, the other still wrapped in worn bandages. He didn't look at her. Just sat, his posture steady. Balanced.

After a while, he offered a flask.

"Coffee," he said.

She took it. Gave him a curious look.

Drank.

Didn't speak.

Didn't have to.

They sat in silence for a while. Long enough that the light began to shift through the trees.

Finally, Kemp exhaled. It wasn't a sigh. Just breath let go slowly.

"Vaelthys couldn't fly for six months after his first rider fell."

Ruiha turned, slightly. Not all the way. Just enough.

"You didn't talk about that."

"Didn't need to," he said. "Not until now."

More silence.

It stretched, comfortable and aching.

"You think it ever stops hurting?" she asked.

"No," he said.

A pause.

"But it changes."

She let out a breath through her nose. Not quite a laugh. Not quite a sob.

"That's not very comforting."

Kemp gave her a slow shrug.

"Comfort wasn't what you needed. Just the truth."

They sat together a little longer.

Not touching. Not leaning. Just two people whose fires had burned through too much, left with ash and memory.

Then Ruiha's hand moved.

It didn't reach for him.

It just found his.

Fingers brushing, then resting. Still.

And they stayed like that.

Beneath a whitebark tree.

MARK STANLEY

In the peace carved from ruin.

Epilogue

The Sacred Tree looked different now.
    Not taller. Not brighter. But heavier, somehow.
    Like it had taken on something it would never speak of, and was choosing to carry it anyway.

Karl stood at its base, staring at the place where the roots had closed over the tankard.

His tankard.

Forged in a haze of half-mad inspiration, or desperation, he wasn't sure anymore, with guidance he hadn't asked for and shards he'd hammered by instinct more than understanding. Meant to hold ale. Maybe stew.

Not the end of the bloody world.

He folded his arms, grunted. "Could've made a sword. Or a throne. Or a damned relic."

A beat.

Then a grin.

"But no. A tankard. And they laughed."

A breeze stirred the leaves above, rustling like breath over old parchment. Somewhere behind him, birdsong returned to the canopy. Sunlight flickered through the boughs.

"Holds darkness better than it holds mead," he muttered. "Not bad, really."

He turned, about to find someone to gloat to—

And there she was.

Dreyna.

Hair the colour of dying starlight. Cloak like smoke. Boots that didn't bend grass when she walked. The forest seemed to hush itself as she stepped toward him.

She stopped a pace away. Looked him over. Smirked.

"You saved Vellhor," she said.

Karl puffed up.

She didn't say anymore. Just leaned forward and kissed him once, soft and dry, on the cheek.

Then turned and walked past him.

Karl blinked.

Then turned to the nearest person—a confused young elf trying to re-stack offering stones.

"Did you see that?"

The elf opened his mouth. Thought better of it. Walked away.

Karl nodded to himself.

"Aye. Thought so."

He stood there a moment longer, hands on hips, chin high, gaze sweeping the clearing like it was a kingdom.

He turned back to the Tree.

Watched the wind slide through its branches.

Didn't speak.

Didn't move.

Then, almost to himself—

"And they'll say I was drunk."

He smiled.

And let the world be still.

Printed in Dunstable, United Kingdom